MADAME TESSIER KNOWS ALL

KNOWS ALL

MOLLY SUTTON MYSTERIES
BOOK XIII

NELL GODDIN

Goddin
Books

ISBN: 978-1-949841-27-5

I

JANUARY 18, 2009

A cold night in Castillac. Sliver of a moon. Cloudless.
The streets empty, nothing stirring.

Two a.m.

Just enough light that he could see where he was going without a flashlight.

He was nimble, and made his way down *rue* Tabac with almost no sound. He wore leather boots with worn, soft soles—soles that could have used a visit to the cobbler, his wool sock showing through in several places.

He reached the front door of Madame Lagasse's house and put his bare hand on the latch.

He stood for a long moment, arguing with himself. The latch was freezing cold.

And then—a deep breath—no more hesitation. He tried the latch, and when it was locked, he pulled out a wire and a screwdriver, and in less than a minute slipped, unseen, inside the house.

. . .

"It's a glorious day to waddle around doing nothing," said Molly, pouring a glass of orange juice as Ben came through the kitchen with his toolbox. She was—not to mince words—colossally pregnant, due to give birth at any moment.

"Carry on with your glorious waddling," he said. "I'm headed to the *pigeonnier* to make sure the rathole is still plugged up."

Molly put her hands on the counter and leaned on them, trying to take some weight off her feet. "Oh, Ben," she said. "I want tourists staying there, not rats."

"I know what you mean. It's so depressing to have the gîtes sitting empty like this. I feel like I just need to do *some*thing."

"Things have been slow before, of course. We have to expect ups and downs. But not like this. Not just an off month, but *zero* reservations on the books. Nothing. And no one even emails with random questions about whether Castillac has any decent restaurants or whether there are any bilingual babysitters available."

Ben nodded, shaking his head. They had talked it all over, many times—how the world financial crisis had made its effects felt in Castillac, even deep in the Périgord, far from Wall Street and American bankers. How tourists were not touring. Not while everyone, rich and poor and in-between, felt so insecure about the future.

And for far too many—insecure about the present.

"We have much to be grateful for," he said, putting the toolbox down and wrapping his arms around Molly as best he could, given her girth.

"Absolutely," she said, hugging him back. "I'm not that worried about getting along, day to day." She hugged him again. "Well, actually? I *am* a little worried about that. But I do have confidence that if the gîte business never revives, and you don't get any surveillance work, and our investigation business is dead—um, what was I saying?"

"You have confidence? And then you said a lot of terrible things."

She laughed. "What I mean is—if everything that we've been doing goes belly-up, we'll just figure something else out. I'll learn how to fix cars or something. You can be a plumber."

Ben cocked his head, imagining this. Then he kissed the top of her head, gave her belly a rub, and took off for the pigeonnier.

W ednesday, lunchtime. Chez Papa had a lone customer, Madame Tessier, who was having a *salade* with a poached egg, and a glass of red wine (local, out of a large jug—the cheapest available—but still good).

Nico Bartolucci wiped the bar down for the tenth time that day. He considered sliding into the banquette across from Madame Tessier because he felt lonely and thought it possible she might want to chat as well. She was known to be the font of all Castillac gossip and in nice weather installed herself in a folding chair in front of her house, so that she could chat with any and all who passed by. Usually when she came in, she was with Madame Lagasse—maybe, since she was alone, she might not mind an intrusion? But the mood was different now. People in the village seemed more closed up, less welcoming. Nico decided not to press himself on her.

It was a strange time in the village; people were on edge. Now that Lehman Brothers in New York had collapsed, sending world stock markets plunging, Castillacois—along with much of the world—had lost the feeling of relative economic safety they had been taking for granted. They didn't need to have an investment portfolio themselves to feel the frightening chill.

It was so quiet in the bistro that Nico could hear Madame Tessier chewing.

He checked to make sure the glasses were stocked, the refrigerator was sparkling clean, the ice machine humming along and full. All the supplies for making cocktails topped up and fresh, ready for the evening, when, if recent past was prologue, very few people would be coming in to order anything anyway.

If he owned the place, he might consider closing it temporarily, at least until the economy showed some sign of life. But Alphonse, the owner of Chez Papa, wouldn't hear of it. Not because he was optimistic about turning a profit, but because he did not want to take away a valuable place for villagers to socialize and connect with each other, not in these unsettled times.

With a sigh, Nico looked out the window, hoping his wife Frances might stop by with baby Luka. Hoping, really, for *anybody* to stop by; at this point, he would be glad to see even someone he did not like. Anything to break up the day, filled as it was with nothing to do, no one to talk to, and nothing to think about except the various anxieties that flooded into his mind when he considered that he had a wife and baby to support, and how long could Alphonse really afford to keep the place open, with so few customers?

THROWING financial caution to the wind, Molly asked Lawrence to lunch. Spending money at a restaurant was perhaps not the most prudent decision; she had a number of rationalizations ready. But Ben did not raise an eyebrow, only said he was going to be repairing the door to an armoire that wasn't closing properly.

Lawrence did raise an eyebrow, however, after settling into his chair at the Café de la Place. He was wearing a charcoal gray wool suit with a pale yellow pocket square. "Did you unearth some hidden jewels at La Baraque?" he said. "To what do I owe this delicious extravagance? I'm grateful, of course. But aren't we all afraid of going broke in the next five minutes?"

Molly shrugged. "It's only lunch. Not like we're chowing down on seven courses at La Metairie."

"I can't remember the last time I ate there," said Lawrence mournfully. "I heard the owner is thinking of closing it temporarily."

Molly shook her head as though to deny that possibility. "Things aren't even that bad, here in France. All those government protections come in handy when disasters like this hit, right? What's bad is everyone expecting things to get much worse."

"Well, they very well may, Molly. You know better than anyone how much we depend on those travel dollars, especially American ones. And the Americans all appear to be hunkering down at home, not that I blame them."

Molly shrugged, "Yes, believe me, I'm well aware. But see—I can't do anything about that. It's utterly out of my control. So my idea is that all of us simply carry on and hope for the best, instead of hiding at home worrying about everything. What good does worrying ever do?"

Lawrence looked askance. "You want to take away one of my main hobbies? If you snatch worrying away, whatever will I do all day? And since when are you so devil-may-care, especially with *le bébé* on the way?"

Molly shrugged again. But Lawrence, who knew Molly very well, noticed a quick expression on her face that made him think she was not quite so fancy-free as she pretended.

"Well, what then?" he said.

"Huh?"

"There's—oh, here comes Pascal," said Lawrence, literally licking his chops.

Pascal, handsome and cheerful as ever, took their orders and disappeared into the kitchen.

"You're not as blasé as you seem, that's all I'm saying," said Lawrence.

Molly avoided eye contact. She did a thing with her lips that she did when a thought bothered her.

"Out with it," said Lawrence. He poured himself a glass of red from the *pichet* Pascal had brought, but did not take a sip.

"I can't say this to anyone but you."

"Well, that pleases me, I have to admit." He looked at her carefully. Molly was in the fullest bloom of pregnancy, her face round with healthy color, her hair impossibly bounteous and glossy and even more out of control than ever. But in her eyes, there was…not quite fear, but something…

"There are things you can't know until you go through them," she said. "Being pregnant…it feels a little like you've been placed on a conveyor belt," she said, still looking out of the window. "Inexorably, day by day, you move forward to the day of the birth, not that you have any idea when that is. You have no say in what comes next. You're just riding on that belt as it goes along, hoping for the best. You're at the mercy of your body as it does what it does, you know?"

Lawrence looked skeptical. "I can't imagine this is news, Molly. What—"

"Well, it's one thing to know a thing is true and an entirely different thing to experience it. That's all I'm saying. Physically— and emotionally—it's—"

Just then Pascal appeared at the table with their bowls of stew, and set them on the placemats. "Enjoy your lunch," he said, and hurried off.

"We're the only ones in here," said Molly. "What's he in such a hurry about?"

"Everyone's a little off lately. You were saying? About how I couldn't possibly understand?" Lawrence dipped his spoon into the stew and couldn't help smiling at it, the sauce a rich brown with nuggets of glossy onion and carrot showing through.

Molly was back to looking out of the window. "What I'm trying to say—and breathe not a word to anyone, of course—"

"—of course—"

"—is that I have this feeling of not being in control of *anything*. All I wanted was a baby. Of course I'm thrilled to pieces that I'm about to have one. But also it feels like...the baby is going to do what it's going to do and I have no say in it at all. Once it's here, what will that be like? Will I ever have a moment to myself again? Will I even be the same person? Now that I finally got those horrible implants removed, will I be able to nurse my baby? And what about Dufort/Sutton Investigations? Is that a closed chapter, because I won't have time or energy to put into it, and maybe it's simply not a suitable job for the mother of an infant? What about Ben? Will our relationship suffer? Will he feel burdened? What in the world is my life going to turn into?"

Lawrence spooned in a mouthful of stew and sighed, then leaned back in his chair. "That's a lot of questions," he said finally.

"That all you got?"

"Well, for a number of those questions, I'm not in any position to comment. I will say this though, based on my observations of other new parents. No, you won't be the same. The entire enterprise will be too much for your old self to take in, and so you change. You have to, to accommodate the new person who will, of course, be the center of your life for some years."

"And Ben? What's the baby going to do—"

"Molly. I don't think I have ever seen you this lacking in confidence. May I say, gently and with love: pull yourself together? Ben will be supremely happy. He was made to be a father and he very much wishes to be a father. I don't think you have a thing to worry about in that department."

"Thank you," said Molly softly. Her belly was so large she had to sit away from the table and had dribbled some stew on her shirt. "Look at this," she said, pointing at the stain. "I'm not in any condition to be out in public."

Lawrence looked at her sternly. She held his gaze and then they both burst out laughing.

"I'm a mess," she said, still laughing. "But okay. I just...I just needed to say those things out loud and now I have. That old aphorism 'be careful what you wish for' kept repeating in my ear and maybe now it will leave me alone."

"I never thought of you as so interested in controlling things," he said, trying to get Pascal's attention so he could order dessert.

Molly shrugged. "Me neither. And that's part of what's so unsettling. The baby's not even here and already I'm not feeling myself."

"When's your due date again?"

"Day after tomorrow," said Molly.

"I can understand why you'd be feeling some trepidation. Are you nervous about the birth itself?"

"Of course I am! I'm old to be doing this, you know, as that unpleasant Dr. Boulet is constantly reminding me."

"I have a feeling it's all going to go very smoothly. The birth, and years of childhood, the marriage, the work, all of it."

"That's awfully rosy," said Molly. "What if something goes wrong, what if the baby..."

"Molly, for God's sake, stop it. You're letting your monkey brain run away with you," said Lawrence. "And, uh, if anything does go wrong? You'll simply deal with it, as we always do."

Molly felt fragile. Just hearing her friend say the words "go wrong" was enough to make her stomach clench. She took a deep breath, and then ate a big spoonful of stew, and did her best to govern her ungovernable mind.

PAUL-HENRI MONSOUR, junior officer at the Castillac *gendarmerie*, was accomplishing that Wednesday what he accomplished every other work day: walking the streets, ears and eyes open, alert for any sign that someone needed help. In the back of his mind, he was considering his own situation with a newfound worry: when he started his training, the gendarmerie had seemed the safest of careers—France would always need gendarmes, *n'est-ce pas?* But with the global financial collapse, anything seemed possible. No one's job was safe. He could easily imagine the conversations taking place in the upper echelons of government, officials frantic over the budget musing that surely insignificant little Castillac could get along without a junior officer at all. Best case, he was transferred someplace interesting. Worst case...he imagined handing over his uniform, out of work, with no prospects. He shuddered.

Paul-Henri walked the length of the village, seeing no one on the street. That would be unusual were it not for the cold, he thought. Lately, people stayed inside more, they weren't shopping as much, and he had noticed a current of...not quite anti-social sentiment, but something near to it...in which villagers were more likely to turn away when they saw him coming. Less likely to have a chat on the street corner than they used to.

His belly was rumbling and he decided to go to the *épicerie* and pick up a little something. His mother would say—especially in these uncertain times—that chocolate was an extravagance, but Paul-Henri believed it to be a nearly perfect antidote to malaise. And surely he was old enough not to follow every bit of advice his mother gave him, even if all those bits were forever repeating in his head and showed no sign of abating.

"Bonjour, Ninette," he said, carefully closing the door behind him against the draft (as his mother had taught him). "I heard you had been forced into taking all the shifts here at the épicerie when Simonette took off for—where exactly did she go? Off to find herself, did she?" He smirked and then tried to soften his expression.

"Bonjour, Paul-Henri. She's gone to India for six months. Not a crime, I don't believe?" Ninette was in her early forties but looked younger; her figure was trim from being on her feet all day, and she took care with her hair and makeup, going with the latest styles without being too trendy.

Paul-Henri pulled the back of the jacket of his uniform down and rolled his eyes. He liked Ninette and felt an attraction to her. But every time he came into the épicerie, they seemed to get off on the wrong foot.

"So tell me, what's the state of the village this morning?" she said.

"Quiet. Perhaps too quiet. It's rare—possibly it has never happened even once—that in mid-morning, on a day without rain or snow, I walked from one end of the village to the other and did not see another soul."

"Been slow here too. Even the regulars haven't been coming in. Madame Tessier and Madame Lagasse, they come in every Wednesday like clockwork, and I hold their bags for them while they have lunch at Chez Papa. Not today though."

Paul-Henri pretended to focus his attention on the display of chocolates. "Tell me," he said, "hazelnuts or walnuts?"

Ninette looked at him like he was crazy. "Walnuts. Of course."

"Belgian or French?"

Ninette did not dignify this with an answer. "I heard a fight broke out at the market on Saturday. Never in my life. Were you there?"

"Of course I was there. Saturday is my day off, but you know I like to be present during much of the market hours, in case I am needed. I'll have these, if you please," he said, putting a Cote d'Or Praliné and a dark chocolate with almonds on the counter.

"Did you arrest anyone?"

"No need. It was just a scrap between some teenagers. Nothing to get upset about." He had an urge to magnify the danger of the encounter but could not, in the moment, think of a believable way to do so.

"Since when do we have fistfights at the Saturday market? It feels as though the world has gone mad," said Ninette.

Paul-Henri shrugged. "With the youngsters, sometimes tempers get high. Always been that way, don't you think?"

Ninette started a story about her teenage years and the time that guy with the broken nose kept picking on her best friend, whose family eventually moved away. To Perpignan? Or was it Narbonne?

This is the slowest story ever told, Paul-Henri thought, then grinned at the prospect of eating his chocolate bars. He waved, thanked her, and went back to the street, shivering against the cold, and almost walked straight into Edmond Nugent.

Strange, thought Paul-Henri. Edmond never ventures out of the *pâtisserie* at this hour.

❧ 3 ❧

"Honestly, Jules—you're fretful as a baby with colic. Just talk to me. What is the matter?"

Jules jumped up from the chair he had just sat down in. The room was cold and he rubbed his hands together. He was thin and his sweater was worn.

"You already know what the matter is. Those debts are killing us and we're running out of money. The social services aren't enough. We're cold, we could use more nutritious food, and—" he stared at her belly, which was seven months into a pregnancy. "I wish I had never borrowed that money," he said in a low voice.

Amelie went to him. She put her arms around his neck and pressed herself against him so that he felt her warmth. "Things will work out," she said. "They always do." She put the back of her hand against his cheek.

"Your hand feels like a slab of ice," he said, summoning up a smile. He leaned down and kissed her.

In the bedroom, they could hear their son talking to himself. "Put it back, put it back, put it back," he said, in a monotone. He paused, and said it again. And again.

Amelie shook her head slowly. "It's been the same for hours."

"He needs help," said Jules quietly. "But from who? Doctor Boulet has been totally useless."

"I'm sorry I didn't get him to school this morning," she said, looking at the floor. "He flat-out refused. Lay down on the floor and wouldn't budge. I didn't have the heart to force him."

Jules rubbed her arm and looked away.

"Where were you, anyway?" she said, looking into his eyes, and wondering if he was going to tell her the truth.

"Couldn't sleep," he said. He turned away from her. "Well, I'm going to go talk to Monsieur Marks and see if he could use any more help. He's doing a renovation out at that falling-down house on route de Périgueux. At least those Americans seem to have a bit of money. For now, anyway."

"Good idea," said Amelie. She smiled at her husband. She loved him so much. But also, she couldn't help feeling, in that cold January of 2009, that love was wonderful—all fine and well—but perhaps, tragically, not enough to survive on.

MOLLY HEARD a faint knock and went to the door. "My gracious, Constance," she said. "You knocked so quietly I would never have guessed it was you."

"Your detective skills are rusty," said Constance glumly.

"To be fair, you usually arrive with a bit more...fanfare."

Constance shrugged. "Make me a coffee? I could use some cheering up."

"Along with the rest of the world, it seems. Sure, come on in."

Constance stood in the front of the woodstove and baked the backs of her legs. She looked on the verge of tears.

"Here you go," said Molly, handing her a cup. "So tell me. What's going on? Is something the matter?"

"What *isn't* the matter?" said Constance, and took a large glug of the coffee.

They spent the next half hour discussing which shops had

closed, which marriages were on the point of failing, what recipes for cheap meals they had discovered.

"I don't even like beans," Constance said, making a face. "Is there…is there any good news at all?"

"The baby is due anytime," said Molly. She put her hands on her belly and smiled so broadly that Constance did too.

"Well, not to be a downer, but—okay, I already *am* a downer, I'm like the heavenly *incarnation* of a downer, so please just completely ignore everything I say—but—are you worried at all, Molly? About having a baby when everything in the world is so… hideous?"

Molly did not answer for a moment. Then she took Constance's hand and held it. "It's true that some things, as we were just saying, aren't so hot. But. But. But. It's also true that much of what has us so frightened hasn't even happened. When you got here just now—both of us jumped with both feet straight into the future, and got busy imagining how horrible everything's going to be, eating nothing but beans for eternity and all the rest of it. Well, the future isn't here yet. Things are how they are right now. And right now? We're two friends having a lovely cup of coffee together in front of a warm fire. That's pretty good—better than good, wouldn't you agree? I think the more we can focus on *right now*—instead of next week or next month—the better off we'll be."

"Okay so you've turned into some kind of monk now?"

Molly laughed.

"You got anything to eat?" said Constance quietly.

Molly jumped up—well, perhaps more like she rolled up, rather like a sea-going vessel cresting a swell—and went into the kitchen to put together a plate. Constance was no longer cleaning for Molly since there were no gîte guests, and even though the circumstances were obviously beyond her control, still, Molly felt guilty about taking away her friend's job. The idea of Constance going hungry even for a second filled Molly with all kinds of feelings: fury at the bankers who had brought this state of affairs on, anxiety that her own larder might not stay full forever—in short, she was sent straight into the terrifying future that only the moment before she had insisted they ignore.

In a few minutes, Molly set down a plate with slices of *jambon*, olives, and a hefty hunk of Cantal. Constance fell on it as though she hadn't eaten in days, which was not exactly the case.

"Mfph," said Constance.

"Indeed," said Molly. "How's Thomas?"

"He's good."

Molly looked askance. Good? Since when did Constance not have some kind of story about Thomas—how other women were trying to steal him, how he had taken her cycling which was a nightmare, how besotted she was with him and was he ever going to propose or was she going to die a spinster?

"Anybody die lately?" Constance asked.

"Not that I know of."

"Well, that's some good news right there."

"Yes," said Molly, admittedly feeling a bit conflicted. It wasn't that she hoped for someone to get murdered so she could investigate it—she certainly wasn't that craven—but at the same time, she had learned about herself that the peace and quiet she had moved to France looking for wasn't exactly what she wanted after all.

She had found out that she very much liked to feel useful. And so far, the best way she had found to be useful was helping put criminals where they belonged.

I wonder if the financial pressure will lead to some burglaries, she thought, and then shook her head and tried to stop guessing what the future would bring.

❧ 4 ❧

Edmond Nugent, award-winning *pâtissier* and owner of pâtisserie Bujold, slid the enormous tray of almond croissants out of the oven, deeply inhaling the buttery aroma as he did so.

His life was a life of routine, as it was for all bakers. Up at three a.m., check the sourdough, make a batch of puff pastry, check inventory.

Make custard, make rolls, put rolls in oven, form baguettes for next rising.

Grind pistachios. Make icing, two kinds. Take trays of croissants from the cooler, where they had an overnight rising, and put them in the oven.

Set timers as he went along. Sweep.

Allow himself a moment's rest, sitting on a stool next to the cash register, enjoying a *petit café* and a day-old croissant.

Before the debacle in the U.S., there were rarely any leftover croissants. Edmond could practically cook as many trays as he wanted, and somehow they would all get sold, all get gobbled up by a steady stream of customers that began the minute the shop opened at six-thirty in the morning. He had considered buying another oven, the demand was that solid, despite the size of the village not growing much. But it was not—understatement of the year—solid any longer. He never would have guessed that croissants, that staple of France, would fall into the category of luxury item. He only charged a euro-fifty! But the reality was, demand had fallen off, and now he sustained his business by selling baguettes.

Yes, baguettes, too, were cheap, and his were very, very good. And of course, Edmond treasured his baguettes and was proud of the perfectly shattered crust, the soft and chewy inside, the adaptability for making sandwiches, slathering with butter, or mopping up sauces, making croutons, toast, or a base for virtually anything one could think of to put on a plate or in one's mouth.

But baking almost nothing but baguettes, day after day after day? It is murderous to the spirit, Edmond thought, sitting on his stool by the register since the immediate tasks were finished for the moment and there were no customers to talk to. He loved experimenting with new pastries, trying combinations no one else had thought of, and amazing his customers with these innovations. Sometimes he used an unexpected ingredient, like sumac. Sometimes the shape was new, sometimes the texture.

Sometimes he liked his pastries to surprise...and sometimes to give the comfort of familiarity.

With baguettes, the wondrous glory of them was that you knew exactly what you were getting, no surprises. Which was a lovely thing, the comfort of an expectation being met, without fail. However, there was no room for innovation, which made for a boring professional life.

Edmond sighed a grand sigh and took the last sip of his coffee. He tapped his fingertips on the counter and thought of another favorite pastime of Frenchmen, after eating bread....

He had expected to be married with a family by now. And here he was, on the downward slope of his life—unfortunate and difficult to face, but that was the reality—living alone in his small apartment, with no one else to care for and love. He couldn't even have a dog because his hours didn't allow it. And a cat...well, he wasn't that desperate.

But lately—incredibly—his fortunes had changed.

A flicker of desire had sparked in the most unlikely place. Not only desire, but a warmth in his heart—and that warmth was beginning to burn hot.

Edmond allowed himself to get so deep into memories of her and what had happened at their last meeting that he nearly burned the croissants.

"WELL, look at you in a brown study!" boomed Lapin as he burst through the door of pâtisserie Bujold, seeing Edmond staring off into space.

Edmond leapt up from the stool, his face turning pink. "A person is allowed a break." He sniffed. "I have been up since three, a time of the morning I don't believe your aged carcass has witnessed lately. If ever."

"We're the same age, so I don't know about throwing around 'aged,'" said Lapin, grinning.

"The usual?"

"*Bien sûr*," said Lapin. "Actually I'll have a Napoléon too. I'm feeling...I don't know...."

"Everyone's depressed. You would think that would lead to more pastry-eating, as it has in your case. But alas, that has not been the widespread effect. We live in a village filled with penny-pinchers with a great deal of resolve, I'm sad to say."

"Sorry to hear it, my friend. As you can imagine, my shop isn't doing much business either, except for the most worn and utilitarian pieces. Just had a fellow come in, wanted a bed—and believe me, I have some beautiful beds, Louis Quinze, with gorgeous carved headboards, or a sturdy, gleaming brass for something less rococo...but the fellow took the cheapest one, low-grade materials, barely even looked at it. The economy has killed people's sense of aesthetics, just killed it dead."

"I'm selling nearly half as many croissants as last summer. *Half.* And the pastries? *Mon Dieu!*" said Edmond, shaking his head and putting his hand to his forehead.

"Well, I've been thinking this whole thing—I mean the financial mess—maybe just maybe—could be a gold mine for me, in disguise."

Edmond brought a plate with the Napoleon and a cup of coffee to a table and Lapin sat down.

"Mm?" he said.

"Well, what happens when money is tight? And you're working the same job, your salary or whatever isn't going to change, so maybe you look around your house, and you see that console table that you got from Great-Aunt Lucille and you think 'I never liked Great-Aunt Lucille, she was an overbearing, bossy old crank, I think I'll see what I can get for it.' See what I mean?"

"You're thinking you'll scoop up a lot of inventory in the down times and then sell it when things turn back around?"

"Exactly!" said Lapin, beaming at the prospect.

Edmond shrugged. "You might be a little over-optimistic, Lapin. This village is beloved to me, of course, but I doubt it's packed with that many hidden treasures."

Lapin scowled. "We had the jewels from the Château that one time."

Edmond shrugged again. They sat, looking out of the window. No one walked by.

"I still lament that desk," said Lapin.

"What Molly calls the 'jillion-dollar desk'?"

"The very one. I finally did sell it, to some Americans who fell in love with the idea of the forgery. But not for a jillion dollars, or even close."

Edmond got up and checked the croissants.

MADAME TESSIER KNOWS ALL

"What about Lili Lagasse?" said Lapin. "I heard she has a necklace, worth a fortune."

"Says who?"

"You never heard that?"

"Well...yes, I have," said Edmond begrudgingly. "But that doesn't mean I believe it."

"I think I'll pay her a visit. If she does have it, maybe she'll be proud enough to want to show it off to me."

"Is it that thing she wears, that has the odd little ball hanging on a gold chain?"

"Edmond, I'm shocked. You go around looking down old ladies' dresses?"

"Get out of here, you old goat," said Edmond, laughing. "You know perfectly well what I'm talking about."

"Well, if *I* had a really valuable necklace, I'd wear it all the time too," said Lapin. "That way, you'd have to knock me on the head to get your mitts on it. Much better than letting it languish in a safe-deposit box or some such."

Edmond waved goodbye and went into the back, and Lapin left the pâtisserie. He stood for a long moment on the sidewalk trying to decide whether he should go back to his shop, or to Madame Lagasse's. It would be so delightful to come back and tell Edmond how wrong he was about the necklace—and the anticipation of doing so led him to take off across the village, hoping he had the correct address in mind.

5

"Well, I don't understand why you think it's a bad idea. Americans do it all the time," said Molly, hands on hips.

"We're not in America," said Ben with a shrug. "I'm not saying you shouldn't, or I forbid it, or anything like that. I'm only...look, people have babies in France! There's an accepted way of doing things. You don't have to figure everything out from scratch or borrow all kinds of American practices. Everything will be fine."

"I'm only talking about getting a group of women with babies together, so we can give each other support and have a few laughs. I don't see the harm."

"I didn't say anything about harm. Only that I've never heard of anyone around here doing such a thing. I'm not criticizing you. By all means, Molly, do what you like! I'm going to go check the rathole in the pigeonnier."

"Didn't you just do that a few days ago? Have you seen any indication any rats are still getting in?"

"Just keeping an eye out," said Ben.

He was annoyed, she could hear it in his tone. And she was annoyed too. Molly opened her mouth to say something but

27

managed to stop herself, and Ben slipped out the terrace door without another word.

They were both on edge, of course they were. The longed-for and completely unexpected baby was due any moment; they were going to be new parents and had no idea what to expect. Oh of course, they expected to be joyful—but they were also, rather embarrassingly to themselves, a little bit scared.

Molly decided to talk to Frances, so she hopped on the scooter and sped away—helmet on, at a low-to-moderate speed—and within minutes was ringing her friend's doorbell.

There was bedlam inside.

Luka was having another bout of digestive problems and the apartment's smell was...unfortunate. Frances hadn't had a good night's sleep in recent memory and looked haggard and on her last nerve.

"This isn't the vision of motherhood I was hoping for," said Molly, managing to scrounge up a halfhearted laugh.

"It is dire," said Frances, shaking her head. "This motherhood thing...it is absolutely *dire*. We had no idea what our mothers went through! It's like running marathons back-to-back and then standing on your head while cooking soufflés and learning a new language. It's—"

"Here, let me take her." Molly reached for the squalling Luka and cradled her across her round belly. She murmured to her, jostling her gently, but the baby screwed up her red face and shrieked even louder.

"Gotta say, if you had been able to quiet her right down, I might have jumped out the window and run away and never come back." Frances had to raise her voice over the crying. "I feel like such a failure. She's been at this for a solid hour. Plus, in the middle of the night. Wit's end doesn't begin to cover it."

"Let's go outside," said Molly, and quickly they put Luka in a little jacket and hat, slid her into the carrier, and went out. The air was cold and the sky overcast.

And just like that, Luka stopped crying. She looked up at Molly, blinked, then closed her eyes and fell asleep before they had gotten to the end of the block.

"Thanks," said Frances in a small voice. She reached her hand to Luka's face and smiled at her daughter. "Did we really punish our mothers this way? And...why am I so bad at this?"

"Yes, and you aren't. It's just...it's hard. Always has been. You've got this little person who needs you every second of the day and night and can't tell you what the matter is." Molly felt her stomach drop at her own words. "Honestly, Franny? I'm terrified."

Frances started laughing. "You? You can't fool me, Molls, you're not scared of anything. Never have been. Not when you were a kid and in really big trouble for doing something terrible. Still not scared."

"I never did anything terrible."

Frances just laughed. They walked for a few blocks, Molly feeling the weight of the baby on her chest and finding it a very nice feeling. "I've got an idea. Ben thinks it's a bad idea, but he's wrong."

"Of course he is."

"So there's you with Luka, and me, any minute now, with Baby X. I was thinking—partly from seeing you go through it—mothering a baby is so hard and exhausting and lonely. What if we had a group of mothers who could hang out together? The babies will still cry, but at least we'd have company. Of people who really get it."

"Sure, I guess. It does seem like a lot of the time when Luka is really upset, having someone else pick her up helps. Like the newness distracts her for a second and she forgets to be miserable. Do you know any other new mothers?"

"No. But we could ask around, if you think it's a decent idea?"

"Yeah, okay, Molly, sure. I don't think it'll be a magic bullet, but I'm willing to give it a try. I'm so beaten down at this point,

NELL GODDIN

I'd agree to rent some penguins and build an igloo if it would keep Luka happy. So a mother's group? Why not?"

It was not a rousing endorsement of the idea, but good enough for Molly, and she decided to swing by the épicerie on her way home to consult Ninette, who was almost as good a source of village intel as the formidable Madame Tessier.

"I FEEL LIKE A TEENAGER CUTTING SCHOOL," said Edmond, leaning over to kiss the neck of his beloved. "I never leave Pâtisserie Bujold at this hour."

She giggled, then took his chin in her hand and kissed him hard on the mouth.

They heard footsteps on the sidewalk and sprang apart.

Madame Tessier came into the épicerie, eyes bright, her graying hair permed and bouncing. "Well, bonjour Edmond, bonjour Ninette!" she said, looking from one to the other.

They bonjoured back, making only fleeting eye contact.

"So you don't have any sugar sprinkles at all?" said Edmond to Ninette.

"I'm afraid not. Don't you order them wholesale from somewhere?" said Ninette, dropping down out of sight to straighten up something on the shelf under the cash register.

Madame Tessier peered over the counter. "Sugar sprinkles?" she said to Edmond, eyebrows raised.

"All right then, I'll have to change my pastry plan," said Edmond. "Au revoir, you two," he added, on his way out.

Madame Tessier watched Ninette with amusement. She hadn't actually seen anything between them, but she was expert at reading a room and she knew there was *something*. She had heard the note of falsity in Edmond's voice. And the more nervous Ninette behaved, the surer Madame Tessier was.

Edmond, the old bachelor, and Ninette, the spinster—had known each other their entire lives—would wonders never cease?

"Got a problem down there?" Madame Tessier asked, looking at the top of Ninette's head.

"Just neatening up. I don't like mess," said Ninette. "I'm not used to seeing you without Madame Lagasse on a Wednesday, is she ill?"

Madame Tessier shrugged. "I'm headed over to see her after this, she didn't answer her phone, probably stayed up too late watching one of those detective shows she adores. I've been feeling the chill, as we all have, and so I thought, I know what I need, some cocoa! It's been an age since I've had any. Maybe since I was a child."

She bustled down the aisle to fetch the cocoa, while wondering just how far the situation with Edmond had gotten. Was it simply a mild flirtation? Or was it possible she was completely off-base and they were only old friends?

The inquiring mind of Madame Tessier wanted to know.

She was a scrupulous sort of gossip, with strict ideas about what she was allowed to pass on to others and what she was not. So even though she would bet a hundred euros that Edmond and Ninette were having a romance—against all odds, at their age!— she did not yet have proof, and so would keep her suspicions to herself.

For the moment.

❧ 6 ❧

January 18

The night was cold and Lili Lagasse was sleeping deeply under an eiderdown quilt she had made herself many years ago. She was lucky to be a good sleeper as she got older; many of her friends continually lamented that they were not, and she was grateful not to be among them.

Despite this, just before two a.m. her eyes flew open. What was that noise? Instantly she was wide awake.

Not only did she sleep well, Madame Lagasse still had her hearing. She heard—unmistakably—the sound of the front door closing, the lock clicking back into place. And then, footsteps. Someone coming upstairs.

Lili listened. She listened with wonder rather than fright. In a flash—the instant she had awakened to the sound of someone jiggling the lock on the front door—she had known what was about to happen. And she did not fight against it.

He was taking his time.

She felt a chill go through her, but strangely, fear was not the main thing she was feeling. It was...curiosity. Who would dare break into her house? Who was after her necklace?

She reached one hand to her neck and caressed the chain with the gold cross, then took the filigreed ball with the jewel inside between her fingertips. She murmured to herself, a prayer. Tears sprang to her eyes, not tears of sorrow but a much broader swath of emotion—she was feeling everything, in that last moment before death—joy, fear, humility, regret, love—

She waited.

The creak of the stair, almost melodic.

She found that time did a funny thing when you were about to die. It did not rush by, as she would have expected, but slowed down to a snail's pace, which made her think of escargot, one of her favorite dishes, and for a moment—a long, stretched-out moment—she reminisced about her favorite dishes and considered how much pleasure they had given her over a decently long life. She could almost taste the garlic and parsley and butter.

She thought of her great friend, Hélène Tessier, who had shared many of these meals with her.

She thought of eating a bowl of fresh peaches with whipped cream, her favorite since childhood, and imagined licking the whipped cream off the top.

When the man reached her door and pushed it open, he saw Lili smiling, with one hand at her throat, holding the jewel.

Lili watched the door swing open, so slowly it was as though her last moments were stretched out to an hour or more, she was still practically tasting the whipped cream, and marveling at how unafraid she was. It felt to her as though what was happening was preordained to happen, and there was no chance of changing the outcome, which allowed her to witness it and go through it free of torment.

"Ah, bonsoir," she said, with a bit of bravado, on the verge of laughing because she understood how ridiculous it was to greet politely the man who was there to steal her most precious necklace and who was going to kill her once he had it.

He nodded, momentarily confused, and then strode to the side of the bed, his expression distorted by the violence he had in mind.

❧ 7 ❧

"Bonjour, Ninette!" said Molly, bursting into the épicerie in all her pregnant glory.

"Bonjour, Molly. My heavens, you look about to explode at any second."

Molly grinned. "Doc says anytime now, I'm so excited!—and also terrified." She started to go on but remembered Ninette had never married and had no children, and thought it might be rude to natter on about pregnancy and childbirth.

She stood for a moment, distracted by a vision of all the groups: people with children, people who have children but didn't want them, people who don't have children and did want them, people who don't have children because they didn't want them... and of course sometimes people start in one group and hop to another, as Molly knew as well as anyone.

"Molly?" said Ninette. "Did you want something?"

"Yes! Sorry. I find lately that my tendency to daydream has gotten a little out of hand. I came to ask you, since you have your finger on the pulse of the village—do you know anyone with a new baby, or about to have one? I'm looking to connect with others in the same boat. I know about Selma," she added with a big grin, "but is there anyone else?"

Ninette looked up at the ceiling while she thought. "It's true, nearly everyone in the village comes in here, over the course of a month. I think Madame Tessier would like to set up a winter outpost in here, so she can gather information where it's warm," she said, with a laugh. "But okay, let me think, babies, babies…I don't know of any besides Luka, whom of course you already know. There's Amelie Bresson. Lives over on rue Camus? You know her?"

"No, I don't. I'm continually shocked at how many people this village can hide who are new to me."

"It's not that small," said Ninette with a sniff.

Molly heard the door open behind her and felt a blast of cold air on her legs.

"Bonjour, Edmond," said Ninette, her face composed.

Molly said her bonjour and looked at Edmond curiously. "What in the world are you doing away from Pâtisserie Bujold?" she said.

"Am I not allowed freedom of movement, like any other civilian?"

"No, of course you absolutely are not. You should be imprisoned in your shop during the entire day and night, making all the treats we require for our happiness," said Molly.

Edmond made a face and turned to Ninette. "Do you have any sugar sprinkles?" he asked. "I want to make something new but to my surprise I don't have enough sprinkles."

Later on, Molly laughed about Edmond and the sprinkles, and how she had simply accepted his question as legitimate instead of understanding it as the ridiculously weak cover that it was. She blamed her obtuseness on her pregnancy, because how many balls was a person supposed to juggle in the air at once, after all? She couldn't be attuned to every nuance, all the time. There were limits, even for Molly.

. . .

AMELIE HAD ALLOWED Laurent to stay home from school for yet another day. The boy hated school so desperately, and his hatred was not like the usual sort of distaste that children often have for school or being told what to do. It was more visceral. It was as though his small body—not his conscious mind—knew that school was all wrong for him, and consequently he would put up any amount of fuss to be excused from it.

"You know you're going to get me in so much trouble with *Le Maitre*," she said, ruffling his hair. Laurent cringed at her touch and she drew her hand back.

"Put it back," he whispered. "Put it back, put it back, put it back."

"So you say," said Amelie, sitting down next to him on his bedroom floor. "How about these guys?" she said, picking up a toy soldier in a red helmet. "What's his name?"

Laurent shook his head.

"What does he do? What's his job, then?"

"He shoots," said Laurent. He paused, then picked up another soldier and a small plastic dinosaur. He put them in his mother's hands. "Make them talk," he said. He collected some pieces of train track and put them in a shoebox along with some train cars.

Amelie felt a twinge in her belly, which she knew to be advance notice of labor—but the event could be many days away, even weeks—at least that was how it happened last time, so she wasn't worried. She breathed in, then out; the twinge didn't really hurt. She wondered if Jules had managed to get any work from the Americans out on route de Périgueux.

After the twinge passed, she picked up the dinosaur and marched it over the rug towards Laurent. "Here I come," she said in a squeaky voice. "I want to have a party. Do you know anyone we could invite?"

Laurent looked at her with an expression of disgust. "That's not what he would say."

Amelie sighed.

"Do it again," said Laurent. "Make him talk the right way."

"You say that as though I know what the right way is. If there's a right way for dinosaurs to talk, maybe you could show me what that is?"

Laurent's face was stony. He shook his head and then turned his back, putting the soldiers and dinosaurs in a row, and all of them, plus a number of pirates and robots, stayed in his bedroom for another half hour, saying nothing.

$\gtrsim$ 8 $\precsim$

After his conversation with Edmond, and then getting another cup of coffee at the hole-in-wall across the street, and organizing the display in his window for the second time in an attempt to draw in new customers, Lapin felt restless and out of sorts.

He wanted some good news for a change.

And so he was led, impulsively, to put the CLOSED sign on the shop door and take off for rue Tabac.

He understood that it would be rude of him to bang on Lili Lagasse's door and ask her point blank about the valuable necklace and how much she wanted for it. It wasn't as though they were close friends, where sometimes you could go too far and then be forgiven for it. Perhaps he could figure out a sneaky way of getting the information out of her. First, he needed to know the state of her finances before making an offer; obviously that would be crucial for how good a bargain he might be able to strike. This was only a first pass, and if Lili wasn't forthcoming, for whatever reason, he could always revisit the subject some other day.

So often in these matters, the long game with a patient attitude wins the day, Lapin thought to himself.

There was absolutely no hurry, he added to himself to underscore the point, as he arrived on Madame Lagasse's doorstep and rang the bell. His mind was, of course, on the necklace, which Lili wore all the time, though he had never seen more than the chain upon which it hung, as the bauble itself was usually tucked into her décolletage, hidden under her clothing. He tried to remember if anyone had reported seeing it up close, and described it, but couldn't remember. Which made him think that no one had, Lapin being especially tuned to such pieces of information—he would certainly have tucked such a description away for another time.

It is possible, he thought with a sinking feeling, that the existence of the necklace was only a rumor with no basis in fact—that there was no necklace at all, outside of the imaginations of chatty villagers. With a grimace, he shook off that thought.

He rang the bell a second time. To his ear, the bell sounded only like the faintest tinkle, so he went to knock. Still no answer. And it was then—in a strange sort of flash that he felt in the center of his chest, as he described it later—that he had the feeling something was very wrong at the house of Lili Lagasse.

He went to the window and tried to look in, but the curtains were pulled and he couldn't see much of anything. Lapin's heart was racing. He trotted down the narrow alley between the Lagasse house and the neighbor's—it was something of a tight fit, bringing on a wave of claustrophobia, and Lapin's heart beat even faster—and he came out in the back of Lagasse's house, into a small garden.

The garden was surrounded by a stone wall about five feet high. Scrambling over it were climbing roses, the leaves dull from the cold. Lapin tried the back door; it was locked.

He peered through the window on the back door, into the

MADAME TESSIER KNOWS ALL

kitchen. It looked unremarkable, nothing out of place, a few dishes in the drainer.

Lapin started to go back down the alley but then stopped again. He was not a superstitious man, not a man who believed in the supernatural or anything of the sort. But he felt in that moment—something he never told anyone, ever, even allowing everyone to believe that he had broken into Lagasse's house searching for that stupid necklace—he believed something tapped on his shoulder.

It tapped with some insistence. And the thought came into his mind that he needed to get inside that house, no matter how.

Lapin did not hesitate but looked around and found a brick that Madame Lagasse probably used as a doorstop when the weather was warm. Lapin used his coat sleeve to wrap around his hand, then picked up the brick and punched out the window on the door, grimacing at the sound of broken glass, which was sure to raise an alarm.

He dropped the brick, reached in through the jagged hole, and unlocked the door.

For a few seconds, he waited, listening. Then he turned the latch and went inside.

"Lili?" he called.

The house was still. It was cold.

Too cold, thought Lapin. As though someone had turned the heat down before bed and then never turned it back up when morning came.

That was the moment—which he never told anyone about either—when he felt the second sharp stab of anxiety.

"Lili!" he called.

Quickly he glanced in the living room. Empty.

He ran upstairs, arriving at the bedroom door, his chest heaving.

Madame Lagasse was in bed, lying still, the covers pulled up to her chin.

Lapin held his breath. Slowly he walked in. "Lili? Are you all right?"

When he got closer, he could see by the color of her skin that Lili Lagasse had breathed her last. He stood by her bed, blinking back sudden tears and feeling a wave of sorrow even though she had never been more to him than an acquaintance.

🍂 9 🍂

Florian Nagrand, coroner of Castillac, arrived at the house in under an hour. His reluctant assistant, Matthias de Clare, was with him.

They stood at Lili Lagasse's bedside, making visual observations only while waiting for Chief Charlot to arrive. Lapin, shaken by the sight of the body, had taken off the second they arrived, wanting to get back to the safety and comfort of his shop.

"She looks peaceful," said Matthias. "By the way, did you say you had asked Peter Bonheur about moving me to a different position?"

"Supposedly she owned some valuable jewelry," said Florian. "That's the rumor anyway, and all I know about her. Never married. Quiet."

"People in this village know way too much about each other," grumbled Matthias.

"People know things because people talk. If she didn't want anyone to know about the jewelry, she didn't have to say one word about it. Could have kept it as her little secret. I wouldn't be at all surprised to find out that Lapin was here sniffing around after it."

Matthias shrugged. "And about Bonheur?"

"For God's sake, man, I've told you a hundred times, any move is very unlikely to happen, not these days. Best thing you can do, in these uncertain times? Put your head down, do your work, wait for a more propitious moment to ask for favors. You've got to be patient. You don't know Peter Bonheur like I do. Believe me, he is not going to put himself to any trouble on your account. Or anyone else's, unless there's something in it for him."

They heard the Chief come in the front door.

"Up here, Chief!" called Florian, and then he stepped aside to make room for her and Paul-Henri.

"She looks so peaceful," said Paul-Henri.

"That's what I said," said Matthias.

"Gentlemen," said Chief Charlot. "Do your jobs if you please, and spare us the sentimentality. Can you identify her?"

Paul-Henri looked as though he'd been slapped. "I was most certainly not being sentimental," he said. "The victim's name is Lili Lagasse. My observation was simply that it appears Madame Lagasse died in her sleep, and there is no sign of violence."

"Any relation to Léo Lagasse, of the Bergerac gendarmerie?"

"Not that I'm aware," said Florian.

Charlot peeled the eiderdown quilt back. All four of them reacted in some way—Matthias gasped, Florian's and Paul-Henri's eyes widened, Charlot's eyes narrowed.

"Still think that?" said Charlot.

Madame Lagasse's facial expression, of course, had not changed—but now her neck was exposed, and they could see bruises in several places, and a thin line of dark bruising just above her Adam's apple.

"Looks like someone tried to yank a chain right through her neck," said Florian. "And these bruises along the side appear to be in the shape of thumbprints."

"So peaceful," said Charlot, with heavy sarcasm.

She stepped away from the bed and called Bergerac, asking them to send forensics on the double.

"Don't touch anything," she barked to the others.

Florian scowled. "Wrong side of the bed this morning?" he said.

"Of all people, I shouldn't have to explain to you that the gendarmerie and your coroner's office have taken hits to reputation lately. So let's be professional about this, no mistakes, no corner-cutting, and keep emotions out of it. If you *please*," she added.

Matthias rolled his eyes to Paul-Henri out of sight of Chief Charlot, and Paul-Henri started to laugh but turned it into a cough just in time.

"Take her to the morgue and do the autopsy right away, no lollygagging. The faster you get me the report with the cause of death, the better. And—it goes without saying—not a word to anyone." Charlot felt compelled to say this though she knew they would ignore her, and by lunchtime the entire village would be abuzz and that damned Molly Sutton would be sniffing around where she didn't belong.

Unless, she thought—with a prayer—Sutton pops out that baby. A baby should take her off our hands for a little while, right?

THE HOUSE on route de Périgueux was beautiful, or at least it had once been, made of golden Dordogne limestone with pleasing proportions, tucked against a small hill. Now the left wing was a jumble of crumbled stone with no roof, and the right wing had an alarming sag at one corner. Jules could see at a glance that there was plenty of opportunity for work, and he allowed himself to feel hopeful.

A man dressed in chinos and a flannel shirt stood looking at the house, and turned when he heard Jules coming.

"Bonjour!" Jules said, sticking out his hand in what he believed was the American way.

"Bonjour to you!" said Johnny Marks, owner of the crumbled

house. "What can I do for you?" His French was quite good and Jules was relieved about that.

"I'm Jules Bresson. Looking for work, and I'm guessing you could use some help," he said. "Part-time, whatever suits you. I've done plenty of roofing," he added, not entirely truthfully.

Johnny stroked his chin, gazing at his house. "She's a mess, isn't she," he said, grinning. "My wife thinks I've lost my mind. I bought the place on a whim, you know—we weren't even looking for a house, just happened to drive through Castillac, saw it...do you believe in fate, Jules?"

Jules shrugged.

"I keep telling her, look, it was built in the early 1700s. That's an awful long time ago—before America was even a country! And sure, she looks a little ragged right now. But she's still standing! More or less. To me, that's quite a recommendation. It means we don't have to hurry, feeling desperately rushed. The house has endurance. She has resilience. And so we can take our time as we make repairs thoughtfully."

Jules did not know what to make of this speech. Did the man want to start repairs or not?

"Put another way, I spent most of my money just buying the place, so I'm afraid I'm going to have to do the work myself, at least for now. The central section is watertight at least, and we've got a woodstove that keeps us warm enough. It's a bit like camping, but my dear, understanding wife is thankfully up for adventure."

Jules and Johnny stood with their arms crossed, looking at the house. Jules's apartment was the cheapest Castillac offered, but he didn't think he would trade with Johnny, not with the roof looking the way it did. He thought it would be a good idea to offer some kind of compliment. "It's a handsome house," he said, awkwardly. "Or it will be," he couldn't help adding.

"Well, my income situation...without going into a lot of boring personal detail...my income fluctuates rather a lot. Some months are lean, and others fat. I'm in sales, you know what that's like, feast or famine, no rhyme or reason to it. How about I get your number and if I have a good month and have a little extra cash, I'll give you a call? You've got some construction skills, do you?"

Jules nodded, though the nod was perhaps a bit of an exaggeration. As a teenager, he had helped his father repair a shed roof. That roof had been just a rectangle of tin, not clay tiles, but learning new things was what the internet was for, so Jules wasn't worried. He gave Johnny Marks his number and headed back to the village, still with no work, his mind on his impossible debt as it almost always was.

THE MINUTE they got back to the coroner's office, Florian had hurried Madame Lagasse and Matthias straight to the autopsy room. Matthias was glad he had managed to text Molly the details since once back at the office, he was not allowed even a moment to himself.

"Is it that baby coming that has you so, uh, how should I put it—conscientious, lately?" he groused to Florian.

"Might as well get the autopsy out of the way," said Florian cheerfully. "Then we can enjoy our lunch in peace, knowing that we've completed our duties like the good public servants we are. It's a simple case, at least as far as we're concerned," said Florian. "Now tell me, what do you see?" He gestured at the body of Lili Lagasse, laid out on the examining table.

"Finger marks on her neck." Matthias closed his eyes and shuddered. "It's so cold in here, can't we turn the heat up a little?"

Florian did not dignify this with an answer. "Yes, and even the nails made marks here, and here," said Florian. "You are probably not aware that in some cases of strangulation, the bruises and contusions do not show up until the next day. That could well be the case here, since we did not collect the body until several days after the time of death."

49

Matthias shuddered again.

"Good thing it's been so cold—"

"Please! I don't need any extra details, really I don't! If this is a simple case as you say, let's fill out the forms and be done with it, then."

"You can't rush training, Matthias. Now, please. One more thing before we go to lunch."

"Don't talk about lunch in here!"

Florian smirked. "You'll be interested to know that finger-prints can, in fact, be recovered from skin. So if that woman from Bergerac forensics knew what she was about, right here is all the evidence anyone would need to convict a murderer. You can't exactly make an argument that your fingerprints are on a stran-gled person's neck by chance!" Florian chuckled. "Now come on, get the camera ready. Charlot needs whatever we can give her as soon as possible—and if we drag our feet, believe me, she'll be over here hounding us to our last nerve." Florian gave him a quick smile and adjusted Madame Lagasse's arm so that she was lying symmetrically on the table.

Matthias tried not to make a face. Cheerful Florian was way, way worse than grouchy Florian. And Matthias hated the autopsy room. It was cold, all the surfaces hard. The whole enterprise made his stomach heave.

"Maybe Peter Bonheur will be pleased with my good citizen-ship when you tell him about it, and he'll move me to a position more suited to my—"

"Don't even put a big toe on that path," interrupted Florian. He walked around the table, looking carefully at the corpse of Lili Lagasse. "Take photos of her neck, front and sides," he said.

Matthias opened a drawer and took out the camera, did what he was told. He played a little game with himself, telling himself that the body was just a mannikin, stuffed with wool. But he did not fall for his own trick.

"Note the abrasions and contusions on the neck and nowhere

else," said Florian. "The ligature marks, most likely from Madame Lagasse's own necklace..."

"What is this necklace everyone is going on about?" muttered Matthias. The flash when he took the photos made them blink.

"Oh, some trinket Madame Lagasse liked to brag about. It's childish, that's my opinion on it. People like to feel they're part of a fairy tale, complete with granted wishes from a genie and instant wealth. They like to believe in magic, that a precious stone will save them from...well, I would say what they're looking for is protection from death. Maybe that's only my line of work talking. But still, I think it's correct. What good is some valuable stone really going to do for anybody? Is it going to bring actual happiness? I don't think so."

Matthias snapped a few more pictures and put the camera down. "So this one is open-and-shut?" he said. "Strangulation, no other possibilities?"

"Now you're thinking like a coroner," said Florian. "It is true that sometimes the appearance of a specific cause of death can be quite convincing, and yet deceiving. Until we get further along in the process, we don't know much of anything, no matter how it looks. Could be that Madame Lagasse had taken an overdose of opium before the robber even entered her house. A host of causes of death are still possible, as far as we know. And that is why the process of the autopsy is always paramount," he said. "And why we cannot allow ourselves to fall prey to making assumptions, no matter how warranted they may seem."

Matthias couldn't help it: he rolled his eyes.

Florian noted the eyeroll but did not respond. Selma was nearing her due date, his baby would soon be born, and there was nothing, absolutely nothing that could dim his happiness at what was coming.

Matthias, meanwhile was praying: Please Lord, let me have another job. Any job. I will happily, gratefully be a sewer cleaner for the rest of my life. Amen.

❧ 10 ❧

"I'm undone about the whole thing, completely *undone!*"
Madame Tessier was walking back and forth in her small
living room, dabbing her eyes with a linen handkerchief, while
Molly sat in an armchair and watched her with a sympathetic
expression. "My dear, dear friend—murdered! What has
happened to this world of ours?"

"I know you were very close," she said.

"Lili and I...a lifelong friendship...we had a standing date,
every week we did our shopping at the épicerie and then lunch at
Chez Papa. These kinds of rituals are...they are the backbone of a
life, you understand?"

"Yes. I really do."

"It's the routine, the rhythm it gives. And of course, the inti-
macy. All those lunches—oh, we talked about everything under
the sun! The good, the bad, the ugly. The embarrassing. The
shameful. And of course, the wonderful things too." She sat on
the edge of the sofa and put her face in her hands. "Lili...like all of
us, she was imperfect." Madame Tessier choked out a sort of
laugh, and shook her head. "Had some blind spots, for certain.

Some complications. But a lovely, lovely heart." She bent her head and gripped the edge of the sofa.

Molly could see her shoulders shaking and felt the deep sorrow of her friend.

"I told her a million times, 'take that necklace off and put it somewhere safe!' She worked at the bank for years, you would think of all people she would understand about keeping valuable things safe. But she would just laugh. Absolutely refused. And now look. Some ruffian—no, far worse, some *murdering bastard*—excuse my language—has forced his way into her house, and robbed and killed her. What is wrong with people, Molly? Why do so many put material things ahead of people, even to the point of killing them?"

"I wish I knew."

"And this is rude of me, and selfish—but I'm not at all pleased that you're having that baby any second and won't be able to do anything to bring this particular murdering bastard to justice."

Molly shrugged. Privately, she wasn't on maternity leave. Not yet.

"This necklace—what sort of thing was it? Can you describe it to me?"

Madame Tessier waved her hand dismissively. "Oh, I don't know, some bauble Lili put great store by. She said her mother left it to her. It wasn't really a necklace, it was a...a sort of ball, made of gold, filigreed gold, and the ball opened up and there was a jewel inside, dangling from a very thin gold chain. She wore the ball on a chain around her neck, but it was a long chain, so the ball was hidden under her dress. And you know, thinking about it now—the fact that the thing was hidden probably added to the allure, you know what I mean? People didn't forget about it because most people had never actually seen the thing. Kept the curiosity alive, you know? Like an endless tease. Oh, Lili!"

"What sort of jewel was it? Did she ever show it to people?"

"Oh, she was very proud of it, no question about that. Like I said, she completely refused to consider her own safety and put it away. No, she had to wear it around her neck every single day. And also—like I said—Lili had some blind spots. And this one, oh boy. Killed her, that's what."

"You don't know what kind of jewel?"

"Like a dog with a bone, you are. What difference does it make? I think it was a ruby. She showed it to me many years ago but I don't really remember. Jewels, necklaces—not really what I'm interested in, you know? I didn't pay any attention."

"I do know," said Molly, smiling. "You're interested in people."

Madame Tessier nodded, then jumped up and began to pace again. "I don't know what to do with myself. Obviously I know Lili is dead. But some part of my mind will not accept it. Will not believe it. And I keep thinking, okay, we've gone through all this grief, this terrible thing, whew, so can she come back now?" She shook her head again. "Would you like some coffee?"

Molly patted her gargantuan belly. "I better not. Though it pains me to refuse."

"You look like you're going to have that baby right on my sofa. It would certainly be exciting but I'd really rather you not. I'm already at my limit."

Molly took this as the hint to leave that it was. She kissed Madame Tessier on both cheeks and left.

It hurt to see her friend in such pain. She felt a surge of determination that she would see the murdering bastard who killed Lili Lagasse sent to prison—baby or no baby.

THAT SURGE of determination made her hungry, so Molly's next stop was pâtisserie Bujold.

Edmond was in a state.

"What in the world?" said Molly, watching him literally wring his hands as he paced back and forth.

"My *oven*," he said, closing his eyes and putting his hands on either side of his head. "The idiot repairman keeps saying he has fixed it, but it is *not* fixed, it is overheating—just barely, you understand, but the world of pastry requires precision, Molly, not temperatures in some vague range!"

"I'm sure it does."

"I just cannot today. Just cannot."

"Cannot what?"

"Cannot anything! For heaven's sakes, I would think you of all people would be more comforting!"

"You would?"

"You, who loves pastry more than life itself!"

"Oh. Well, yes, I do. I'm sorry your oven is misbehaving. Does that mean there aren't any croissants?"

"Almond or regular?"

"I'll take whatever you got. Six. If you please."

And in a moment she had collected her little white box, paid, offered more condolences over the state of the oven, and skedaddled back into the cold. It made sense that people were on edge: a Castillacois had just been murdered, if the reports were correct, and she had no reason to think they were not. But Molly felt calm and focused. The pattern of bruises, described to her by Matthias in some detail, made it clear that the killer was intent on stealing the famous necklace. And as far as Matthias knew, no necklace was recovered from the scene.

She wondered if the robber had decided to kill Lagasse so she couldn't point the finger at him, or whether her death had been an unintended consequence of the robbery.

She wondered—

—suddenly a force unlike anything she had ever felt gripped her abdomen. She put her hands on the wall of the nearest building and stood there, holding her breath, in a state of shock.

Was this...labor?

Then, bit by bit, the force eased off. Molly stood up, straightened her back, remembering to breathe. Then she burst out laughing, because the thought she had had was: oh, I really am having a baby? This is actually real? Some part of her mind still didn't believe it was going to happen, the same as Madame Tessier not being completely able to accept the death of her friend.

At the same time—another part of her mind was resisting and frightened of the impending inevitability.

Our minds are funny, she thought, the way they try to protect us from the truth.

Molly was still holding the little white box; she was tempted to eat a croissant right there on the sidewalk while she figured out next steps. Her beloved scooter was parked, waiting—but Molly had finally, in that moment of her first real contraction, arrived at the conclusion Ben had been urging her toward for months, which was that she was in no condition to be riding any scooters.

It was freezing and the sky was gray. Molly wished she were home at La Baraque in front of the woodstove. She considered calling Ben, or Christophe's taxi. But after standing on the sidewalk for several minutes, the world began to right itself and she felt like herself again, no more contractions, and decided that the baby had only given her a wave and was not actually, not in that moment anyway, ready to be born. She could carry on as usual.

One more errand. Molly left the scooter and walked to rue Camus to introduce herself to Amelie Bresson, a prospect for the mother's group. The streets were empty. She listened to a few birds as she walked but even their songs sounded cold.

The Bressons lived in a building with two apartments; theirs was in the back. The building was a little dilapidated, but in the charming way of much of Castillac—the old stones glowing, and crumbling a bit at the edges. Molly made her way past some garbage bins and knocked on the door.

She heard Amelie's voice, then the door swung open. Amelie took in Molly's belly and grinned.

"Bonjour, Molly," she said. "I know we haven't met, but I'd recognize you anywhere. Please, come in!"

Molly smiled, a little uncomfortable at being recognized but put at ease by Amelie's warmth.

"I was just doing some housework," said Amelie, slipping off a dusty housecoat. "Can I get you anything? Some tea?"

Molly shook her head. Amelie looked to be at a similar stage in her pregnancy, which felt somehow reassuring. Ninette had mentioned a young boy but hadn't mentioned his name or age. Molly noticed a toy train next to the sofa.

The two women sat on the sofa together, almost instantly forming a connection—laughing over the indignities of pregnancy, the odd mixture of fear and relief women have when the due date gets close, the daily grind and joys of taking care of a baby. Amelie was curious about the mother's group and readily agreed to be part of it.

So that's three of us, thought Molly later, as she waited on a street corner for Ben to pick her up. I guess I'll have to ask Selma, she thought, feeling resistance to the idea for some reason. Florian would get his nose out of joint if I didn't. And anyway, four is usually better than three.

She shivered in the cold, one hand holding the little white box and the other absently rubbing her belly. She realized she should have offered Amelie a croissant and shook her head at her absent-mindedness. When the baby comes, she thought...and then shook her head. She knew from all the stories women had told her that the absent-mindedness was only going to get worse, from lack of sleep if nothing else.

A working brain is a necessity for detective work, a mean voice said to her, and she shook her head again as if to exorcise it.

Her baby was due "at any moment," the doctor had said.

But the baby was not what she was thinking about. No, as she texted Ben for a ride and walked back towards the center of the village, Molly was picturing a filigreed ball of gold, with a tiny clasp, and how it opened to reveal a round ruby, glinting in the light, hanging from a gold chain no bigger than a spider's web.

11

At the gendarmerie, Chief Charlot was giving Paul-Henri his orders.

"Now, the Lagasse case. Forensics, as you know, is painfully slow. I've tried over the years to pressure them into getting results back faster, but have not found that to be helpful. These days, with looming budget cuts—no doubt there's a backlog and a personnel shortage and nothing we can do about any of that.

"And even if forensics gives us prints, DNA, the whole shebang—the killer could have sold the necklace and be gone from France long before those results get to us. So: first thing is to track that necklace," she said. "Get on the phone, call the usual places in Périgueux and Bergerac, make some calls to Bordeaux and Ângoulème as well. These thieves can move fast and we want to do our utmost to get on it before that necklace changes hands and we lose it entirely."

"What if the thief wants to keep the necklace for himself?"

Charlot looked at Paul-Henri. A long pause. "You mean, and not sell it?"

"Yes."

"That's idiotic, Paul-Henri. Sometimes I wonder if your mother dropped you on your head."

"Or maybe the thief is experienced, a real pro—he knows we'll be making those calls, knows if he sells, he risks getting reported and nabbed—and decides to sit on it for a good long while, just tuck that necklace away, and wait to sell it until we've given up. Could wait a few years even."

Charlot narrowed her eyes at the junior officer and shook her head. "Get on the phone," she said, with a sigh.

They had searched Madame Lagasse's house thoroughly and turned up no necklace nor anything else of value. To Charlot's mind, the situation was crystal clear: Lagasse had talked about that necklace too much, word of it got to the wrong person, and that person finally decided to make sure the necklace had a change of ownership. With the shaky financial circumstances affecting nearly everyone, she guessed any number of people might have had designs on that necklace. As for the killing of Lagasse, Charlot was sure that had been accomplished to cover the tracks of the thief, because obviously what good would stealing the necklace do if Lagasse could alert the police to who had stolen it?

Paul-Henri spent the morning dutifully making calls. Charlot sat at her desk, leaning on her elbows, running through the list in her mind of Castillac's less principled members, and then jumped up and went to pay a few of them a visit.

12

He was freezing and wanted to go home, wanted more than anything to enter his home and experience the pleasure of Amelie's warm greeting, then stand by the fire watching Laurent play with his toys, confident that his family was happy and well taken care of.

But Jules knew these were wishes, nothing but fantasy. He couldn't go home until...until what? He had found some way to bring in some money? Found some way to redeem himself, to be able to face his wife with an open, guiltless heart?

How was any of that possible now?

He thought of his son and his chest constricted. For several years now, Laurent had struggled with almost everything, including simply playing, which Jules would have thought natural to every child. The boy was, for lack of a precise or medical way to say it, tormented in some way, almost never happy, even though his mother did her very best, which in Amelie's case was exceptional. But nothing she did seemed to help very much, or for very long.

Instead of turning down rue Camus, Jules kept walking, as

NELL GODDIN

though the movement of his legs would bring new answers to his problems.

The night at Madame Lagasse's house had obviously gone very, very wrong. And he understood that there was nothing he could do to fix any of that. It was too late. All he could do was try to figure out the next step to take, a step in the right direction for once. Jules was a man who, despite his circumstances, had an optimistic nature, so when he had an idea, he often believed it would be the solution to everything—and so both the night at Madame Lagasse's house and the attempt to get hired by Johnny Marks had surprised him when they failed. And the disappointment at these failures was that much more acute, because he had believed in the ideas and in himself right up to the moment when everything fizzled into nothing.

Worse than nothing, he thought, seeing Lili Lagasse in his mind, every detail of her nightgown, her hair, and the tiny pink roses on her sheets. He stood on the cold, empty street and put his face in his hands.

AMELIE WAS MAKING LUNCH. She was in the phase of pregnancy during which eating is a distinct pleasure, and so she smiled at the plates of food as she arranged them: some slices of dry sausage, thick slices of Tomme, a small cluster of grapes. A baguette to share, and a pot of Normandy butter.

Jules had told her not to try to save money on food, that in her condition she needed nourishment more than anything else, and so did Laurent, who had sometimes dramatic problems with his digestion. Amelie was grateful, though she found small ways to economize that needn't be shared with her husband.

"Laurent, *à table!*" she called.

He was in his parents' bedroom, going through their drawers. It was a thing he did, a habit, and neither Jules nor Amelie could figure out his reasons or devise a way to stop him. It seemed as though he were searching for something, something he couldn't even name but which he would know when he finally saw it.

The Bressons did not have a lot of furniture. In the bedroom, there was a bureau with four drawers; Laurent found nothing but clothes in them and so he searched those less often. On each side of the bed was a small table, each with its own drawer. On his father's side, he found some toothpicks, that was all. On his mother's side, a small pot of ointment, some hairpins, a cotton handkerchief.

He took out the handkerchief and smelled it. He inhaled again. Then he put the handkerchief back and started to close the drawer.

"Laurent!" said his mother from the doorway, and he startled violently. "I've told you a thousand times to keep out of those drawers! There is nothing in there for you, nothing to interest a child! All of your toys are in your room, where they belong. Now come on, it's time to eat."

With a sigh, she hustled the boy into the kitchen and into his chair. Why is it that motherhood is all about repetition, she wondered. I say the same things to Laurent, day in and day out. Is it the same for all mothers? On some days, it felt unbearable.

She slid into her chair and ate a piece of sausage, trying to smile at her son, and feeling glad that Molly Sutton had invited her to this odd thing she was calling a mother's group. Maybe it will be just the thing, Amelie thought, while also thinking that the piece of *Trappe d'Échourgnac* she was eating was the best piece of cheese she had ever eaten in her life.

Laurent nibbled at a piece of sausage. Amelie could read his lips: he wasn't making any sound, but saying, "Put it back, put it back, put it back" in what felt to her like an endless, meaningless loop.

She rubbed her eyes, took a deep breath, and wondered when Jules was coming home.

❧ 13 ❧

"It is difficult, as you can well imagine, for me to leave pâtisserie Bujold overnight," Edmond said. "Even though, chérie, what you describe is delectable, positively glorious. I have never spent a night away from the shop, not even once since the doors opened fourteen years ago." He reached a finger to the tip of her nose and gave it a boop.

"Just think," Ninette said, eyes bright. "First of all—*privacy*. No villagers coming through the door any minute. We could really and truly relax. Enjoy each other," she added, with a slow smile, tilting her head down and looking up at him.

To Edmond's great pleasure, he saw a blush color Ninette's cheeks.

"I've invited you over many times," he murmured. "It's true that I have to go to sleep very early—"

Ninette laughed. "So early there's not really any point, I don't close up here until six-thirty."

"What has happened to us?" he laughed. "We are old, that's what, and cannot let go of practical considerations. If we were still twenty, what outstandingly pleasurable mischief might we have gotten up to?" Ninette laughed with him and for the moment, they did feel twenty. "I just...again, your proposal is wonderful, it's magnificent! But...I don't think there is a single soul in the village I could trust to run things in my absence."

"What if you simply closed for a day? Or if that's unimaginable, how about a pâtissier in Bergerac or Périgueux? How about Fillon, right here in Castillac—"

Edmond was shocked. "You can't be suggesting I allow that cretinous—"

Footsteps. Quickly Edmond came around the side of the counter and said a too-loud bonjour to the young woman coming inside the épicerie.

"My suppliers are—I don't know what to say about them, they're just a mess," he said, still too loud.

Ninette giggled. She saw that Edmond enjoyed pretending there was nothing going on between them, but rather than take offense, it amused her.

Paul-Henri burst through the door, and the cold draft made Edmond and Ninette shiver.

He looked from one to the other, then smirked. "Well, bonjour to you both and what in the world, Edmond, I must say that these continual sightings of you out and about instead of behind the counter at pâtisserie Bujold—it's unsettling, is what it is, and don't we have enough upheaval worldwide without this too?"

"Bonjour, Paul-Henri. My, you're a delicate soul. I merely stepped out for a moment to get some extra butter for a thing I'm devising—"

He nodded to Ninette and left—with no butter—letting the cold air in once again.

Paul-Henri eyed Ninette, who was pretending to be busy with something under the counter. "You might as well let the cat out of the bag," he said, while looking at the display of chocolate bars.

"What cat?" said Ninette.

"You know."

"Well, if you already know, there's nothing to say, is there?"

The door opened and yet another blast of cold air came in.

"Bonjour, Amelie," said Ninette. "Bonjour, Laurent."

Laurent glowered and stared at the floor. Amelie squeezed his hand to let him know it was all right not to answer (though it had taken her many months to get to this point of allowing him to opt out of what was commonly considered good manners).

Ninette smiled at Laurent. "I see your daily quota is expanding," she said to Paul-Henri, who had placed five chocolate bars on the counter.

"One needs sustenance in the cold, don't you agree, Laurent?"

Laurent did not make any sign of hearing what the gendarme said to him. He stared at the floor, his expression stony, until his mother pulled him down an aisle so she could get the coffee she came for.

CHIEF CHARLOT RAPPED on the door of the Barstow's shabby house and turned her head to listen for any sound inside, guessing that if anyone was home, they would check to see who was knocking before opening the door. And seeing it was the Chief, they might try to pretend there was no one home. So she listened and watched the window for any movement of the curtain.

As far as she knew, the inhabitants of the seedy little house were Madame Barstow, her son Malcolm, the two younger girls, and a younger son. Fletcher Barstow was still in prison, thanks be to God.

She rapped again but her gloves muffled the sound, so she peeled them off and knocked very hard with her knuckles and then banged her hand against the door.

"You could just ring the bell," said Mrs. Barstow, opening the door. "Come on in then, the cold is frightening today."

"Ah, thank you, bonjour Madame Barstow, and I'm sorry to

trouble you. If I might have a word?" Charlot sometimes used excessive politeness as a way to disarm someone she wanted information from.

Mrs. Barstow stood with her arms crossed, waiting. She had big bags under her eyes and her skin was tinged with yellow. She did not expect whatever Charlot had to say to be good news. With cops, it never was.

"No doubt you've heard about Madame Lagasse?"

Madame Barstow shrugged. "Don't know her." A girl shrieked in the next room and Charlot heard a second girl shush her.

"Come on, Madame Barstow, you must have at least heard of her. Lili Lagasse, famously the owner of a very valuable necklace?"

Madame Barstow shrugged again and puffed her cheeks out. "I don't know why you think I pal around with such as that. I lead a quiet life, especially since Fletcher's been gone."

Charlot walked past her and looked around the room, which was spacious and messy, magazines on the floor, toys scattered about, a sweater in a heap on the rug. "I know your husband had a fondness for jewels. So I thought I'd drop by, see if you'd heard anything."

"You think he did a burglary from prison? He's got talents, my Fletcher, but I don't think he could quite manage that."

"Perhaps—same as the murder he's in prison for—he put someone else up to it."

Madame Barstow shrugged yet again, communicating just how lame she thought this suggestion was. "And I would know about that how? My Fletcher is dear to me," she said—Charlot remembered reports of the beatings he gave her—"but I'm not getting letters from him telling me to go around stealing and murdering."

Charlot gave her a penetrating look. She raised one eyebrow.

"He cares about me too much for that."

Charlot smirked. "No doubt. Well, if you do happen to hear anything...if any of Fletcher's friends come around, if they happen to mention...I could put in a word at the prison, make things a little easier for your husband."

Madame Barstow didn't buy this for a second. All she wanted was for the cop to get out of her house and leave her be. She smiled a false smile as she walked Charlot to the door, and slammed it once the cop was out on the street.

The night was even colder.

Clear. The half-moon casting shadows.

Three a.m.

A man walked through the center of the village, through the Place, in no hurry. He ambled, taking his time, despite the intense cold. His jacket was zipped all the way up; he wore a black wool cap pulled down to his eyebrows. Insulated boots. Outside the coroner's office, he stopped, appeared to consider, then kept going, through the rabbit warren of streets until he reached rue Camus.

The neighborhood was residential. There were no lights on in any houses, no people on the street, and as the man stood next to an alley, absolute quiet.

No dog barked, no cat complained, no night bird had a word to say.

One streetlight made a faint glow and the man looked about for a rock, found one, and with a quick flick of his arm, threw the rock and extinguished the light.

He walked past the Bresson place, turned around and walked toward it again. He would need to find out who lived in the adjoining apartment. The moon allowed him to see without using a flashlight. He noted the windows, the garbage bins, the type of lock on the door.

He took all this information in and filed it away, then walked back the way he had come.

❊ II ❊

❧ 15 ❧

Molly kept looking out of the living room window at La Baraque, expecting to see Frances, Selma, and Amelie Bresson coming any minute. She was as excited as a child waiting for her birthday party to begin, and she supposed, in a way, it *was* a sort of birthday party, though the birth wasn't hers, and it hadn't even happened yet. Molly had always liked people, liked being in company, and the impending birth had intensified that feeling. She wanted to talk about the experience, hear what other women had to say about it; plus, she knew the other mothers would be more interested in some of the minutiae than Ben, no matter how forbearing he was.

Glancing longingly at the coffeepot, Molly poured herself a glass of orange juice while she waited. Her doctor—that horrid man—had warned her off coffee in these final days of her pregnancy, and even though she had a rock-solid belief that coffee could never, ever be harmful to her, she didn't dare give Dr. Boulet the satisfaction of going against his directions and God forbid, something going wrong.

Nothing was going to go wrong.

Right??

Ben said so. And Ben was nothing if not a reasonable and cautious man, not given to wild optimisms about anything.

Then—with plenty of noise—Amelie, Laurent, Selma, Frances, and Luka came spilling through the door. Bonjours and *bisous* exchanged, Laurent shrinking back and looking at the floor, Luka howling.

"Well, this group is starting off with a bang." Molly laughed, lifting Luka out of her carrier.

Frances immediately flopped on the sofa with a hand to her forehead, moaning.

"I hope it's all right that I brought Laurent," said Amelie.

"Of course, of course!" said Molly. "Would you like some apple juice?" she asked the boy.

He kept his eyes on the floor but nodded his head with some enthusiasm. Molly smiled and went to the refrigerator to get the juice and a plate of charcuterie she had already prepared, figuring no matter what the time of day or how strict the French food rules, the women would be starving.

They sat in the living room with the woodstove jacked up to maximum heat, discussing the various vagaries of late pregnancy, the way one never actually got used to the lack of sleep, and Luka's progress on all matters digestive. Molly found a toy truck to give to Laurent that he showed no interest in. He was using his finger to trace the patterns in the old rug.

"Should I get more food?" asked Molly, looking at the bare platter where the sausage, Camembert, and prosciutto had been.

Frances and Amelie shook their heads. Luka was asleep on the sofa. For a few moments, no one spoke. A feeling of warmth and camaraderie was already present in the group and there was no pressure to fill the silence.

Without intending to, Molly blurted out, "I didn't have a great relationship with my mother. And now I'm afraid I'll have no idea how to be one."

Amelie's eyes widened. Frances laughed a little. "Is it time for the group therapy portion of our meeting?" she said. "Good, because I could use a little myself. But let's begin with you," she said to Molly. "Say more. What's this you're thinking about?"

"Well, that's it, really." Molly rubbed a palm over her belly. "This kid is arriving any minute now, and it's just starting to occur to me that I'm going to be doing a job I never expected to do and I have no earthly idea *how* to do. I know, I babysat—but it's not the same. You know it's not." Molly looked from Frances to Amelie. "I guess most women just more or less do what their mothers did? Is that how it's been for you?"

"More or less," said Amelie. "My mother lives on the other side of the village, and she helps out some. But—she is a vital woman, still young—not even sixty—working, and involved with all kinds of projects of her own."

"Is she head over heels for her grandson?"

Amelie hesitated. "Of course she loves him very much," she said quietly, reaching to stroke Laurent on his neck. He did not flinch but leaned into her like a dog might.

"And—really, please excuse me, I didn't intend to open up this conversation when we barely know each other," said Molly.

"Not at all," said Amelie, smiling.

"Please, say what's on your mind!" said Selma.

"All right, I'll ask some more nosy questions then," Molly said, with a smile. "So you and your mother...your relationship is good?" Molly continued. "Do you want to be the same kind of mother she was?"

Amelie nodded. "More or less," she said. "Obviously there are some things I have a more modern approach for. But the main thing—and I say this to reassure you, Molly, about this job you didn't expect—the main thing is just to communicate love and acceptance. Everything else will fall into place if you just do that. Don't you think, Frances?"

Frances laughed. "Well, that's sensible, of course. It *sounds* good. But when you haven't slept in pretty close to an eternity and there is never-ending explosive pooping and crying and nothing you do seems to make any difference at all—" Frances moved closer to Molly, who was holding Luka now that she had woken up. She smoothed her hand over the baby's head. "I don't mean to sound...it's just...there have been a lot of moments when the love I feel for her doesn't seem to count for much."

The women sat, pondering this.

"It's a hard job," said Amelie. "A *really* hard job," her voice cracking a little.

Laurent had been quiet, what Molly's mother would have called "good as gold," and he continued to trace the pattern in the rug with his finger, over and over.

"So your mother..." started Frances.

Molly shook her head slowly. "I'm not saying she was terrible. She didn't abuse me or anything like that. It was just..."

Molly got a faraway look in her eye and the others waited. But she shook her head, unable to find the right words.

"I wouldn't say she was warm," said Frances finally.

"Oh! You knew her?" said Amelie.

"Molly and I grew up together," said Frances with a grin. "I know all the down and dirty on our girl here! There isn't that much, to be honest. Sad to say. But anyway—I spent plenty of time at the Sutton house and got to know her family—I was about to say I got to know them pretty well, but the thing about the Suttons...they didn't really *let* you get to know them well. They were nice enough. But they didn't go in for closeness, if you know what I mean?"

Molly was looking at the floor.

"I'm sorry, my English is only so-so," said Amelie. "But I think I follow. They were... a little closed up, is that how you say it?"

"Yes," said Frances. "Molls, do you mind me talking about your family like this?"

"Of course not," said Molly.

"Actually—it's occurred to me before that the reason you're

such an incredible detective is that you learned that skill growing up in your family. No one said what they really thought or felt about anything, so you were left to deduce it, to look for signs."

"What in the world. Why didn't you tell me that before?"

Frances jumped up and took a bow. "Look, people are messed up in a million different ways that they never intended or chose. I can say this though: if your mother was still alive, she'd be super excited about this baby. No question about that."

Molly wasn't so sure, but she *was* sure that Frances was a great friend who was doing her best to reassure her. And Amelie...just being in her presence made Molly feel better. Amelie was the human version of the best baguette you ever had—soft on the inside, comforting, sustaining, not trying to be something it wasn't, a giver of life.

Could I be any more dramatic? Molly snickered to herself, wondering who goes around comparing their friends to kinds of bread. But while she was at it...her mother? Her mother had been a slice of Wonder Bread. White, flavorless, barely nutritive, with a dry crust you couldn't get down without a lot of water. But better than starving, a lot better.

"Let me get another platter of food," she said, with a shrug at her own thoughts. The other women did not protest.

"This gathering was a good idea, Molly," said Selma. "Florian is really happy—but that doesn't mean he wants to talk about it."

"Oh, believe me, Nico got *so* sick of hearing me blather on about labor and how scared I was. I give him massive credit for never objecting. But he would get this look on his face." Frances laughed. "Sort of like I was offering to light his hair on fire or feed him a plate of worms."

"A mixture of terror and disgust?" said Molly with a laugh. "Sounds about right. And sort of how I feel about it too."

Selma was polishing off some amazing Italian sausage, *cacio et pepe*, and cocked her head. "Well. let's talk about something else, how about it? The only way I can manage to deal with my fear is to distract myself as much as possible."

"Sounds like a plan," said Molly.

Luka started to cry and Frances went to pick her up.

"I'm trying just to keep reminding myself how lucky I am," Molly said, almost to herself.

Laurent continued to trace the pattern on the rug, over and over, with an expression of deep concentration. Amelie mustered a wan smile. She loved Laurent with every fiber of her being—of course—but she did not exactly feel that she, or more importantly, Laurent himself, was especially lucky. Autism was difficult and there was no pretending it was not.

"WE JUST—I don't see where in the budget that money would come from," said Ben.

"I know. Like squeezing cabernet from a stone, right? So yeah, I hear you, but let's see if we can figure out something. I really want to help Amelie and Jules. I think money—or lack of it—is causing major stress for them. She didn't ask me for help or anything like that, it's just what I noticed in conversation. She's... she's really wonderful, Ben. Just the loveliest person. And they've got this son...I'm not sure...anyway, if we could just hire Jules to...I don't know, we always have a bunch of projects floating around in our heads, let's pick one! I think it would do so much for them."

"I'm sure it would," said Ben. "But can we afford to?"

"My feeling about money is that when you spend it, more appears from somewhere."

Ben did a double take. "How did I not know this before I married you?"

Molly shrugged and laughed. "That I'm a spendthrift? You did know. What about that natural pool I had to have, that sits unused because it needs more work and I haven't gotten around to it?"

"Mm," said Ben.

"And of course my monthly cheese expenditure…"

"Cheese is not a luxury."

"Spoken like a true Frenchman."

Ben made a small bow. "Actually, I have been thinking…it would be smart to use this time, this period when we don't have guests, to make some improvements around the place. So once tourism is back on track, we'll be ready. More than ready—much improved, with the possibility of a more secure income."

Molly clapped her hands. "Now we're talking! What have you been thinking about? Because that shed—you know, the broken-down one not far from the pigeonnier—it's got possibilities."

"Turn it into a gîte?"

"It'll be a job—plumbing, electrics, the works."

"And it's so small."

"A lover's hideaway?"

"For a detective with a logical brain, you have a romantic streak a kilometer wide," said Ben.

Molly started to answer but suddenly her abdomen gripped with a force unlike anything she had ever felt and she stood rooted to the spot, her mouth open, unable to speak.

"Molly?"

She shook her head and bent over, putting her hands on her knees. "Ouch," she said softly.

"I'll call the midwife! I'll call Boulet!"

Molly shook her head again. She huffed out some loud, slow breaths, and finally stood up. "No, no, don't call. It's not time yet. But maybe…soon? These are like warm-up contractions."

Though if these are only the warmup, she thought to herself, *heaven help me.*

✦ 16 ✦

"The usual?" Edmond didn't wait to hear Lapin's answer but reached into the pastry case with a pair of tongs for Lapin's favorite *réligieuse*.

"No, thank you," said Lapin, a bit prissily.

"What?"

"I said, no thank you. Not today. Just espresso, if you please."

"Why are you talking to me like that?"

"Like what?"

"Like I haven't known you your entire life and can hear a mile away when you've got something to say that you're not saying. Are you on a *diet* or something, heaven forbid?" He let the empty tongs drop to the counter with a clatter.

"Oh for heaven's sake, Edmond."

"I'm waiting."

"It's only...there are pressures..."

"Still waiting."

"I'm saving money, okay? You're being awfully pushy this morning."

"I'm about to go broke, is what I am, with everyone in the

village suddenly doing all this belt-tightening or whatever you want to call it, as though eating a simple pastry every so often is going to send them to the poorhouse. It's ridiculous! We shouldn't be deforming our lives on purpose this way, refusing the pleasures that are the very essence of daily life!"

"Why don't you bang your fist on the counter while you're at it."

"Maybe I will," said Edmond, and banged his fist. "Ow."

There was no one else in the shop and the two friends sat at a table to drink their espressos.

"Dare I ask how business is?" said Edmond. "You doing Lagasse's estate at least?

"Pfft," said Lapin. "I haven't heard a word about it and no idea whom to contact. I think she's got some relatives...somewhere nearby? Maybe Périgueux? Just between you and me, without the necklace, what good is her estate going to do me?"

"You're a mercenary lad."

"Says the man making a fuss when I didn't buy one little pastry. Anyway—business is terrible. I do wonder if she had any other jewels tucked away somewhere."

"A man can dream," said Edmond with a smirk.

"Ever since last Wednesday, I've been in a complete funk. Finding Lili like that...my nerves can't take it."

"Oh, get out of here with your nerves. Your nerves are just annoyed that you didn't get your paws on that necklace."

"You paint a rather greedy and heartless picture of me," sniffed Lapin.

Edmond shrugged. "We have to be greedy these days, with business how it is," he said, by way of softening his insult.

"So who *does* have the necklace," said Lapin. "That's what I'd like to know."

"That necklace is probably already in some out-of-the-way Paris shop," said Edmond. "Or it's been privately sold. Some sheik's wife is wearing it this very minute, swanning around in the desert, momentarily diverted by her new bauble."

Lapin made a face. "That necklace belongs in Castillac."

"Huh?"

"That necklace has been here since...forever, and if Lili is no longer able to wear it, then it should belong to another woman in Castillac. Not in Kuwait, or whatever it is you've got in your head."

"You're telling me if you had the necklace in your shop, and a rich American came in and wanted to buy it, you'd tell her oh no, that necklace is reserved for one of the villagers, I won't take your money?" Edmond let out a cackle.

Lapin pursed his lips. "What's the latest from America, anyway? Are they sorting out their banking problems? Is there any end in sight to all the tourists staying home?"

Edmond shrugged. "Nothing we can do about that. I'm not even reading the papers anymore. Point is, we should be worrying about what's under our noses, not across the Atlantic. And one thing that's under our noses—obviously—is someone is willing to kill for a necklace. Someone, I dare say, who lives right here in Castillac."

"We don't know that," said Lapin. "Gossip spreads all over, could be someone from Bergerac or even Bordeaux heard about the necklace."

"Maybe. But far less likely."

"Or if it *was* someone local, sometimes people get desperate, they do things they wouldn't have dreamed of doing if the circumstances had been different."

"So what? What does it matter what they might or might not have done some other day, when the weather was different?"

"You don't have to jump down my throat, I'm just thinking the thing over."

They sipped the last of their espressos. Lapin allowed himself to take a peek at the pastry case, his stomach growling.

"Well, I'm sure Molly—" Edmond started.

"Are you joking? Have you seen her lately? That baby is going to burst out any second. She's not going to be fit to investigate anything, not for the foreseeable future. Too bad for Lili."

"Too bad for all of us," said Edmond mournfully. He very nearly offered Lapin a pastry for free, but stopped himself before getting carried away.

JUST AFTER LUNCH, Madame Tessier took a deep breath outside the gendarmerie, then pushed open the door and went inside. Chief Charlot and Paul-Henri were both at their desks.

"Well, this is a pretty sight," said Madame Tessier.

"Bonjour, Madame Tessier," said Charlot. "Is there something we can do for you?"

"If you don't know the answer to that question, your detective skills are sorely lacking."

Charlot searched for an answer that was not rude but came up with nothing.

Madame Tessier came to Charlot's desk and rapped on it sharply three times. "You can arrest whoever murdered my dear friend Lili Lagasse."

Paul-Henri came over to Madame Tessier and took her hand. "I'm so very sorry for your loss," he said.

Madame Tessier rolled her eyes and took her hand back.

"It's a terrible thing," said Charlot. "Of course we're doing all we can."

"Really? It looks to me like you're lazing around inside, probably playing solitaire on your computers."

"Now, Madame Tessier—"

"You do know about the necklace?"

"Of course," said Charlot.

"Where would a stolen thing like that be sold? How do you track these things?" asked Tessier.

"I assure you, we're on it," said Charlot. "Now please, go about your day and leave us to it."

"Or maybe it's poker you're playing on there?" she said bitterly, pointing at Paul-Henri's computer. "Lili didn't deserve this. Even if it was...ill-advised to go around talking about that idiotic neck-lace—she didn't deserve to die over it," blurted out Madame Tessier, waving her hands in the air. Tears glinted in the corners of her eyes.

"Of course she didn't," said Paul-Henri soothingly, as he guided her to the door. "We'll find whoever did it, I promise you."

Madame Tessier let out a strangled noise of disbelief. "Or—maybe you lot are just waiting around for Sutton to do your work for you?"

"Rather a low blow," Paul-Henri muttered, as he closed the door after her.

Charlot and Paul-Henri exchanged a look. Charlot shook her head. "Anybody get back to you?" she asked.

"Yes. All of them have. But so far...no necklace seen anywhere by anyone."

"You've contacted Paris?"

"Yes, Chief. It's on the list of stolen goods." Paul-Henri still held onto the idea that the thief might keep the necklace until he thought it was safe to try to sell it. But he didn't say so.

"What about the neighbors?"

"I'll go around again. On my earlier attempt, many of them weren't home. Or they didn't answer. I'm finding that people are skittish these days. They don't want to come to the door, even for an officer. In general? People don't feel safe anymore. It's this financial trouble, so much anxiety—"

"All right, no need to give me your interpretation of international matters, Paul-Henri. Go talk to the neighbors again. Somebody may have seen something, heard something, and not remembered it until later."

Paul-Henri was more than happy to have a reason to leave the gendarmerie and Chief Charlot. He moved down the street with a sense of purpose, whistling, and thinking about what kind of chocolate he was going to get. So far, it was a three-chocolate-bar day, and who knew, that number might climb even higher, depending on what happened in the afternoon.

❦ 17 ❦

Molly felt restless. They hadn't made a final decision about hiring Jules, but she guessed Ben would come around. Now what to do for the rest of the afternoon?

Thoughts of the baby—anxiety about labor—the murder of Lili Lagasse—all of it swirled around in her head without any organization, making her jumpy and at loose ends. She was not much good at waiting, she knew this about herself. And waiting to go into labor was the worst waiting she had ever faced.

The scooter was parked for the duration in a barely used garage, and Molly set off for the village on foot, smiling to herself about the vision she presented, making her way down rue de Chêne like an ocean-going vessel, heavy and not exactly nimble, but chugging along with slow, steady progress.

As she walked, her thoughts turned back to Lili Lagasse. Molly hadn't known her except as a companion to her friend Madame Tessier—a familiar face, but not someone she had ever really talked to, not beyond pleasantries at a village fête. The idea of this made Molly sad, as though she had missed out on knowing a person she should have known, and now it was too late—as though it were possible to know and value everyone, and as though Castillacois should be immortal.

Death, thought Molly, and then held her breath, letting the word sit there, taking up all the space in her mind. My mother—

A small truck whizzed by and Molly waved at the driver though she didn't recognize him. The houses of the village came into view and she plodded on, noticing again how much energy it took to move, even slowly. With a pang, she hoped that labor waited until she was home again—what was she thinking, walking down the road by herself, when she was already getting those random contractions? What in the world would she do, give birth alone—lying in a ditch—if no one happened to drive by?

All through the pregnancy, in a way, she had continued to act as though she were not pregnant, because some part of her consciousness did not accept that it was real. Sure, she gave up her kirs and eventually the scooter, and now her beloved coffee. But these acts almost felt like token offerings, not decisions made out of knowing—really believing—she was going to have a baby.

An actual, live, not imaginary baby.

And now, even though labor was imminent, she continued to make decisions as though labor wasn't real either. Why was it taking so long for reality to catch up? Our minds are so mysterious. We choose what to believe not based on the evidence in front of us—or, sometimes we do and sometimes we don't. We're not consistent. Maybe there are reasons for this?

At the edge of the village was a small park with a basketball court and a couple of benches. Molly sank gratefully onto one of the benches, wishing she had brought something to drink, not feeling the cold because her pregnant body put out the heat of a blast furnace. After this little stroll, she told herself, I'm going home and not budging until the baby is born.

Having made that promise to herself, her thoughts turned to the murder. The name Lili Lagasse went through her mind again and again, as though all by itself, the name would conjure some

MADAME TESSIER KNOWS ALL

vision or idea about what had happened to the unlucky woman on her last night on earth.

After she felt rested, Molly made her way to rue Tabac. It was sunny and cold and no one was on the street. Under her breath, she sang Tobacco Road as she went:

I was born in a trunk.
Mama died and my daddy got drunk.
Left me here to die alone
in the middle of Tobacco Road.

SHE TOOK HER TIME. Walking slowly, watching and listening in case anyone came outside she could talk to. When Molly got to Madame Lagasse's house, she knocked on the door and then felt foolish, because Madame Lagasse had lived alone, so obviously there was no one to answer.

Without thinking about it, she pushed the latch, and the door eased open. Quickly Molly looked up and down the street—still empty. She slipped inside.

Yes, of course, there was no one to lock up either, she thought, standing in the foyer and taking a deep breath. She wondered if Madame Lagasse had any relatives nearby.

The house smelled of dried lavender. The wallpaper was sophisticated and faded, a pattern of leaves with many shades of green. A grand hall tree was just inside the door, which featured a central mirror with beveled edges and ornate carvings of leaves and branches. An umbrella was in the stand, and a wool coat hung on a hook.

The sight of the coat, hung there by an owner no longer alive, was moving to Molly. She imagined Madame Lagasse shrugging off the coat only a few days ago, reaching up to the hook to hang it, never a thought that it would be the last time she performed this everyday act. Had she looked at herself in the mirror afterward? Smoothed her hair? Smiled? Or simply gone on about her business in the half-absent way most of us get through the day?

Molly walked into the kitchen. It was tidy, except for the glass where Lapin had broken the window in the door. A few plates in a drainer. Nothing on the wooden table. A frigid draft sweeping through that hole in the glass—Molly moved on to the next room.

The living room: ashes in the fireplace, a worn armchair with a standing lamp behind it, a stack of books on a small table by the chair. The sun came in strong through the window and Molly saw a little glimmer underneath the table. She knelt—no small feat— and saw that it was a piece of pottery with a bottle-green glaze. Something had obviously broken, and this scrap, a little bigger than a bottle cap, had been left behind in the clean-up. Carefully she picked it up by its edges. Had it been a vase? A candy dish?

With a groan, Molly got back to her feet and looked at the green chunk. She gnawed on her upper lip, as she often did when she was trying to see a situation clearly, wondering if whatever had broken had been treasured by Madame Lagasse; the glaze was the most beautiful color. She slipped it into her pocket.

Molly thought how sometimes to solve a murder, the more you know about a victim, the more you know about who killed her. But was that true in this case? Wasn't this situation perfectly plain—a woman owned a valuable necklace, this fact was widely known, now the necklace was gone and the woman had been strangled.

The motive was patently clear. Find the necklace and you'll find the murderer. The murder—it was nothing personal. Just means to an end.

Was there any other way to see it?

Molly automatically distrusted the obvious. But that didn't mean it wasn't correct.

She went upstairs, holding onto the railing and breathing heavily. The house was narrow and the ceilings high. On the next floor was only a bathroom and Madame Lagasse's bedroom, and a small room, barely bigger than a closet, where a sewing machine sat on a small table that had a stool tucked under it.

The bedroom had large windows with thick damask curtains pulled to the sides—also green—and held with gold tasseled sashes. On one curtain, the sash had loosened and was on the floor. Molly stood for a long time looking out at the street, pondering life, death, and the last moments of Lili Lagasse.

"I ALMOST DIDN'T COME, thinking the place would be empty," said Lapin to Nico, who was in his usual spot behind the bar at Chez Papa. "Has something happened? Is there some good news at last?"

Nico shrugged. "Maybe people got tired of sitting home alone. What about you? Haven't seen you in weeks."

"Well, I—maybe what happened to Lili Lagasse got people thinking: life's too short to stay home doing nothing."

Nico shrugged again. He was just grateful not to be tending an empty bar.

You still wouldn't call Chez Papa packed, but the barstools were filled, along with two of the banquettes, and there was a congenial murmur of voices. Lapin ordered a beer and turned around to face the room. A pretty young woman came in and his eyes lit up. Out of old habit, he smiled an ingratiating smile and started off in her direction, but she slid into a banquette with a man much younger than Lapin, kissed him on both cheeks, and started talking animatedly.

Lapin remembered he was married, pulled himself together, and got back on his stool. I don't know what comes over me, he thought to himself. As he sipped his beer with no one to talk to— his wife Anne-Marie was home with a cold—his eyes glazed over as his thoughts returned to Madame Lagasse's necklace. He could practically feel the weight of it in his pocket, and he sorely regretted never asking Madame Lagasse outright if he could see it and hold it in his hand.

Someone jostled him and Lapin snapped out of his daydream to see Edmond Nugent, of all people, standing in front of him with an exasperated expression. "What planet are you on?" said Edmond.

"Earth, you ninny," Lapin shot back. "What are *you* doing here? You're supposed to be asleep by this time of night. Always. Without exception."

Edmond shrugged, did not answer, and asked Nico for a *pineau*. He perched on the stool next to Lapin, and Lapin could sense his friend's anxiety.

"So?" Lapin said.

"So what?"

"So what are doing here? Don't you have to get up and bake bread in about five minutes?"

"It's not that late."

"I don't like it when routines are disrupted. Not when I don't know why."

"You don't have to know everything, Lapin. You're not the king of the village whom everyone has to report to." Edmond scanned the room and sat on his stool facing the door.

Lapin grinned. "You sly old fox."

Edmond sipped his drink, did not answer.

"You're meeting somebody. A *woman*. I'm right, aren't I?! You old dog. Why didn't tell me? Who on earth is she?"

Edmond pursed his lips but his eyes were smiling. He drank his drink and did not throw Lapin so much as a crumb.

The door opened and everyone shivered against the frigid draft. In swept Paul-Henri, not in uniform but wearing a smart cashmere scarf that he had saved up for, finally choosing the navy over maroon. He was not on duty, not technically, but had thought it a good idea to get out and about at night in case he chanced into some information pertinent to the Lagasse case.

Alcohol made tongues wag, he knew that much, so Chez Papa on a Friday night seemed a good choice.

He was doing his best not to dwell on it, but he could not let go of the idea that he was on the verge of being transferred—shocking, considering his coup when he had saved Molly Sutton's behind only a few months ago! Such transfers were the norm at the gendarmerie and had nothing to do with performance. The reasoning behind the practice was that officers could get too cozy with their constituents, and it was best to move them around a bit to keep up objectivity. But he reasoned that if he nailed the Lagasse murderer, his preference for where he was posted might carry some weight. He took up a station at the end of the bar, ears open for any morsels.

Nico served Paul-Henri and then swung to the other end of the bar, where Frances sat with Luka asleep in a carrier.

"How are my favorite girls?" he said, leaning over for a kiss.

"Bored out of our skulls," said Frances congenially. "I'm sorry to whine, but it's just not the same without Molly."

"Isn't her baby due—"

"—any second now. Maybe she's having it this very minute!"

"Oh!"

"What?" Frances swiveled on her stool to see what Nico was looking at. "Madame Tessier? Has she ever been in here before at night?"

"No. Not that I've ever seen."

Madame Tessier strode up to the bar and placed her handbag on it. "What do you suggest?" she said to Nico.

"I—you mean, to drink?" said Nico. "Bonsoir, Madame Tessier, it's good to see you."

She waved her hand as though to brush off his politeness. "Yes, to drink. I only keep wine at home. And right now, I'm...I'd like something a little stronger."

Nico poured an Irish whiskey, neat, and slid the glass in front of Madame Tessier. Frances's eyebrows were raised; she felt dislocated, even though there was nothing so radical about a villager coming in to Chez Papa for a drink on a Friday night.

But one of the main things about Castillac was: there were *routines*. There were *expectations*. And part of the foundation for the general contentment of the villagers—the reason they felt safe, more or less—was that these routines were respected and followed and one could count on them.

Edmond Nugent, in a bar at ten o'clock at night? Not part of the routine.

Madame Tessier—same.

What had been an agreeable murmur in Chez Papa shifted. Voices got higher, chairs scraped, a girl in one of the banquettes stood up suddenly and knocked over a glass of wine.

It was not that anyone in the bar blamed Edmond or Madame Tessier; they were not conscious of why they suddenly felt like everything was all wrong, and nothing good was going to happen that night, and they should have stayed home after all.

❦ 18 ❦

"Get the door, willya Malcolm!" said Madame Barstow, who was stretched out nearly horizontal on the sofa, having followed the bottle of wine she drank with dinner with a large glass of whiskey.

Malcolm got up from the floor where he had been playing a game of Parcheesi with his younger sister. He cracked open the door to see who it was.

A big man pushed his way in, bringing a stream of cold air with him, followed by a small man who was thin and wearing a coat that had seen better days.

"Is that Shane Fowler I see with my very own eyes?" said Madame Barstow, laughing as though she had uttered a piercing witticism.

"Thought we'd pay a visit, out of respect for your husband," said Shane, taking off his coat and throwing it on a chair. He sported a black mustache that looked like it came from the costume department from an old Western—the ends swooped out and ended in points that drooped down.

"Lovely," said Malcolm under his breath. These friends of his

NELL GODDIN

father's—they were nothing but trouble and he didn't like them coming around. His mother was problem enough.

Madame Barstow hoisted herself up off the sofa to get the men a drink. The little sister whispered in Malcolm's ear that they'd finish their game later and skedaddled out of sight.

"Why you look so unfriendly," said the little man to Malcolm.

Malcolm gave him a look—as unfriendly as he could make it— and did not answer.

Madame Barstow and Shane were laughing uproariously in the kitchen. The sound of breaking glass, then more laughter.

"Heard about poor Madame Lagasse," said the little man, making an exaggerated sad face.

"I don't even know you," said Malcolm.

"Rodney Smith," he said, holding out his hand.

"Sure," said Malcolm, giving the man's hand the barest shake.

"So Shane and I were wondering—"

"I don't know anything about it," said Malcolm. "Neither does my mother. You got no reason to come bothering us."

"I heard the necklace held a jewel."

Malcolm rolled his eyes.

"I heard it was a jewel the size of a quail egg. You ever seen a quail egg?"

Malcolm shrugged.

"Shane and I were just saying, this is exactly the kind of thing that gets Fletcher excited. Your dear Papa, he loves a jewel, am I right? And so we thought—"

"—I wouldn't guess thinking is your strong suit," said Malcolm.

"No need to bring out the insults," said Rodney, making a comical hurt expression. "Men have feelings, you know."

Malcolm was trying to figure out a way to remove the creeps from the house without causing too much of a ruckus. His sisters were tucked away safely in their bedroom. His mother...his mother, as usual, was hindering more than she helped. More cackling from the kitchen, along with the sound of something else being dropped on the floor.

"All I'm saying is, if Fletcher is up to his usual tricks, and he pulled off this sweet little heist from the inside…if he could use any help, with uh, with getting that quail egg sold or moved or whatnot—"

"I told you, we had nothing to do with any of this. I'm pleased you think my father has such powers," he said sarcastically. "But he's spending his days breaking rocks, not masterminding jewel heists. Good night." Malcolm had had enough. He glanced into the kitchen and saw his mother dancing with Shane Fowler, laughing with her head tipped back. Malcolm heard the crunch of broken glass as they stepped on it.

If it weren't for his sisters, he'd have left this house long ago. He heaved a big, sorry-for-himself sigh, and went to the girls' room to check on them before getting into bed.

"How are you feeling tonight, dear mother of my child?"

"A little superstitious, so don't be jumping the gun like that."

Ben smiled. He and Molly were in bed. She was lying on her side, facing him, but kept squirming, unable to find a comfortable position.

"I thought a little more about Jules," said Ben.

"And?"

"Ah, let's do it. I think we can keep an eye on the budget and help the guy out at the same time. We'll end up making the money back once we start having guests again. This situation in the U.S.—it's got to resolve eventually, don't you think?"

"Well, it will or it won't, without our help. But I guess I feel like it's better to go forward expecting the best instead of the worst."

Ben smiled and smoothed a crazy curl off Molly's face. "So we're set on the names?"

Molly nodded.

"The nursery is all ready?"

Molly nodded.

"There's nothing for me to do?"

"Just hold my hand. I'm new at this, remember?"

"And you're sure you want to have the baby at home? French hospitals have a wonderful reputation when it comes to childbirth, they really do."

"Oh, I know." Molly struggled to sit up and fluffed her pillows. "It's not...I've got nothing against French hospitals, it's...it's this other thing. I haven't really told you about my mother's death, have I?"

"Only a little, about the car accident."

"Yeah. Well, she didn't die at the scene. Unfortunately. Because she ended up being helicoptered to a hospital, what they call a trauma center, and she lived for another week." Molly ran her hands over her belly. "It was not a good week," she added, brushing tears from her eyes.

Ben slipped his arm around her and hugged her closer.

"Well, and it's complicated. I wasn't very close to my mother. As I've told you, she wasn't terrible. She didn't beat me, she wasn't cruel or anything like that. But...she was...a little...chilly. Didn't show her emotions much. I sat next to her hospital bed during that terrible week, talking and talking to her, even though she wasn't conscious. I said everything I had held back my whole life —the good, the bad, the ugly. I guess you don't have to be close to a parent for their death to wreck you? The nurses were wonderful, I guess the doctors did their best...but it was without question the worst week of my life. If I could live the rest of my life and never set foot in a hospital again, I would be very glad. And I trust Louise, our midwife.

"Anyway—I don't want to dwell on what happened with my mother. But also—for certain—the last thing I want is to be in a hospital where all those bad memories will be flooding me when I go into labor. I want to bring this baby into the world in the place I have been the happiest of my life, right here at La Baraque, with you."

The prospect of his child being born any minute had Ben feeling emotional all the time lately, and he felt tears well up at this. "That sentiment is wonderful, it really is. And thank you. I only...well, I don't want to pressure you to do something you don't want to do. The birth is your show, Molly."

"But...?"

"I...well, you know me," he laughed, a little self-consciously. "I worry, especially when...it's you I'm worrying about. And so, it's reassuring to think of you having the baby all safe and sound in a hospital, with a lot of experienced hands on deck."

Molly nodded. But she was not going to change her mind. If she imagined walking into a hospital, it felt as though a chill went through her body. No, her place was right here at La Baraque, with a fire in the woodstove and Bobo and Ben at her side. "How about if I ask Louise if she could bring someone with her? Would that help, having more hands? Though I'm not sure what there really is to do beyond listen to me yell. And you know—if anything does happen, you can whisk me straight to the hospital in Bergerac. I'm not saying I won't go no matter what. Just hoping I get through the whole thing right here."

The whole thing was finally beginning to be real for Ben, too, and he felt a flash of fear that anything bad could possibly happen to Molly or the baby.

"It's just crazy that this new person is about to arrive and be a huge part of our life, and we haven't even met him," murmured Molly. "Or her," she added. She lay with her head on Ben's chest. Bobo jumped up on the bed and stretched along Molly's back.

All of them were deeply content, for the moment, and at the same time, nearly overcome by anticipation. Even Bobo, in her genius doggy way, knew something big was up.

19

Meanwhile, across town, Florian and Selma were getting ready for bed and continuing their endless argument about where to live.

"But Castillac is my *home*, dearest darling!" said Florian. "My work is here, my life..."

"You say that as though I don't also have a home or a life."

"Of course that's not what I mean. My impression was...I thought, last summer, that you were ready to leave England? You were so critical of your life there, and so enthusiastic about Castillac. I thought—"

"Well, it's one thing to leave your country for a vacation, and another, *entirely different* thing, to leave for good. We're not so young, after all, to make such a big change."

"You *are* young," he said, and reached to caress her belly. "And so beautiful," he said, actually choking up.

Selma leaned her head back and laughed her braying laugh, which Florian also found beautiful.

"You going over to Sutton's next time they get together?" he said, getting up to get a drink of water.

"I certainly am," said Selma. "I was so pleased that she included me, and sorry to miss the first one."

Well, if anyone can convince Selma that moving to Castillac is a good idea, it's Sutton, thought Florian, glugging down the water and jumping happily into bed with his very pregnant fiancée.

FIRST THING SATURDAY MORNING, Ben called Jules and asked him to come over so they could talk about possibilities for work. Jules hopped on a rickety bicycle and came right away.

Ben offered coffee, which Jules refused. Ben had the idea that Jules didn't want to take anything extra, even a cup of coffee— that he was uncomfortable enough with the offer of work, possibly thinking it was part charity.

Well, it *was* part charity, thought Ben. He's not altogether wrong. But it's also legit, and hopefully once the work begins, Jules will feel all right about it.

"We've got, oh let's see, seven beds right now for gîte rental," said Ben. "Pigeonnier, cottage, and the annex on the back of the house. Right now everything is empty, not a single guest. Business is dead." He shrugged and managed a smile. Jules was listening intently but did not react.

"So Molly and I were thinking, why not use this time, when no one's around to bother, to expand and make improvements? And then, once the Americans get their act together and things return to normal, we'll be better positioned than we were."

Jules made a quick nod.

Quiet fellow, thought Ben. "So, two things are at the top of the list. The shed that I'm about to show you, which we want to turn into a cozy gîte with one bed, suitable for a single or couple. And then we've got this natural pool that's got some problems that need addressing—though that work's going to have to wait until the weather turns. Frozen over now, of course, depending on the day."

Again, the quick nod, without eye contact.

They reached the shed, which was in worse shape than Ben remembered. The roof had a big hole on one side, the floor was dirt, and the whole structure did not look stable. The walls were wood and light shone through various holes.

"Huh," said Ben. The two men stood for a long moment, looking at it. They walked around back, checked out both sides.

"I don't see..." said Jules slowly.

Ben laughed. "Neither do I! It's Molly who has the imagination around here. This thing looks like a—"

"—perhaps a bit of a mess—"

"—complete disaster—"

"—total shambles—"

"—utter ruin—"

The men cracked up, shaking their heads.

"Glad we see eye-to-eye," said Ben. "Well, so tell me. Do you think you have the skills to turn this ungodly mess into something habitable? It seems roomy enough, at least. One room, with a kitchen alcove. We can always add on to make space for a bathroom. Everything very simple. Sort of a rustic hideaway. But maybe it's too far gone? I can do small repairs but a project like this is way over my pay grade."

Jules nodded. "Sure," he said. "I think I can do it." He paused. "I can absolutely do it."

Ben knew Jules's wife was about to have another baby, and he could only imagine how stressed Jules must be to find some way to provide for his family. He clapped Jules on the shoulder and said, "All right then! Let's go forward. How about we start by you making a list of what materials you need to get started. I won't buy everything at first, just what you'll need for, say, the next couple of weeks? That sound okay?"

Jules nodded and tried to seem confident. He was a quick learner, he said to himself. All he had to do was find somewhere that had the information he needed, and he could figure it out.

The project was just a broken-down shack that had to be transformed into a livable space for a short-term visitor. He didn't have to build Notre Dame.

I can do this, he said to himself, as he got back on the rickety bike. And repeated, privately of course, many hundreds of times over the days to come.

MOLLY WAS IN A STATE.

Dr. Boulet had said that Sunday, January 25—*tomorrow*—was her due date. Though he had emphasized that, as with all things in nature, you couldn't be precisely 100 percent certain about the exact moment it would happen. Well, she would appreciate some precision and certainty, thank you very much. Plus the doctor was given to continually droning on about "advanced maternal age," giving Molly one more thing to try to block from her mind, a process she had no talent for.

And now it was Market Day, when for several years she had gone into the village each week in what was a deeply pleasurable routine. She had promised herself to stay home, so staying home was what she was doing. But she was not resting and contemplating—she was climbing the walls.

"I can do that, Molly," said Ben, finding her on her hands and knees scrubbing the bathroom floor.

"I know you can," she snapped. "Oh. I'm sorry, that came out wrong. Help me up."

The space was small and it was hard for Ben to get into a useful position. His wife was heavy, her shape awkward, and it was only with quite a bit of huffing and puffing on both their parts that they managed to get her upright again.

"I'm a living, breathing Humpty Dumpty. Maybe I should avoid the floor in the near future," she said, once she caught her breath, and they looked at each other and broke up laughing.

"How about you just lie on the sofa with Bobo and daydream for the rest of the day? I know the waiting is rough on you."

"As I've said a million times, this is not your average, everyday anticipation. This is wishing desperately for something to happen that I'm terrified of."

"You're going to do great," said Ben, taking her hand and sitting down with her on the sofa.

And because Ben was Ben, his reassurance did help.

She jumped up again.

"You're like, what is it the Americans say? A Mexican hopper bean?"

"Jumping bean," said Molly, without cracking a smile—and if a language mistake didn't make her laugh, she was clearly not herself. "It's Changeover Day! I want guests on the way and Constance coming in with a clatter and a million personal problems, and I want to take the scooter into the village and go to the market and pick up some croissants from Edmond and—"

"You want everything to stay the same."

"Is that so wrong? When 'the same' was so, so good?"

"Of course not—"

A knock at the door.

"Expecting anyone?" Ben asked. Molly shook her head.

He opened the door to find Madame Tessier standing there, shivering.

"Madame Tessier, come in! Bonjour," cried Ben, ushering the half-frozen woman to a spot in front of the woodstove.

"I wonder if I might have a word with Molly," Madame Tessier said, rather formally.

Ben wasted no time making himself scarce.

Molly started to offer something to drink but the older woman cut her off. "Listen Molly, I'm not here on a social call. Some other time, let's do that."

Molly nodded. They had always spoken frankly to one another, and she knew that whatever Madame Tessier had to say, she would not beat around the bush. They sat down. Madame Tessier put her large handbag on the floor, then brought it to her lap.

"This is business," she said.

Molly thought she heard a tremble in her voice.

"It's about Lili."

Molly waited. Madame Tessier seemed to be working to master her emotions. Molly looked at the flower print of her dress and then at her sensible brown shoes. She was wearing an odd brooch, shaped like leaves, made of green enamel. Interesting that she stopped to put on jewelry before leaving the house, thought Molly.

"I cannot *stand* what has happened to her," Madame Tessier said. "I know everyone in the village is saying she got what she deserved—"

"—I haven't heard anyone—"

"—and maybe in some way it is even true. At the very least, Lili acted rashly. She put her own ego, if I may say so, ahead of her well-being and safety."

"—I don't—"

"All right, Molly. All right. Then tell me: what would you say the chance is that she would be lying in the morgue right now if there had been no necklace?"

Molly looked down at the floor.

"This is my point," said Madame Tessier.

The two women looked at the smudged window of the wood-stove where they could see flames dancing. They considered.

"Very simply: I want the person or persons who did this to be brought to justice," said Madame Tessier.

"Of course," said Molly. "I know you were great friends."

"We were." Madame Tessier breathed a long, long breath, in and then out, as she fought back tears. "Obviously you have something else on your plate just at the moment," Madame Tessier said, looking at Molly's belly. She tried to summon a smile, to appear that she didn't consider Molly's pregnancy to be an impediment to her wishes, but she did not entirely succeed. "If I may ask—when are you due?"

"Dr. Boulet says tomorrow. But that I mustn't place bets on it."

Madame Tessier sighed. "It's most inconvenient. I know how selfish that sounds, and I hope you know that I am pleased about your blessed event and wish you every happiness, which I'm sure you will have in abundance."

Molly cocked her head. Madame Tessier did not sound like herself. It was almost as though she were reading from a script, as though she were acting, and the character she was playing was quite formal, punctilious, and self-centered. Not at all the more informal, gossipy, even jolly Madame Tessier Molly knew.

"At any rate, there's nothing else for me to do but plunge forward with my proposal. Understand that I, again, am aware of the circumstances and realize that you will not be able to give the case the attention you normally would."

Molly did not like where this was going.

Madame Tessier reached into her capacious handbag and pulled out a stack of euros, in a bank wrapper, and put it on the sofa next to Molly. Then she reached in and pulled out another, and another.

"There's quite a bit there," she said, with a note of triumph. "I haven't any idea what you normally charge, and of course, as I said, I am cognizant of the special circumstance of this baby's imminent arrival. Whatever it costs, it is worth it to me, and I am very confident in the quality of your work. You see, obviously, that I want to hire you to find Lili's murderer. Obviously, the timing is terrible—but! The baby is not here yet. Maybe it will not arrive for another week. So I believe it is possible that you could get a great deal of the investigation finished beforehand. Are you feeling well? No, uh, complications, at your age?"

Molly shook her head. Would people please stop talking about how old she was?

"A woman of your talents, Molly—you might well be able to wrap the whole thing up in a few days, before the baby even has an idea about arriving. And then you can enjoy motherhood and recover from the birth with the contentment that comes from justice served and a murderer no longer roaming free in our village."

That last bit was something of a low blow, playing on Molly's fears about safety as a new mother. And sure, Molly herself had designs on the case, and only the other day had been in Madame Lagasse's house sniffing around. But that was entirely informal. Certainly not worth being paid for. And her due date was *tomorrow*.

Molly rubbed her eyes and tried to think. She did not want to refuse her friend. And of course, if there was a killer in Castillac, she wanted to be the one to catch him.

But this was not an ordinary time.

"Madame Tessier. Please. I know how much this means to you," Molly said, picking up the stacks of bills and handing them back. "I will, of course, keep my eyes and ears open. You can always count on that. But I'm afraid that this time, we are going to have to rely primarily on Chief Charlot to get the job done."

Madame Tessier got a sour look on her face and started to speak but Molly interrupted her. "I know, I know, the gendarmerie hasn't been...lately...I mean...look, this case has the probability of being an easy one. The most likely explanation, as you yourself said, is that someone stole Madame Lagasse's necklace and then killed her to avoid being identified. So all Charlot has to do is find the necklace, and she'll have the perpetrator."

"You make it sound oh so simple. But how is finding a necklace easy? In the wide, wide world, this small thing you can slip into a pocket? Needle in a haystack, Molly. It could have been smuggled out of the country by now. Or it could stay hidden, not for sale, for years, because the murderer knows full well the gendarmes will be looking for it. Or—he might want to keep it for himself, might give it to his girlfriend—"

"Oh, Madame Tessier, you know that is not how criminals work. The killer took the necklace for the money. He's hoping—lots and lots of money. That is the beginning and end of it. He is very unlikely to be able to hold on the necklace for very long, because the desire for that money will win out over caution. Thieves, by and large, are not blessed with restraint. Or brains either, usually."

Madame Tessier was not cheered by any of this and looked as though something had let all the air out of her. She seemed to have shrunk, sitting on the edge of her chair, her hope collapsed.

"Oh, Lili, what did you do?" she said softly, and put her face in her hands.

Molly started to cry. Her emotions were already running at a fever pitch and seeing her usually composed friend break down pushed her right over the edge.

Ben came in to ask if he could make them lunch and found the two women holding hands and crying. He paused a moment and slipped back out of the room.

Suddenly Molly gripped Madame Tessier's hand with such force the older woman cried out. Molly bent forward and moaned, an animal sound from deep within.

"Oh my," said Madame Tessier. "Ben!" she called out.

Ben had not gotten far down the hallway and he ran back to the living room. "What's the matter?"

Molly moaned again. She had both hands on her belly now, and was bent over, eyes squeezed shut.

"Chérie," said Ben, kneeling down beside her. "Remember to breathe."

"I *am* breathing," Molly said through clenched teeth. "For crying out loud." She did not move for another few moments, eyes still closed. Then, gingerly, she sat up and looked around the room, blinking and massaging her back. "My God, that hurts," she said, putting both palms over her belly.

"Perhaps Dr. Boulet was correct," said Madame Tessier.

"We'll see," said Molly. "I've been getting these contractions for days, off and on. At first I thought okay, here we go! But then nothing progresses. I get one, and...nothing."

Ben smoothed the hair away from Molly's face. "What can I get you? Some tea?"

"You know I despise tea," said Molly.

Madame Tessier shot Ben a look. Neither of them had ever seen Molly this grouchy.

"I wouldn't mind a piece of cheese," Molly said in a softer tone, and Ben scrambled into the kitchen to make her a plate.

"As you know, I never had children," said Madame Tessier. "So I don't know a thing about this experience you're about to have except what people have told me over the years. All I can say is, apparently no matter how difficult the process is, you soon forget all about it. That's what I've been told, at any rate. Of course, don't hesitate to call if there is anything I can do to help you." With a sigh, she stood and collected her handbag with the euros stuffed back inside.

Molly stood, grimacing because of her aching back, and walked her friend to the door. "I'm sorry I disappointed you," she said.

Madame Tessier shrugged and shook her head.

"But let me suggest this," said Molly. "As you know, the necklace must be found. If it was taken by someone in the village—and this seems likely, since knowledge of its existence was Castillac news—then it's possible the person who took it might tell someone. Remember what I said about criminals not being very bright. They blab when they should keep their mouths shut. And once that happens, you know exactly how things work. The news will travel. And who is better at keeping her finger on the pulse of village news than you, Madame Tessier?"

20

"Thanks for letting Laurent come along," Jules said to Ben, as they walked out to the shed, the boy close behind them, his gaze on the ground.

"Happy to have him," said Ben. He smiled at Laurent, who was walking rather stiffly through the frost-withered grass of the meadow. Bobo was up to her usual antics, bounding after rodents and leaping joyfully in the air, but Laurent paid her no attention.

"I'm working on that list of materials," said Jules. "I thought today I'd clear the place out, do some more detailed assessment. Laurent's going to be my right-hand man."

Ben smiled again at Laurent but the boy kept his face turned to the ground.

"You like to do construction like your Papa?" Ben asked him.

Laurent showed no sign of hearing.

Jules shrugged at Ben with a sort of smile.

"Okay then," Ben said, understanding that this day of work might go on more easily without him, "I'll head back to the house. Let me know if you need anything. Come on, Bobo!"

When he got about fifty yards away, he turned around and saw Laurent carrying a load of old, unusable planks out of the shed.

The boy walked over next to some bushes and set them down carefully. Ben smiled and waved but Laurent had run back to his father.

All of a sudden, the prospect of having a son who ran to him that way, with trust—Ben was nearly overcome with feelings of happy expectation and also, a vague sort of fear, barely acknowledged, about whether he would be up to the job of father.

"SHAKE A LEG, HOW ABOUT IT," Shane whispered to Rodney, who was carrying the implements of his trade, which were quite heavy.

Rodney did not protest aloud but he wished Shane would trip and smash his face on the pavement.

They were sneaking through the early morning light of Sunday dawn, on their way to Lapin's shop, having hatched the idea to break in and steal Madame Lagasse's necklace, which they were almost certain was inside.

Rodney had been the first to suggest it. "Why wouldn't the thief take the easiest way out?" he argued. "Steal the thing and move it as quick as possible, that's how to do it," he said. "Everybody knows that. And with the thing attached to a murder? Even more so," he added, with the satisfaction of believing he was right and had beaten Shane to it.

The street was quiet in the faint, washed-out light. Very cold. It was not exactly early, because in January, in Castillac, the sun didn't come up until eight-thirty. The village, as far as the men could tell, was still fast asleep.

"I don't even hear a bird," said Rodney as they approached the shop.

"Will you shut up," said Shane.

They tried the front door, just for kicks, and when it was locked, went down a narrow alley to the back. There was an open area behind the shop where trucks could pull up to load and unload. Some wooden pallets were stacked to one side, an empty garbage bin. Shane looked all around, checking the windows of other buildings that faced this open space. He saw no one; the windows were mostly shuttered.

"All right, move along," he said, pointing at the door and then the tools.

"You not gonna lift a finger?" said Rodney.

Shane just smirked and crossed his arms. "I'm on lookout," he said.

Rodney and Shane had known each other a long time. They had gotten into trouble together as teenagers, had nearly been arrested several times for petty theft, and it was something of a miracle neither had spent any time in jail. When Fletcher Barstow was in charge, they had gotten along better, but with Fletcher in prison, when it was just the two of them—they were like oil and water.

As soon as they had the necklace, thought Rodney, he'd never do another job with Shane again. And oh what a happy day that will be.

He drove the crowbar into the slit between the door and the sill. It shrieked as it moved against the metal plate and Shane quickly looked up to the windows to see if the noise would bring anyone to a window.

In another moment, Rodney having some talent (and practice) in the breaking-in department, they were inside the shop.

"What a pile of junk," said Shane, moving down an aisle as Rodney closed the door behind them.

"Hope the fat bloke doesn't have a safe," said Rodney.

"Bloody hell," said Shane.

They spread out to search the shop as quickly as possible. The necklace wasn't in the display case with the other jewels. And it wasn't—as far as they could tell—in the small space that served as Lapin's office. Not tucked away in his messy desk with layers of papers strewn across it, not in the drawers, not in a box of candy sitting on the desk, which contained only candy.

"Maybe the problem is, we're looking for something which we don't properly know what it even looks like," said Shane.

"A chain with a jewel hanging off it. Size of a quail egg is what I heard."

"Never seen any quail egg."

"Me neither. But I can deduce," said Rodney. "And I don't see any necklace, period."

Shane looked dissatisfied, and Rodney knew that how that feeling in Shane usually played out was he got smacked in the back of the head or shoved into a wall. So he stayed light on his feet, ready to dodge if Shane made any sudden moves.

Then they froze. Someone was coming in the front door to the shop, whistling.

21

"—So unless it was a passel of raccoons who scampered out before I could catch them—and who smoked a cigar and got ashes all over my desk—somebody was in my shop. And that somebody used a crowbar on my back door, which is going to cost a bundle to repair. My shop isn't secure. Anyone could sashay in there, right through the back, with the door already busted open."

"And steal all those museum-quality pieces."

"I'm not in the mood, not this morning," said Lapin. "I'm distraught. I feel violated."

Edmond snickered but he took Lapin's plate and put another religieuse on it without charging him. "This village is going to hell in a handbasket," he said. "At least they didn't take anything."

"Who knows what they might have taken? It's not as though my inventory...I mean, it's not..."

"You mean to say it's an unholy mess in there. Did you call Charlot?"

Lapin looked away. It wasn't that he was engaged in anything criminal, nothing like that, but did that mean he wanted gendarmes snooping all around his place? No, no, he did not. "I'll take care of it myself," said Lapin, and Edmond wondered exactly how he thought to accomplish that, but said nothing.

Lapin sighed. "Can't we have some good news for a change? Why is it nothing but bad, bad, bad, day in and day out?"

Edmond perched on his chair and sipped his coffee. He did not look remotely depressed but smiled to himself.

"I did get one little smidgen of good news," said Lapin. "The nephew of Madame Lagasse, a *mec* who lives in Bordeaux, contacted me to do the cleanout of her house."

"You think there might be something good?"

Lapin shrugged. "I'm not getting my hopes up, for once. I sort of expect that the famous necklace was more or less all she had of any real value. I wonder how she even came by that thing in the first place."

Edmond shrugged. He sipped his espresso and smiled to himself again.

"What are you grinning your fool head off about? You might as well tell me, I know you've been up to something. Or *someone*," Lapin added with a smirk.

Edmond started to tell him, then changed his mind. "Are we not allowed a secret now and then?"

"Oh, whatever, don't tell me then. I'm sure whoever it is will be telling her girlfriends and I'll find out soon enough. If you want your oldest friend to find out from village gossip instead of from your own lips."

"When you get sullen, it's really something to witness," said Edmond. "Now, be serious for a moment. I do want to talk to you about this—but I will tell you right now, if you start passing out smart remarks, I'm going to clam up and that's it."

"Ah, all right."

"It's you in particular I want to talk to," said Edmond. "Because you got married sort of late in the game."

Lapin's eyebrows flew up. *"Married?"*

Edmond nodded. To his horror, he felt a blush creeping up his neck.

"Who is she?"

Edmond shook his head slightly. "What I want to ask you is... did you feel...was there some amount of...how did you determine whether you were ready for marriage, financially speaking?"

Lapin looked at his friend. "What, is this woman some kind of high maintenance type? Is she from the village?"

"Can't you just answer a simple question?"

"Oh, calm down. Honestly, I didn't give finances any thought at all. Maybe I should have. When my relationship with Anne-Marie started to...to progress, I suppose you could say, I knew I was going to marry her. So I did. Money didn't come into it at all. She works, I work, we share expenses. I don't—are you saying you think you need to be able to afford to support both of you? Who *is* this person?"

"Well, she has a job. Actually, she has...we'll call them... resources, of a certain kind. But I would like it if I could provide for her so that she could quit working, if she wanted to."

"You want to know what I think? I think you're dragging your feet, coming up with a bunch of nonsense, because you don't actually want to get married."

Edmond blanched. Was Lapin right?

"What does she say?" asked Lapin. "Is it her idea that you make all the money so that she can...what? Have babies, is *that* what you're thinking?" And then Lapin, unable to stop himself, dissolved into laughter.

Edmond crossed his arms and very much regretted giving him that free réligieuse.

THE MUCH-ANTICIPATED due date had arrived. Molly lay in bed, scanning her body for any changes. She felt like a whale but more or less the same whale as yesterday and the day before. She could feel the baby move just a bit, not as much now because there was no room. "Hello in there," Molly murmured. "I'm ready if you are."

Ben stirred and rolled over. He smiled and reached his hand to her belly and patted it.

And then they were up and making breakfast and showering and doing their best to pretend it was a day like any other, which maybe it would be. Ben went out to meet Jules at the shed for some heavy-duty destruction, and Molly...well, she did not know what to do with herself, and wandered from one room to another, hoping to find something to distract her.

Finally, she decided to do a load of laundry, might as well make herself useful. Going through pockets, she found the small bit of pottery she had taken from Madame Lagasse's house. She looked at it in her palm, thinking.

Then put on her coat and walked out to the shed, where the men were taking turns with a sledgehammer and enjoying themselves mightily.

"Nothing like causing ruin to really bring pleasure," said Ben with a broad smile. Then he remembered what day it was. "What's up? You...feeling anything?"

"Nope. Bonjour, Jules," she said, and Jules came over to kiss cheeks.

"Amelie had a good time yesterday, thank you for including her," he said.

"My pleasure! We all get along like gangbusters. So, Ben—can you get away just for half hour or so? I've got some business at the gendarmerie."

Jules stepped away. He picked up the sledgehammer and bounced it a little in his hands.

"Business? I thought the only business for today was having that baby." Ben laughed, sounding nervous.

"I'll tell you about it in the car," said Molly. Ben nodded and the two of them walked away through the meadow.

Jules watched them until they were out of sight. And then he smashed the sledgehammer into a section of the dilapidated foundation so that it sprayed rocks and debris twenty feet away.

BEN DROPPED Molly off and said he would come back for her in fifteen minutes.

"I'm sure Charlot will kick me out long before then," said Molly, and managed, with some wiggling and grunting, to get herself out of the car.

She rapped on the door and then went inside.

"Good heavens, Molly, don't have that baby right here at the gendarmerie," said Charlot.

"I don't intend to. I dropped by because I found something I thought might interest you. It's probably nothing. But I...I went over to Madame Lagasse's house the other day...I...well, I was just having a look around, the door was open..."

"And?"

"I found this little chunk of pottery under a table in the living room." She brought it out of her pocket, having put it in a small glassine envelope. "Of course I have no idea what the story behind it is. But I wondered whether it might be something you could test for prints? Madame Lagasse's house...felt so peaceful. So calm. Didn't you think so? Not a place where a brutal murder had occurred. The only evidence of any disorder was this broken pottery. Is it possible someone threw something in a fit of rage—a murderous rage? A vase, a dish, whatever it was? Threw it and broke it and then hastily cleaned up before making his escape?"

Charlot looked at Molly with pity. "All right," she said softly, politely taking the glassine envelope from Molly's hand. "The murder occurred upstairs, for one thing, with Madame Lagasse being strangled in her bed. Not after some sort of brawl in the living room."

She shook her head and then gave Molly the side-eye,

thinking pregnancy might have damaged her ability to think clearly.

"And anyway, what would the murderer have to be in a rage about? He got away with the necklace. He made sure there were no witnesses. So far, he's getting away with it. What reason would he have for throwing vases?"

"Well," said Molly, "strictly speaking, we don't know if he has the necklace. We only know we haven't found it."

Charlot pressed her lips together. "Sometimes the most obvious thing is the thing that happened," she said. "We don't have to chase after every possibility in the universe to get to the truth."

"Okay, well, the idea occurred to me and I thought I'd pass it along. It's probably nothing, I'll give you that."

"The forensics team was fairly confident we will get prints from Lagasse's neck."

Molly was not usually squeamish but she shivered. "Usable prints?"

"Yes."

"Well, that would be something," said Molly. "Do you have any suspects—"

"Goodbye, Molly," said Charlot. "I hope you have an easy labor and enjoy your baby."

Molly started to press for more information but decided perhaps, on her due date, this wasn't the moment. She waved to Paul-Henri and left the gendarmerie. Ben was waiting with the engine running, and Molly plopped heavily into the passenger seat.

"Well, that's that," she said. "Probably my last act as an investigator for...will it be years?"

Ben laughed and shook his head. "Unlikely, Molly. Very unlikely. Now, let's go home and watch a movie and try to take our minds off everything."

Molly leaned her head on Ben's shoulder as he drove to La

Baraque. Her thoughts drifted back to Madame Lagasse's house, and her feeling that there was a story there that they hadn't discovered yet. Or maybe she was wrong, and it *was* as simple as a theft and a murder to cover up that theft.

That did make the most sense, she thought. And she was so relaxed on Ben's shoulder that she nearly nodded off before they got home.

🦋 22 🦋

Paul-Henri came into the épicerie and quickly closed the door behind him. He greeted Ninette, who was wearing a thick Icelandic sweater against the drafts every time a customer came inside, and leaned across the counter to kiss cheeks.

"Is this cold snap ever going to end?" she said.

"Feel my hands," he said, taking one of hers and holding it, and looking into her eyes with a sly smile.

"My gracious, Paul-Henri, you're going to give me frostbite!" She snatched her hand back and saw that Paul-Henri was giving her...the look.

The look—unmistakable to any woman—that meant: I am interested in you *that way*.

She stepped back. To say that she did not feel about Paul-Henri *that way* was a massive, hilarious understatement.

Another blast of cold air as the door opened and Madame Tessier came in.

"Bonjour, Madame Tessier," said Ninette, relieved that some-one, anyone, had come into the épicerie. "It's not your regular day, I'm surprised to see you."

"My regular day was my habit with Lili," said Madame Tessier.

"So I thought...it would be best if I started to do my shopping on a different day."

Paul-Henri had no toe-hold to get into this conversation and turned his attention to the chocolate bars.

"Have you heard anything?" said Ninette. "About the investigation, I mean. Maybe you can chime in, Paul-Henri. Has the Chief—"

"I don't know how she lives with herself," snapped Madame Tessier. "What murderer has she ever caught?"

Paul-Henri jerked his head up. "Madame Tessier, please. You must have some forbearance, some patience! The wheels of criminal investigations do grind slowly. The body was discovered days after her death. You can't expect an instant arrest, given the circumstances."

Ninette rolled her eyes so that Madame Tessier could see.

"Perhaps it would reassure you to know that a forensics team came up from Bergerac and did a very thorough job," he said. "A crack team, I must say, excellent at what they do. It is painstaking, unforgiving work! And you must realize—the lab work, all the tests—it takes time! We can certainly hope for positive results, but we can't expect them to be immediate."

"Well, I suppose that is mildly reassuring," said Madame Tessier. "What I don't understand—how is any kind of forensic evidence going to accomplish anything at all? Let's say they find some DNA of...somebody besides Lili. And fingerprints of...somebody other than Lili. How in the world will they have any idea to whom it belongs? If it doesn't belong to some criminal already in the system, that is?"

"Oh, but Madame Tessier, it very well may! You do realize that thefts and even murders are most often committed by repeat offenders?"

"No, I didn't know that. Is that even correct? Of course you want to defend the gendarmerie, which I don't mind saying, has not exactly been a shining star of efficiency lately."

"Now, now," said Paul-Henri. "I understand how difficult is to wait. Especially when your dear friend was the victim in the case." He motioned to Ninette that he wanted to pay for the stack of chocolate bars he had put on the counter. "I'm sure you'll be hearing some news soon," he said on his way out, though he had no reason to believe that was true.

"That man is a ninny," said Madame Tessier. "How is it possible he passed all the examinations necessary to be the junior officer?"

Ninette just shook her head. "He's been awfully...frisky...with me lately. Coming in here all the time and giving me the eye. I don't even—what in the world is going on, when suddenly at age forty-four I've got multiple suitors coming out of the woodwork?"

Madame Tessier smiled the first real smile she had smiled since Lili's death. "You have a way about you. Age forty-four suits you. It is my observation, over many years, that people have their moment, their season of flowering. For some it is when they are teenagers, for others much later."

"When was yours?"

Madame Tessier smiled and looked up at the ceiling, remembering. "Long gone now," she said. "But that is all right. My life has unfolded as it should, and I would have said I was much happier, and luckier than most...until Lili's murder."

"It's been hardest of all on you."

Madame Tessier drew in a long breath. "I miss her dreadfully," she said, and the two women looked into each other's eyes. Ninette reached for the older woman's hands and held them tight.

"I hope I'm not interrupting?" said Molly to Amelie, having knocked on the Bresson door without calling first—she had impulsively asked Ben to drop her off on his way to do errands. The strain of waiting was getting to her, and Amelie had such a comforting presence. At Molly's age, it was strange having a child for the first time, with no mother of her own to consult. Amelie seemed like the next best thing, always warm and welcoming, and an especially good listener.

"Of course not! Come in out of the cold! Laurent and I have been very busy building a train track," said Amelie, taking Molly by the hand and pulling her inside. "I thought you would be sitting by the fire, waiting..."

"I should be. I'm not good at waiting," Molly said. "Oh, I love trains!" Molly said to Laurent, who was standing in the center of a complicated track with his arms pressed to his sides. There were little wooden trees and houses set up alongside the track, and a red engine and some boxcars lay on their sides. "Is this one of your favorite toys?"

Laurent looked down and did not answer.

A look of anxiety flashed across Amelie's face and was gone.

"Can I make you some tea? Maybe you would like to help us build. We were thinking of sending the track right into the bedroom."

Molly caught a small smile on Laurent's face, his eyes on the jumble of train cars.

"Tea...well, I guess it would be nice on such a cold day," she said. Amelie went into the kitchen and Laurent followed her.

Molly eased herself down to the floor, thinking it was going to take a crane to get her back up again. Idly she picked up a boxcar to set it back on the train track. There was a miniature sliding door on the boxcar and it slid open.

Out tumbled a necklace.

"Do you take sugar?" called Amelie.

"Uh—"

Hold on just a minute.

Was this...*the* necklace?

Molly pulled it the rest of the way out of the boxcar, her heart in her throat.

How was this possible? What sense—

"Or maybe a squeeze of lemon?"

"Uhh, yes—lemon!" called Molly.

Holding her breath, she stared at the necklace in her hand: a gold chain with a round filigreed ball. Quickly she slipped it into her pocket.

Maybe it was the effect of pregnancy, maybe not, but Molly felt her body react violently to the stress of the discovery—her throat was closing up, she was blinking like mad, one leg started shaking and wouldn't stop.

This necklace couldn't possibly be Lili Lagasse's necklace. What in the world would that be doing here?

She was in a full-body sweat. Molly wiped her brow and willed her eyes to stop blinking. She took a long, deep breath.

Madame Tessier's voice came into her head: "a jewel hanging from a thin chain, inside a filigreed gold ball." Desperately Molly wanted to pull the necklace out of her pocket to inspect it, to see if she could open the ball and see if there was a jewel inside—but Amelie would be back any second. How many gold filigreed balls on chains were there in Castillac?

There must be some mistake, she thought, still trying to get control of herself. It's just a bit of costume jewelry, that's all.

Molly knew it was Lili Lagasse's necklace. Not even very deep down, she knew. But she didn't *want* to know.

She heard the teakettle whistle, then the murmur of Amelie talking to Laurent. She wished she could close her eyes and magically turn back time so that she had never left the house, never made this discovery, never sat on the floor next to the train track with the necklace in her pocket.

But Molly didn't put it back. She didn't even consider putting it back.

You can't assume anything, you know that, she told herself.

She managed to swallow though her throat was dry as a bone. Her thoughts were whipping this way and that: defending the Bressons, wondering if Amelie knew, figuring out how she could get the necklace identified in secret—but it was as though each thought shattered into bits as soon as she thought it. It was impossible for her to follow any sort of logic, to proceed from one thought to the next, her emotions causing havoc in a manner she had never experienced before.

The baby squirmed inside her and she put a hand on her belly. "I know," she whispered. "I'm feeling a little...I don't know what to tell you...but everything is all right. Go back to sleep."

The baby got in one more kick to the ribs. Molly winced and looked towards the kitchen. Then she flipped onto all fours and slowly hoisted herself up.

"Amelie!" she called, trying for an easy-going tone. "I'm ridiculous for putting you to all this trouble, but I think actually I need to go home and lie down."

"Is anything happening?" Amelie asked. "Contractions?"

"No, nothing like that. It's only—I'm sure you understand,

sometimes the fatigue of pregnancy comes out of nowhere and hits me like a train."

She wished she hadn't said train. The image of that boxcar with the door slid open and the necklace falling out—

Molly shook her head quickly as if that would make the world make sense. She made her awkward goodbyes and headed outside. Then she texted Christophe and rode home in the luxury of a cab, her head spinning.

So many ugly, difficult, frightening questions.

Once again, she wished she could go back in time and not pick up that boxcar. For once in her life, Molly wished, fervently, for ignorance.

❧ III ❧

❧ 24 ☙

"I'm sorry I can't get any closer," said Ben, furiously working to squeeze his Renault into a tight spot.

"No worries, I can walk," said Molly.

"Looks like everyone in the entire *département* is here," he said. He came around to help Molly get out of the car, and hand in hand, they started down the road to the cemetery.

She thought she saw Lapin up ahead—he was tall, and wearing his signature Russian fur hat with earflaps, which people teased him about. If there were ever a day for a Russian fur hat, this was it. The wind whipped mercilessly through the crowd of people walking to the cemetery from both directions; the sky was clear but the bright sun offered no warmth. She looked for Amelie and Jules but did not see them.

The mourners pulled their coats tight and hunched their shoulders against the cold. Molly had decided, out of necessity, that pregnant women were allowed any violation of the usual sartorial rules—especially when past their due date—and was dressed in the most comfortable and roomiest clothes she owned, which were a pair of men's wool pants meant for grouse hunting and a wool lumberjack shirt. Over that, she had managed to pull on a black cashmere sweater, though it was being disastrously stretched over her belly, and then a black overcoat, which she hoped hid the rest. A pair of comfortable, ugly shoes completed the effect.

Ben leaned close to Molly's ear to talk to her privately as they walked. "As I know you know, in a murder case, it's always a good idea to keep your ears and eyes open at a funeral," he said.

Molly nodded. She hadn't told him about the necklace. She told Ben everything, always.

Always...until now.

If she told Ben, obviously, he would insist she go to the gendarmerie with the necklace and tell them where she found it. Of course he would. That *is* what she should do. But try as she might, she could not force herself to do it. It felt like a betrayal to Amelie and Laurent. How could she be responsible for putting Jules in prison and leaving them alone while she was pregnant?

The wind kept grabbing Molly's hair, and she used her free hand to try to tuck as much of it as she could under her wool cap.

"Not that we're working this case," he added.

"No, of course not," said Molly. *God help me.*

They kept walking.

"Are you sure you can manage?" said Ben. "The cold is making this feel like a trek to the end of the earth. I wish you were at home resting."

"So do I. I admit, I *am* tired," Molly admitted. "I'm sort of hoping that the exertion will get labor started."

"Maybe not in the actual cemetery."

"Or during the actual funeral."

They trudged on.

"Do you think I can take off this coat? I know it's cold, but I guess I overdressed and I'm sweating to death."

"Whatever will make you comfortable," Ben said, reaching around and slipping the coat off Molly's shoulders.

At last, they passed under the iron sign that said "*Priez pour vos morts*," and walked to the higher side of the cemetery so they could see as much as possible.

It looked as though all of Castillac was there.

Molly scanned the crowd looking for the Bressons. Would Jules be so bold as to attend the funeral?

Did Amelie know? That question, foremost, circled through Molly's thoughts, around and around.

A dense throng of mourners huddled in the cold. In the center of the cemetery, the priest stood near the coffin, which was a dark mahogany and sat on a sort of stretcher on wheels. A teenaged boy, dressed in a down coat and a hat with a red tassel, held a processional cross. Everyone's breath came out in white plumes. Next to the priest stood what Molly assumed was Madame Lagasse's family: two couples, older men and women, dressed expensively, plus several others that seemed to be part of the group, perhaps their adult children?

"You're quite a sight," said Lawrence, sliding in beside Molly and kissing her cheek. "I really don't know what comes over you sometimes." He, of course, was dressed impeccably, in a black cashmere overcoat with a black scarf. His black dress loafers gleamed with fresh polish.

Molly laughed. "I literally have nothing I can fit into. Plus this weather! This was the best I could do."

He kissed the side of her head. "Bless your heart. The difficulties and indignities of womanhood, I can't even begin," he said. "Aren't you freezing with your coat off? And by the way, have you figured out yet who killed our dear Lili? Or is that a touchy subject now that you obviously have this enormous life event taking up all your attention?"

Molly froze, a fake smile on her face. It would have been comical had it not been due to a sort of terror that enveloped her as she realized that keeping Jules's secret meant she would be, de facto, lying to everyone she knew—not only Ben, but Lawrence and every other friend she had in the village.

"'Enormous' is a word that keeps popping up for some reason," she said. She patted her belly—which was, to be fair, verging on gigantic—and shook her head. "About the murder," she said, into his ear, "I hope Charlot takes the lead on this one." Molly stood on tiptoe to give the Lagasse family a good look. "I feel so bad for Madame Tessier. I know grief is a natural thing that everyone has to feel sometime or other, but... it's still hard to watch a friend going through it."

"Indeed," said Lawrence. He shivered. "I hope they don't drag the service out, we all need to repair someplace warm and have hot toddies."

"Don't tempt me."

"A hot toddy without whiskey is still worth having," he said, patting her arm. "And just think, soon you'll be able to have a libation again! Isn't a nice glass of wine good for nursing mothers?"

"First of all, how in the world do you know anything about that, and second, I have no idea, experts argue about everything. It's hard to know what to do half the time."

Just to the side of the family, Molly spotted Madame Tessier, whose eyes were fixed on the casket. The older woman usually had the posture of an athletic trainer, but on that day her shoulders slumped and the effect was as though an invisible but terribly heavy weight was pressing her to the ground. Her sorrow was deep and wide and palpable.

Lapin lumbered up behind Molly and put his big paws on her shoulders. "Bonjour, chérie—but what in the world are you doing here? Aren't you supposed to be delivering that baby right now?"

Molly shrugged. She did not feel up to answering all these questions.

"We just want that part over with," said Ben.

"Children are troublesome," said Lapin. "Why does their entrance into the world have to bring so much agony for the poor mothers?"

Ben pushed that thought far, far away.

"And, well, families in general," continued Lapin. "What do you make of the Lagasse clan? Do you know any of them, Ben?"

"I do not."

"I heard they're from Bordeaux," said Molly. "They look rich."

"I guess the family is pretty well off, with Lili inheriting that famous necklace. Too bad she didn't sell it and take a trip on the Orient Express or something," said Lapin.

"Those tickets are outrageous," said Lawrence. "I just saw the other day—4,000 euros to go from Venice to Paris! For one night!"

"A night to remember," said Lapin dreamily. Anne-Marie came up behind him and he smiled and put an arm around her. "It's our dream trip—right, Anne-Marie?"

Molly wasn't interested in going anywhere except to bed. "I'm going to sit down," she told Ben, and then squeezed past Lapin to where a low wall divided one set of graves from another. Slowly she lowered herself down, trying not to groan.

She was *so done* with pregnancy.

Part of her mind was mourning Madame Lagasse. A larger part was imagining the terrible scene of Jules going to prison and leaving Amelie and Laurent to fend for themselves. But even that was almost crowded out by the final part, which was consumed by the discomforts of her body—it felt as though every limb, every organ, every everything ached—and the desire to get the birth over with as soon as possible.

The priest did his priestly work, people cried, someone played a sad song on a French horn, and then the funeral was over. Molly looked again for Jules Bresson as the crowd hustled by—everyone was in a hurry to get somewhere warm—but did not see him.

25

Ben watched the last of the crowd pass through the gate to the cemetery. Molly was still sitting on the low stone wall, apparently impervious to the cold.

"Ready to go?" he asked. "I have some thoughts about lunch."

"I'm sure you do," said Molly, making no move to stand up.

A gust of wind whooshed through and Ben shivered. "Aren't you freezing?"

"This wind actually feels quite nice," she said, lifting her face to the sky and closing her eyes. "I'm coming," she added. "Just one second. I'm suddenly feeling very tired and I need a minute to marshal my forces."

And then, all of a sudden, she cried out in pain.

Ben dropped to his knees beside her. "Molly!"

Molly opened her knees wide and leaned forward. She made an animal sound neither of them had ever heard before, followed that with a long, low groan, and started to breathe strangely, making loud huffing exhalations, her eyes closed.

Ben tried to say comforting things but it was clear to him that Molly was in some place he could not reach. He rubbed her arm, hoping it was not annoying. He was filled with a mixture of joy and dread that he had never felt before.

When it appeared that the contraction was receding, Ben gripped her arm. "Let's get you home," he said. "Can you stand up?"

Molly shook her head. She was still bent forward, breathing hard as though she had just run around the block as fast as she could.

Ben took out his cell and called the midwife, who thankfully answered immediately.

"We're in the cemetery!" said Ben. "Molly just had a whopper. Now what?"

"Can she walk? How fast are the contractions coming?"

"I don't know!"

"Well, get your watch out. We practiced this, Ben. You can do it. It'll take me twenty minutes to get to La Baraque. Do you think Molly can get in the car?"

Ben had wrestled murderers with guns to the ground, had faced any number of dangerous people in dire situations over the course of his career. But this? Boy oh boy.

"Molly? Can you stand up?" he asked again.

"I think so," she said. Her voice was quiet, otherworldly, not what he expected. "But you're going to have to pull me up, my legs feel noodly."

Ben went behind her, put his arms under hers, and hoisted her right up.

"How do you feel, do you think you can walk? I can always call an ambulance, just say the word if that's what you want."

"Let's see," she said, taking a few slow steps. "It's okay. But when the next one comes, I'm gonna be down on the ground. Holy smokes."

"Maybe we can get you home before then," said Ben, praying to God the Father though he was not a religious man.

"Hey, Ben?" said Molly, as they made their way slowly out of the cemetery. She smiled at him. Ben could see sweat on her forehead even in the windy cold. "Pretty sure this is it."

✣ 26 ✣

The next morning, bright and early, Lapin gave Anne-Marie a warm smooch and headed off to Madame Lagasse's house to start work organizing the contents of her house. Her nephew, Philippe Arpin, had made arrangements with him after the funeral and told him roughly what to expect.

Which was not much.

Philippe said that his aunt had lived frugally, and he believed that all her furniture had been inherited from her parents, none of it worth much because it was out of style, though of course, Philippe himself was not an antiques dealer so was only guessing. He instructed Lapin to clear the house and sell what he could; no household items had been mentioned in the will and none of her surviving family wanted anything. Simply on the basis of the quality of their clothing, Lapin had gathered that the Arpins were financially in an entirely different league from Madame Lagasse.

In short: they were rich, and she was not. And so none of them had any wish to come to the dowdy little house and go through her things, and were more than happy to pay Lapin to do it for them. A common circumstance and one which made Lapin's business possible.

Phillippe spoke kindly about his aunt. Lapin gathered there was some estrangement between Lili and her siblings, but she had been affectionate to her nephew—had given him some lovely gifts over the years, Phillipe told him. He had driven over from Bordeaux to see her several times a year, but wished now that he had visited more often. Was that a typical sentiment when an older relative dies? the nephew asked, and Lapin reassured him that it was practically universal.

The house key was under a bit of ivy in a large flowerpot on the front steps, just as Philippe had said, and Lapin got into the house without any trouble. He took a pad of paper out of his briefcase, clicked his pen, and decided to begin in the living room. It was unremarkable in both size and contents, and typical of what Lapin saw in house after house in his line of work: a worn armchair, where it looked as though Madame Lagasse had spent much of her time; a sofa much less used; and the usual lamps, side tables, etc.

A few pictures on the wall, ordinary and not worth anything. Madame Lagasse had not been a woman for knickknacks—the surfaces were clean and entirely clear of souvenirs, tchotchkes, or house plants.

The effect might have been austere were it not for the wallpaper. The many shades of green in the leaves almost gave the room the feeling of being in a forest. The wallpaper had clearly been expensive, which nothing else in the house—so far—seemed to be. Probably a previous owner of the house had installed it.

Lapin ducked into the kitchen and made note of its contents, then went upstairs. The sewing machine would be sellable, at least. Then into Madame Lagasse's bedroom.

Lapin stopped suddenly. He blinked and felt an unexpected sob rise into his throat, but the sob wasn't from grief—he hadn't even known Madame Lagasse well—it was a response to the violence that had taken place so recently in that room. He could sense it. Undeniably, there was a presence in that room, an impression of dark intent, even evil. Lapin did not pretend that he did not feel it.

He swallowed hard and tried to calm down. He held out his hand and inspected it but it did not shake, which surprised him.

The bed was made, though not neatly. Lapin swallowed again as he imagined Madame Lagasse in her final moments. Had she known the man who killed her? Was it definitely a man, he wondered. Oh, I'll leave those questions for Molly, he thought grimly, looking at the notes on his pad and scribbling a little in the margin to get the ink running in his pen again.

He cleared his throat and set about the job at hand. A small, plain bureau, which wouldn't sell for much but would sell easily. A battered armoire with a mirror on the door. He imagined Madame Lagasse looking in that mirror after getting dressed, making sure she had buttoned her buttons in the correct button-holes before leaving the house. Something about this made tears spring to Lapin's eyes, and he cursed out loud before hurrying through the rest of the cataloguing and going straight home to see if Anne-Marie had put any leftovers in the refrigerator that he could eat, and never mind that it was between meals.

NINETTE LIVED in a small apartment over the épicerie. It was sort of bare bones and quite small, just a bedroom, a tiny kitchen, and a cramped sitting room. Too cramped for much of a party, if she had been inclined to throw any. But the place was literally fifteen steps from the shop, and who could argue with the bene-fits of that? Fifteen steps in the morning, when her joints were a little stiff and the last thing she wanted to do was get in a car and drive somewhere. She was—as she thought about more often than was good for her mental health—forty-four years old and single. Any thoughts she had had about being part of a family and having children were long put to rest. She didn't need much, and the shabby little place was comfortable and felt like home.

Her parents had bought the épicerie when she was a little girl —she had grown up running up and down the aisles, hiding behind the counter—and now that her parents were gone, she kept running the business because she couldn't imagine not doing it, and because the village depended on it.

Like nearly everyone in the village, Ninette had her routines, and on that Wednesday morning, she carried them out as usual. Coffee and a croissant for breakfast in her dressing gown. A shower afterwards. A few minutes reading before going downstairs to open the shop for the first visitors, some of whom—in *their* routines—always appeared the minute it was open.

That morning—Ninette always remembered it as the week of Lili Lagasse's funeral—it was time to go downstairs. She put her book aside and stood up. And then she felt...well, she didn't know what she felt. Strange. Not herself. Perhaps...ugh...was that a touch of nausea?

She went into the bathroom and ran cold water on a washrag and held it to her forehead. Unmistakably, a wave of nausea hit and she put her hand over her mouth, looking at herself in the mirror, eyes wide.

It's not possible, thought Ninette. Not at her age. Just...it couldn't be.

Could it?

27

Molly was in bed leaning against a pile of pillows. In her arms, swaddled in flannel, was baby Olivier, his little face rosy, his hair red, his eyes closed.

Ben sat on the edge of the bed, looking at his son with an expression of astonishment and devotion.

"Molly," he said. "I haven't—I feel—" he faltered, unable to find words.

"I know," she murmured, looking up at him. "I know exactly. And there aren't any words to describe it. Any of it, really."

"Can I get you anything? What do you need?"

"Not a thing. I think I will make the trek to the living room and sit by the stove. That will be ambitious enough for the morning," she said with a laugh. All of her muscles ached and she was sore in places she didn't know she had.

Ben reached for the baby, held him close to his chest, and the little family moved to the living room and got settled.

"Coffee?"

"Better not."

"Who are you?"

Molly laughed. "I'm not entirely sure! Magnificently happy, I can say that much."

"Me too."

Ben bustled about the kitchen, making himself coffee and then working on a massive breakfast to feed his wife, while Molly nursed Olivier and stared vacantly and blissfully at the flames dancing in the woodstove.

She did not think about Madame Lagasse or Jules Bresson or murder even once.

"WE'VE GOT NO CHOICE, the tiles have to come off so we can replace the supports," said Jules, pointing at a rotten joist.

"Ah," said Ben. "I was hoping this would be simpler. And cheaper, to be honest."

Jules shrugged.

"This building has stood here for how long? A hundred years, maybe longer? And still dry inside," said Ben.

Jules shrugged again.

"All right, I see your point. We can't have the roof falling in on paying guests. I'll get the ladder."

"And then get back to Molly and Olivier," said Jules. "How is he doing?"

Ben stopped and grinned. "He's beautiful."

"Congratulations."

Ben nodded, instantly feeling choked up. He felt as though having a son had catapulted him into another world that he hadn't known existed before. Now he was part of the club of fatherhood that Jules was already in. But none of this—including his feelings for Olivier—were anything Ben could put into words, or communicate to Jules or even Molly.

He took off to get the ladder, unable to stop smiling, and looked forward to an everyday lunch with Molly and Olivier as though it were lunch with the King and Queen of France. Not that there was any King or Queen anymore, but the point still stood.

Jules watched him go and then set about clearing the brush from all around the structure with some loppers and a pair of pruning shears. He tried to focus on what he was doing, just snip and throw the branch to the side, repeat—but the effort failed, and all his mind could see was Madame Lagasse, the necklace, and himself in prison, unable to help Amelie or Laurent or this godforsaken baby coming in only a few months.

He closed his eyes and the pattern on the wallpaper, those overlapping green leaves, was all he saw. It was cold but his body felt clammy, and he shucked off his coat and kept snipping and cutting, trying to bring himself into the job he was doing and away from the panic and terror of that awful night.

He was going to hell, that much was clear. The only remaining question was, what should he do to help his family before he went? How to sell that cursed necklace and not get caught?

28

"We've got to *think*," said Rodney. He was at Shane's, it was before noon, and they were drinking a rough red wine. "Someone in this village stole that necklace. So who? Let's make a list." He rummaged in a drawer for something to write with.

"Idiot, take your stupid lists and shove them—"

"—*ferme ta gueule*, Shane. This isn't the time to trade insults. We've got to get along and pull together or whoever's got that necklace is going to move it and we won't ever even lay our eyes on it. *Focus*."

Shane stalked over to the window and looked out, crossing his arms. If they did find the stupid necklace, he thought, Rodney is not getting half. No way.

"There's Pip, he lives on Lagasse's block. Maybe we should pay him a visit."

"He's too stupid to pull something like this off. Can't you turn up the heat in this place?"

"Yeah, he's stupid, okay sure, but also he's right there under Lagasse's nose. He mighta been seeing her walk by every damn day wearing that necklace. That's gonna have an effect on a person. Put on your coat, idiot."

Rodney had a gulp of wine and stroked his chin. "There's been no crowing from the gendarmerie, so they haven't arrested anyone. We couldn't find it at Lapin's. So that means—logically— it's most likely still out there, in Castillac, with some lout holding onto it until the time is right."

"Or maybe they've left town, gonna try Bordeaux or even Paris."

"I'd take it to Marseille, if it was me," said Rodney.

"Marseille, yeah. And how about we wait until the weather turns, and we can have a little beach vacation while we're there, swim in that blue water, eat some seafood and all."

"Now you're saying something less dumb," said Shane.

The two men spent the next hour making plans as though the necklace was already in their possession—which hotel would they stay at, what dishes they would order at what restaurant, what women would be falling all over themselves for their attention— and then put on their hats and coats and went to see Pip.

THE COLD WAS UNRELENTING. Ninette was at her post at the épicerie, now wearing a coat over her Icelandic sweater, and a wool cap that tied under her chin like she was a schoolgirl. It was about as unsexy a look as Ninette could imagine, and she was prepared to snatch the hat off if she saw Edmond outside the door.

But on that cold day—no Edmond. Not much of anyone until later in the afternoon when Madame Tessier swept in on a frigid gust.

They greeted each other. Ninette thought Madame Tessier sounded weary. Which she was. She did not bustle down the aisle, chattering away, as she usually did, but stood idly next to the cash register, her shoulders uncharacteristically slumped. Ninette noticed that she had misbuttoned her coat and so one side was hanging longer than the other.

"How did you find the funeral?" asked Ninette.

Madame Tessier shrugged, then sighed. "I don't know. They're supposed to be...comforting, in some way? I did not find it so. I kept my eyes fixed on that coffin the whole time, unable to believe that Lili was inside."

Ninette nodded and patted Madame Tessier on the arm.

"It's a funny thing to know something is true and not believe it, all at the same time."

"I know exactly what you mean. I'm still not over my mother's death and that was nearly twenty years ago," Ninette said. "Sometimes when I walk on certain village streets, where I remember her so clearly, I can't believe she's not about to come around the corner with a couple of baguettes in her arms."

The two women stood in silence for many minutes. Ninette slid one hand under her sweater, to her belly. The nausea had passed and she told herself it was the sardines she had eaten the night before, just before bed, that had brought it on.

Madame Tessier's head was bowed. Ninette shivered a little though there was no draft. "Are you hungry?" she asked finally, thinking they might share a chocolate bar.

But Madame Tessier shook her head. "I'm angry, that's the problem," she said in a quiet voice. "I'm so mad at Lili for bragging about that stupid necklace and no matter how I try, I cannot let that feeling go. It was bad enough she had to bring it out all the time and try to get me to admire it. I never admired it and didn't pretend to. It was an ugly thing, a big lump on a chain—who cares? I didn't. The thing is—with Lili—it's a common enough story, you know..."

Madame Tessier looked away, out at the street. She shook her head.

"What story?"

"Well, Lili had an older sister and an older brother. And the older sister was the apple of her father's eye. The brother less so. But Lili—to hear her tell it—was not beloved by either parent, sort of an outcast, the black sheep, in a way. And I believe her, because of how the parents treated her."

Ninette waited. Madame Tessier appeared to be trying to get control of her emotions.

Finally she continued. "There are inheritance laws, of course, that supposedly prevent this from happening, but apparently the father figured out a way around them—rich people have their ways, you know. They don't believe the rules apply to them, and often enough, they don't—anyway, when the parents died, the sister and brother inherited the money. The sister got the bulk and the brother what was left. As for Lili—she got the necklace." Madame Tessier made a dramatic shrug. "And from what she told me, it was not an inconsiderable sum those siblings got."

Ninette took all this in. "And did the siblings make up for it? Terrible thing, to favor one child like that."

"It is. I think the brother did give Lili something. Pittance, really, a token. It's not as though Lili ever did anything to deserve such treatment—it was a matter of favoritism, pure and simple. Lili did her best to move forward with her life, she worked at the bank and made her way all right...but some part of her heart was always broken."

Ninette pressed her lips together and the two women spent a moment thinking uncharitable thoughts about the meanness of those parents.

"Lili did inherit that one thing, the necklace, and she clung to it as though it would make her as valuable—as a person—as her older sister. And now—it's the ultimate irony, isn't it, that the necklace was responsible for ending her life?

"Almost feels like a curse."

Madame Tessier nodded.

"Families," said Ninette, shaking her head. "When did the parents die?"

"Oh, it was long ago, when Lili was barely an adult. Car crash. You know that road with the poplars, going out of Bordeaux?"

Ninette shuddered. "Once they started putting those road signs with silhouettes of the people who died on that road—I barely drive anywhere anymore. Spooked me."

"I gave up my car years ago. Don't miss it."

Another long silence. Even though Madame Tessier craved company, when she engaged in conversation—even interesting, meaningful conversation—something about it made her grief expand until she felt like she might explode in a torrent of tears. Without buying anything, she said her goodbyes to Ninette and trudged home, buffeted by the wind.

29

Amelie watched Jules as he stood at the kitchen sink, drinking his coffee. He was staring out of the window. Amelie had a feeling he didn't see what he was looking at, but was lost in whatever thoughts had taken hold of him lately. She knew something was wrong, maybe very wrong, but she had no idea what it was, how to reach him, or how to help. Asking directly was not usually the best way with Jules, though she had tried it anyway. He gave up nothing; she was not surprised.

"How is it, working with Ben?" she said, keeping her tone light.

Jules shrugged, did not turn around.

Amelie felt a burst of anger. Her husband could be so closed off, so unreachable. Sometimes she had compassion for him and sometimes she wanted to scream at him to open up and talk to her about what was on his mind.

Laurent was in his room, playing. The house was quiet.

Jules finished his coffee and put the mug in the sink. "Okay, I'm off," he said.

To Amelie, it sounded like he was an actor playing the part of a husband. Everything about his tone of voice and his posture and his expression was false.

But she had no idea at all about how to get through to him, to induce him to share what was bothering him. Over the years she had tried various things, and nothing had worked even a little. There was nothing to do but be patient, and hope that whatever it was would resolve without her help.

She went to him and they kissed cheeks and said goodbye, and with a heavy heart, Amelie went to get Laurent ready for school. It would be a pitched battle, as it always was, but at least it was a battle she understood.

"THE WALLPAPER IS QUITE GOOD, or once was. But obviously I won't be taking that with me," said Lapin to Edmond, as they sat at a table at pâtisserie Bujold drinking espresso.

"So Lili was a woman of small means, is that the upshot?"

"Oh, I wouldn't say that, exactly. The house...well, first of all, she had a house, that's more than plenty of people can say. And maybe I gave the wrong impression—it wasn't...it didn't feel like the house of a poor person. Or—what I mean is, it was comfortable enough, it didn't..." Lapin was frustrated; he had these impressions that were quite clear to him, but when he tried to put them into words, he couldn't do it.

"Well," he said finally, "I guess what I'm saying is, I had this idea about Lili based on that necklace. I thought, okay, she lives on rue Tabac, not the fanciest street in the village, but she must have some money tucked away somewhere since she's got that necklace."

Edmond nodded. "She was a good customer," he said, which coming from Edmond was high praise. "Reliable, with discerning taste. Every week, a *chausson aux pommes*. I always made a batch so she wouldn't be disappointed."

"So you judge people on what they order?"

Edmond was surprised that was even a question. Of course he did. "Well...some people have more patrician tastes than others. Nothing wrong with that," said Edmond, driving in the knife.

But Lapin was still wrapped up in the subject of Lili Lagasse and her necklace. "I wonder," he said, "where she got it? Did someone give it to her, or did she buy it herself? Inherited? And if she bought it, where did she get the money?"

"You sound like Molly."

"Well, Molly finally had that baby, did you hear? So I don't guess she's going to be doing anything for poor Lili anytime soon."

"A toast to the new baby!" said Edmond. They clinked their espresso cups and took sips.

Lapin was lost in his thoughts.

So was Edmond. He was thinking about the night of love he had spent with Ninette, which he had reviewed approximately ten million times since it took place. His happiness was so complete, so abundant, that he couldn't believe Lapin didn't know all about it just by looking at him. But Ninette had asked him not to say anything just yet, to allow them to enjoy each other without the full-voiced commentary of the other villagers, which they knew was coming but wanted to put off, just for a little while. And Edmond was finding that having this secret all to themselves was nearly as delicious as the night of love had been.

Meanwhile, Lapin was thinking about Madame Lagasse's house and the creepy feeling he had gotten when he was in her bedroom. For a moment, he imagined putting his hands around a person's neck. He wondered if he would have the fortitude to squeeze and keep squeezing—if he had a good enough reason to do it, if there were such a thing. What if the person was threatening Anne-Marie, or even worse, had done something terrible to Anne-Marie? Lapin wasn't sure, even then, if he could do it.

Sex and death, the biggest topics, the ones no one can dodge, distracted the two friends so that they barely said a word until it was time for Lapin to get back to his shop, and for Edmond to attend to the almond croissants that were ready to come out of the oven.

❧ 30 ❧

T he night sky was filled with clouds so it was dark as pitch.
Archie Pippin, formerly of Birmingham, UK, slipped out of
his house on rue Tabac and moved down the street with feline
grace. He was a skinny man, flexible and fast, who had something
of a specialty of being able to hide in unlikely places. Over the
course of his career, he had never once been caught by the police
even though he had made his living exclusively from burglary for
fifteen years.

This was not the first time his mark was another burglar, and
he expected it to be one of the easiest jobs he'd ever done. On the
night of Madame Lagasse's murder, Pippin had been up late,
getting through a bottle, feeling bored, and had the extraordinary
luck to glance out of the window to see Jules Bresson breaking
into the old lady's house.

Pippin was pleased that the weather was warming up. He had
no extra fat on his body and the recent cold snap had been deeply
unpleasant; he never felt all the way warm unless he was standing
in front of a fire or a radiator. As he moved noiselessly down the
street, he daydreamed about the flood of money he expected to
have soon, thanks to Madame Lagasse's necklace, and how he

would be able to turn up the heat in his apartment whenever he liked and as high as he liked.

As he approached the Bresson house on rue Camus, Pip turned his thoughts to the practicalities of how to move the necklace. He ran down his list of contacts, narrowing it to the most efficient and least likely to try to cheat him. The next decision was which method of travel was best—he would prefer to rent a car because of the independence and flexibility, but on the other hand, the expense would be considerable and obviously it left a trail a kilometer wide.

For some moments he got lost in thinking about cars, and which models he liked best, and which luxury extras he would opt for if he were buying one.

He stood across the street studying the Bresson's small back apartment. No light was on, or any lights up and down the street except for the streetlamps, minus the one he had broken some nights earlier. He felt as though he were the only person awake in all of Castillac and beyond.

The train would be best, he decided.

Pippin was getting a bit ahead of himself, as he was wont to do. He did not even have possession of the necklace—not yet. It was only a matter of time, he thought, approaching the building and beginning to apply his usual thoroughness to the job of finding the easiest way to enter it. There was a village fête coming up the following week, and Pippin was of course always alert to events that took people out of their houses for a predictable amount of time.

The fête would be perfect. He wouldn't have long to wait, just a handful of days, and everyone in the village went.

Once he saw the family head off to the fête, Pippin would break into the house, toss it until he found the necklace, and be out and on his merry way long before the Bressons came home. It was a shame that Castillac was too small for night train service and he would have to wait until the next morning to abscond, necklace safely tucked into his pocket.

Jewelry is one of the better things, he thought, appreciating that it was logistically so easy to deal with and to hide. The idea that he could stand on the platform waiting for a train and no one would have any idea what was in his pocket—a very appealing idea indeed.

"I don't know why, but I feel a little nervous," said Lawrence to Matthias. They were driving out to La Baraque to see Molly and the baby for the first time.

"Well, it's a big change in your life too."

"*I* didn't have a baby!"

"Well, obviously. But your best pal did. Big changes are always a little unsettling, even happy ones."

"I suppose you're right."

"Of course I'm right," said Matthias with a smile as he turned into Molly's driveway.

Inside, Molly was walking back and forth and back and forth with baby Olivier, who was not having his best moment.

Ben opened the door and Lawrence and Matthias started to come in and then stopped in their tracks when they heard a piercing shriek from Olivier.

"Oh, don't worry," said Ben with a laugh. "Come in, come in, Molly will be so happy to see you. The baby's only two days old and I swear she's already feeling cooped up and like she's missing out on everything."

"Not true!" said Molly, who had miraculously been able to hear what Ben said over the shrieking. She came over and proudly showed Olivier to Lawrence. "Can you believe it?" she whispered, and then began to cry.

"Oh my heavens," said Lawrence, holding out his finger to Olivier, who grasped it right away. "He's ginger! I believe that's a sign of great luck." He looked into the baby's face, tears gathering in his eyes too. Then he wrapped his arms around Molly and the baby and gave them a heartfelt squeeze. "I don't think I've ever met a person who has come into the world so recently."

"Congratulations," said Matthias, handing Ben a bag filled with presents.

"So tell me, how is it going? How are you doing? Is motherhood all you hoped it would be?" asked Lawrence.

"It's only been two days," Molly said with a laugh. "So far? I'm really tired. I'm sore like you wouldn't believe. But so so so happy."

She and Lawerence looked at each other for a long moment, both of them beaming.

"So—tell me everything," Molly said as they got settled in the living room.

"Everything about what?"

"I feel like I've been in seclusion for a month. What's the news?"

"There is no news."

"That can't be true. Matthias, nothing?"

Matthias shrugged. "Nothing at the coroner's office, I can say that at least."

"Well, that's something," said Ben.

"Nothing from the gendarmerie?"

Lawrence shook his head. "Listen, I know I've always been first in line to urge you to get involved in whatever dire events have transpired in the village. But this time? I'm thinking, why not leave this one murder to Charlot for a change? They could use a win, and you've got other fish to fry."

"He just called you a fish," Molly said to Olivier, who was doing that newborn baby thing of looking all around with unfocused eyes and hitting himself in the face. "Honestly, Lawrence— I feel the same. Let Charlot do the work this time."

"Good," Lawrence continued. "It's not like some of those

other times, when we were scared for our lives and had no idea who might be the next target. *This* murder—it was all about that necklace, am I right? I understand that people feel stressed financially, and it's possible that whoever took the necklace might be someone broke enough to believe an extreme act was the only way to survive. And well—but who cares about the motive, really? The point is, if you're not rich, you're not in danger. Maybe it sounds selfish—and I fully accept that it is—but *I* don't have a necklace, or anything else particularly valuable. I do have some nice pieces of furniture, but nothing worth strangling me for."

"I hope all of that is true," Molly said quietly.

Lawrence wiggled his finger and Olivier held on. "And really, if Charlot can't nail this case? We need a new Chief. They've got forensics, they've got a stolen object, how hard can it be?"

Molly barely heard him. She had that expression her friends knew well—brow furrowed, chewing on her lip—when she was thinking hard about something criminal. "And also—do we really *know* it was about the necklace?"

"You have other ideas?" said Matthias.

"Not at all. Only saying—everyone I talk to is making the assumption she was killed to cover up the burglary. But what if that's wrong and the motive was something else entirely?"

"It's always good to question assumptions, no matter how rock-solid they appear," said Lawrence, in the self-satisfied tone of the best student in the class.

Matthias nodded. "You think like a programmer," he said to Molly, giving her his highest praise.

Why am I trying to believe it wasn't about the necklace, when I know it was? Molly thought.

Why am I trying to defend a murderer?

Olivier let out a squawk and all the adults startled.

"I'm still trying to figure out what all these sounds mean," Molly said, half to herself. She started to rummage in the diaper bag.

"I think he means, when are these tiresome old men going to stop taking away my mother's attention." Lawrence laughed. "I think we will see ourselves out. I am so thrilled to meet you," he said to Olivier, leaning down to kiss him on his ginger head. "Open the presents whenever you like, no rush, nothing that needs refrigeration."

Molly walked them to the door and waved as they drove off. There was something bittersweet about how things were now, how even though she expected to have lunch with Lawrence at the Cafe de la Place like she always did, and chat with him over text, meet up at Chez Papa with him and Matthias—that nothing, materially or emotionally, had changed between them—still, things would not be the same. She couldn't really describe how or why, only that the sight of Lawrence's car disappearing around the bend in rue de Chêne made her want to sob.

Though lately, that was not unusual at all, hormones—and continually lying to everyone she loved—being what they were.

31

The Castillac market in January was nothing like the market in July: much less for sale, of course, because the products were mostly seasonal. And even though the weather was warming, no one would have said it was anything approaching pleasant—and that had its effects on people's moods.

Malcolm Barstow was making a delivery from the épicerie, and taking his time about it, going up and down the aisles of the market to see if anyone would offer him a taste of something. No one did.

Johnny Marks, owner of the crumbling house out on route de Périgueux, strolled through the market with his beautiful wife. They hadn't bought anything but seemed happy simply to be there, no matter the weather or the season.

Frances was headed for the cheese vendor. She had worked on her pronunciation for her favorite kinds—though there were so many—and approached the vendor with Luka facing front in her carrier, smiling at everyone.

Manette arranged baskets of potatoes at her stand, along with some avocados imported from Morocco. A paltry offering, she thought, looking at the sky and wondering if it were going to snow.

"Well, a baby's just a little thing, and having one doesn't take away the ability to walk, am I right?" said Paul-Henri to Lela Vidal, who was there selling goat meat instead of cheese. "I'd have thought Molly would want to be here showing off the little tyke."

"Do you have a special interest in babies?" asked Lela, mystified about why Paul-Henri would care if Molly was there or not.

"I didn't mean to sound out of sorts. Though I *am* out of sorts." He had planned to feel out Molly Sutton to see if she had any information or opinions on the murder of Lagasse, believing that something as common as having a baby wouldn't get in the way of her usual sleuthing. He tried to cover his disappointment. "I think, just between you and me, Lela—I am on the very verge of being transferred. Who knows where? With all the uncertainty —the last thing I want to do is start over somewhere unfamiliar. Excuse me, I shouldn't be complaining like this." He gave her a salute and moved on, thinking he might drop by the épicerie to see Ninette.

Jules was standing in line to get a bit of seafood for Amelie when he saw Paul-Henri headed his way. His throat got dry and his ears began ringing. Stop, he murmured, but his body did not stop.

As Paul-Henri approached, Jules turned to the side, away from Paul-Henri and Bedin, the seafood seller, who was asking if he wanted one or two dozen oysters.

"Yes? Jules? You are way out in the cabbages?" said Bedin patiently.

Jules made a strangled noise, in the throes of a panic attack, unable to manage a single word.

Paul-Henri brushed his shoulder on his way past, and Bedin looked closely at Jules, thinking he might be about to have a seizure.

But the sight of Paul-Henri disappearing into the crowd

calmed Jules enough that he managed to collect his oysters and pay for them. He moved out of the way, between Bedin's stall and the next stall, whose proprietor was selling fourteen kinds of flavored salt, and stared down at the pavement, trying to master his emotions, which felt impossible: no matter what he did, he could not shake the vision of himself in prison.

It wasn't that prison itself seemed so terrible. It would be no picnic, obviously. But people endured it somehow and Jules understood that he would too. It was not himself he was worried about, but Amelie and Laurent and the new baby, alone, with no one to care for them, and the debt piling up and up...

"—is Amelie? Jules, are you quite all right?"

He looked up quickly to see Madame Tessier standing in front of him, holding a straw market basket, waiting for an answer.

His hands started to tremble and he gripped the bag of oysters as hard as he could. "I'm—yes, I'm fine," he said, mustering a reasonable facsimile of a smile. "Just trying to remember what Amelie told me to get."

"Cheese! You know it's a very good food for pregnant women. Of course, I never had children myself. But that doesn't mean I'm not an expert." She laughed.

Jules knew he was supposed to laugh, too, but at the moment laughter was a bridge too far.

"All right then," said Madame Tessier. "I'm going to talk to a few people and then get home in front of the fire. Please give Amelie my love. And Laurent as well."

"I will, thank you," he said, and ducked into an alley and headed for home.

He had to make a decision about the necklace, that much was clear. If he could somehow get it sold, then at least if—or when—he was carted off to prison, Amelie would have something to live on.

Jules was not naive or stupid. He knew that a sudden, unusual bank deposit would arouse suspicion—and that once he was convicted of Madame Lagasse's murder, the authorities would be searching his house and accounts for the necklace, or the profits from having sold it. He knew these facts, but in a feat of mental agility, he set them into a sort of black box where they remained true but not acknowledged, so that he could continue to pretend that even if the worst happened and he went to prison—which he believed almost impossible to avoid—Amelie and the children would be sort of all right.

So he could believe that the whole horrendous enterprise had been worth it.

CHEZ PAPA, Saturday night.

"Things are dull around here," grouched Frances from her spot at the end of the bar. "I miss Molly."

"I'm sure in a few weeks she'll be right here with the baby in a carrier, same as you," said Nico. He moved down the bar to take some drink orders, grateful for the customers.

Awkwardly, getting a bit tangled by that baby in the carrier, Frances turned on her stool to watch the door, hoping someone interesting would come in. A few young people pushed through the door—young enough to consider me over the hill, she thought, even more grouchily. And then came Madame Tessier, who marched straight up to the bar next to Frances.

"Bonsoir, Madame Tessier! I have delight with which to see you."

"How your French has improved!" said Madame Tessier kindly, and not entirely truthfully. She motioned to Nico and ordered an Irish whiskey, neat.

"I approve of this new habit of yours," said Nico.

"Well, don't get too pleased," she said. "Eventually, my grief will recede—at least I certainly hope it will—and I won't have any use for this," she said, pointing at her glass. Then she leaned forward so she could speak softly. "I'd like to run something by you, if you'll keep it to yourself? Molly is obviously entirely taken up with her baby, as she should be. So I'm...well, I'm not so arrogant as to think I could take her place. But somebody's got to try. For Lili's sake."

"Oh, Madame Tessier," said Frances, slipping an arm around and hugging her, even though she knew the French were, generally, more kissers than huggers. She searched her French vocabulary and could not find the words to communicate her sympathy to the older woman, and good wishes in her attempt at detective work. "What is to begin?" she finally said, and grimaced.

"Well, information in Castillac does eventually find its way to me," Madame Tessier said with a shrug. "And gathering information—*n'est-ce pas?*—is the entire backbone of an investigation. Molly has consulted with me numerous times in the past. I've joked that Dufort/Sutton Investigations should be Dufort/Sutton/Tessier...but Molly and Ben didn't seem to get the hint." She laughed and smoothed her curly gray hair behind her ears. "The question is—well, there are several questions, so let's start with the first: will I know a valuable piece of information when I hear it? I feel that's one of Molly's talents. I have experience collecting information, but not so much evaluating it."

"She is good at sifting," agreed Frances, switching to English. "Well, what kind of information would be helpful to know?" she added. Frances, to be sure, also had ideas about being part of the investigation team.

"We've got a straightforward situation, is how I see it," said Madame Tessier, in English, taking a swig of her whiskey. "An old woman who lived alone, who wore a valuable necklace. Vulnerable, and an obvious target. Especially these days, with the whole world feeling nervous about money and having enough of it."

"Did she wear the necklace to bed?"

"I believe she did. I imagine that's something the gendarmes must know, because if she hadn't, there would be signs of the house being searched."

"Unless she kept it in a jewelry box on a bureau or someplace obvious."

"True," said Madame Tessier. "But in that case, she might even have slept through the burglary and not have been killed at all. So I tend to think she had it on, which is why the thief had to become a murderer. It's an assumption, which Molly would warn us away from. But I think it's a fairly logical one."

They sat for some moments thinking, imagining Lili waking up at the sound of someone in her house. Had she taken off the necklace then? Or gotten out of bed? Did she try to defend herself? Would they ever know how the terrible night had unfolded?

Madame Tessier slapped one hand on the bar. "I know I'm repeating myself, but I need to say it again: Lili was an idiot. She never made the slightest effort to keep that necklace safe. Oh, if I could go back in time, I would plead with her to sell the damned thing!"

"She wouldn't have though," said Frances. "I mean, I didn't know her, so I could be wrong, but it seems like if she never took it off and kept bragging about it—it meant something to her. Something important."

Madame Tessier waved that away. "What is more important than living?"

"I hope whoever did this gets put away for a long, long time," said Nico. "Someone who would knock off an old lady like that? For a little money? Scum of the earth."

"Maybe I'll have another," said Madame Tessier.

"Me too!" said Frances, pointing at her club soda with a shot of simple syrup and lime juice.

Luka squawked and Frances murmured soothing sounds at her and rocked back and forth.

Ninette appeared at the bar, alone, shivering from the cold.

"Well, this is rare!" said Frances. "What's going on, Chez Papa is dead for weeks and weeks and now all of a sudden people are showing up who never used to come at all!" Ninette didn't understand English very well so she just smiled in reply, and waved to Nico.

"How are you?" she said to Madame Tessier, putting a hand on her arm. "I was thinking of Lili today when I was unpacking a box of those cheese crackers she loved so much."

Madame Tessier's face lit up. "Oh, she did love those crackers," she said, shaking her head, but able for a moment to feel the joy of remembering someone you loved, and some detail about them that made you feel as though they were right there with you, in spirit if not body.

32

"You can consider me valet and butler for the day," said Ben, with a bow. "I know the mothers are coming and I don't want you to run yourself ragged getting ready." He leaned over to kiss Olivier's head.

"You are very sweet. But please—go for a run, you know you want to and I've got things under control. I'm feeling a thousand percent better, practically good as new."

"But you're up half the night—"

"Eh, it's fine. You men have no idea how amazing it is to be up in the middle of the night nursing a baby. It's...it's...well, I can't find the words for it. Anyway—it's not a chore, is what I'm trying to say. It's the absolute best thing in the world and I'm so grateful I can do it. I don't even feel that tired."

They both looked at Olivier, who was sound asleep in Molly's arms. He twitched and then resettled, and the two parents looked on proudly as though the baby had accomplished something marvelous.

"Okay, maybe I will go for a run. I think Jules will probably come with Amelie, so we'll make some progress on the shed later on."

Molly looked away. She swallowed hard.

Her silence was lying, she did not pretend to herself that it wasn't.

Ben took off and left Molly alone with the baby and her guilt. For a moment, she wondered whether leaving Ben alone with Jules was a safety risk, especially since Ben had no idea of the actual situation. Was her lying not only deceitful but putting Ben in danger?

Why were there *so many* questions she could not answer?

When it was nearly time for the women to show up, Molly put the snoozing Olivier in his bassinet and got some plates of charcuterie ready, along with a fresh pot of coffee and a big bowl of fruit salad.

And then in a moment, the living room of La Baraque was filled with chatter and laughing, and the occasional shriek of a baby. They went through the two plates of charcuterie in the blink of an eye, and Molly reheated a pot of soup and ladled out bowls, which were consumed in another blink of an eye.

"Ah, the prodigious hunger of pregnancy and nursing!" said Selma, pushing back her empty bowl, after having seconds.

"I'm sorry I don't have any pastry to give you," said Molly. "I've been feeling...okay I do know this is a little crazy...but feeling a little superstitious about leaving the house. Just haven't wanted to. Even for pastry, and you know for me that's saying something."

"Not crazy," said Amelie. "You want to keep your little one safe. It's just as it should be."

"I think I missed that part," said Frances. "Those early days of being cooped up were hard to take."

"Well, no need to mourn the lack of sweets—I brought some!" said Selma, reaching into her knapsack and triumphantly pulling out a bag of cookies, mostly broken.

The women descended on the bag of crumbs and devoured them.

Then a pause. The babies slept. Laurent was with his father and Ben out by the shed. The women were momentarily sated and content, except for Molly, who kept stealing glances at Amelie and wondering what she knew.

"Okay, so I had a whole list of things to complain about," said Frances. "But I'm not feeling so complainy now."

Selma nodded. "The power of sausage and cookies," she said. "I don't feel like complaining either. Though I will say if any of you want to cast a spell or say a prayer or whatever you do that would urge this baby to be born—I would be eternally grateful." She put her hands on her enormous belly and looked down at it.

"Due dates are a cruel joke," said Amelie.

"Thank you," said Selma. "Molly, if you don't mind my asking, how soon are you planning to go back to work? Florian has given me the long version of your exploits over the last few years, and I imagine it's not easy to sit around eating soup when there's a murderer on the loose."

"It's been surprisingly easy," said Molly. "Even though I wanted a baby more than anything, I'm still surprised by how entertained I am just by doing nothing except looking at him."

The others laughed.

"I'm sure Chief Charlot will handle things," she added.

"Huh?" said Frances. That was...uncharacteristic, she thought, giving Molly the side-eye.

"Charlot's gotten some bad breaks, I think," Molly continued. "This time, she's got forensics on her side. And...well, anyway, I'm confident she's up to the job."

"I really hope so," said Amelie. "And I hope after she catches him, he spends the rest of his life in prison. Just for breaking Madame Tessier's heart, if nothing else."

The others nodded. And then without a word, as a group, got up to rummage in the kitchen for something else to eat.

. . .

SHE HAD PUT it off long enough. Madame Tessier carefully tied on a scarf, in the chic way that all Frenchwomen know, and left the house. It was Sunday; the village was busy with the big meal of the day or spending time with family. Madame Tessier had no family. Lili Lagasse had been the person she spent Sundays with, if she spent them with anyone. The person she ate with on Christmas morning, the person she complained to, exulted with, teased…

She clamped her teeth together so as not to start weeping on the street. She would have thought, before Lili's death, that there was a finite number of tears in response to any event, and that once you cried them, you would be more or less done with the worst of the grief.

That had proven incorrect. Or at any rate, the tears were—so far—endless, and showed no sign of slowing down.

It was not the most propitious time of year for gossip. Too cold to sit in her chair in front of her house, where anyone walking by might stop and toss a juicy tidbit her way. Chez Papa was sort of promising in that alcohol loosened lips, but so far Madame Tessier had found it awkward to approach people there and strike up conversations. In front of her own house, in her familiar chair—the interactions were so much more natural, and people didn't feel as though she were grilling them or trying to extract specific information.

And that was the problem, she thought. I usually am rather passive during the whole enterprise. I sit in the sunshine and listen to the birds, and people come over and stop for a moment and unburden themselves of whatever gossip they might have come across. Sometimes even confess to something they've done that they shouldn't have. That is an entirely different thing from accosting people and interrogating them. Different from needing to know specific facts about a specific circumstance that the person involved does not want anyone to know.

This investigation business—it was harder than it looked.

And something else she had realized: her age made people tell her things more readily. She looked like a gentle old lady, not capable of hurting a fly. Well, she *was* a gentle old lady, that much was true. People in the village sometimes used her as a sort of confessor, now that they rarely went to mass. They told her the bad things other people did, and slipped in a few of their own misdeeds while they were at it. Madame Tessier took it all in. And some of those secrets, she kept forever.

Did anyone see anything the night of Lili's murder? That was the obvious question, the first question that needed an answer.

She turned onto rue Tabac. Instantly she was flooded with memories of what felt like the million times she had turned that same corner on her way to see Lili. Madame Tessier stopped, looked down at the sidewalk, blinked back tears, then straightened her shoulders and kept walking. The street was deserted and she considered whether it was better to loiter around waiting to see if anyone came out, or go ahead and knock on doors.

She decided to knock, and forget the awkwardness of it.

At the first two houses, no answer.

On the third, a young woman opened the door. A small child wearing only a diaper held onto the woman's leg.

"I'm sorry for bothering you," said Madame Tessier. "I'm looking for information about the night of January 18th? When your neighbor was murdered?"

The woman shook her head, made apologies for being no help, and Madame Tessier moved on to the next house. She knocked on door after door, talked to numerous Castillacois, and got exactly nothing for her efforts except for sometimes, a generous helping of sympathy.

Archie Pippin watched Madame Tessier from his window, standing to the side so he couldn't easily be seen from the street. He was not the sharpest knife in the drawer, but he knew of her friendship with Lili Lagasse and guessed what she was up to.

When she knocked on his door, of course he did not answer.

❧ 33 ❧

"I don't want to make a big deal out of it, I'm only saying...Jules seems troubled," said Ben.

"Do you think there's something specific that's bothering him?" Molly said, her throat going dry.

Ben shrugged. "I didn't ask." He shrugged. "He and I barely know each other."

He leaned down and kissed Molly on the cheek. "Let me take him," he said, reaching for his son.

Molly stood and stretched. I'll bet he's troubled, she thought, if he's opened up that boxcar and found it empty. What kind of pathetic hiding place was that, anyway. She was unable to stop wishing she had never seen the necklace at all.

"I'm so fond of Amelie. And Laurent too. So far, I find Jules... harder to get a feel for. You've spent a little time with him—what do you think of him? What kind of person is he?" said Molly.

A deep rumbling sound from Olivier. The baby grimaced, and then...an explosion.

"Don't worry, I'll take care of it," she said. "Your face, though." She was glad for a reason to leave the room.

She had to tell Ben. *Had to.*

NELL GODDIN

When she returned, Ben had disappeared. The day was gray and she figured another day lolling in front of the woodstove sounded like a good idea. "What do you think, Olivier? Shall we just lie here and rot in the lovely heat, and not do a single thing for the good of the world?"

She spread out a quilt and put him on it, and lay down beside him. They both fell asleep, Molly not having a real nap but drifting in and out of consciousness, all the unanswered questions never really gone.

Then, just on the edges of Molly's thoughts, Lili Lagasse appeared. It was sort of a dream, Molly seeing her in the épicerie with Madame Tessier, laughing over a potato that looked like a local politician. Molly could hear Lili's laugh, could remember the green print of the dress she was wearing.

She shook her head to clear the sleepiness, trying to remember if she had seen Lili wearing the famous necklace. She thought not.

And then without any warning, tears were rolling down Molly's cheeks. Seemingly out of nowhere, the emotion of having a baby—this particular beautiful, brilliant, ginger-haired baby—and knowing that her life would never be the same—knowing that everything had changed, even if most of the changes were wonderful—it filled her with a bittersweet sorrow. In the near future, she wouldn't be having spur-of-the-moment lunches with Lawrence, or spending long hours digging into murder cases. She wouldn't be tearing around on her scooter, scaring pedestrians, wasting afternoons gossiping with Madame Tessier and Edmond. And even while she was mourning these changes, she was filled with more joy than she ever knew it was possible to feel. Even with the necklace hidden in the annex with no plan for what to do about it.

It was confusing, to say the least.

It was time to tell Ben, no matter what.

Oh for heaven's sake, she thought, wiping her eyes and sitting up. The sorrow vaporized as quickly as it had arrived.

Hormones, thought Molly, are making me half insane. I need some fresh air.

And with that thought, she got out the brand-new baby carrier and spent a half hour trying to figure out whose limb went where, and set out on rue de Chêne, mom and baby looking for just the smallest sort of adventure, and keeping an eye out for Ben.

THE MOOD at the gendarmerie was bleak. Charlot had exhausted everything she could think of to track the sale of Lagasse's necklace, and all of that effort had produced nothing, not even a single lead. It was a simple case, a vanilla-flavor robbery-murder, a case a rookie should be able to make headway on. Yet here she sat, with her buffoon of a junior officer, with nothing to do but wait for forensics and cross her fingers.

For the first time in her career—in her whole life—she felt like a failure. She *was* a failure.

Paul-Henri sensed something was going on. He had learned at the knee of his overbearing mother to be sensitive to women's moods, and this sensitivity had been the saving grace in his relationship with his boss on more than one occasion. But this...this felt different. Something that a compliment or an afternoon's industriousness was not going to dissipate.

He sat at his desk catching up on paperwork, France's favorite pastime after eating cheese. Charlot appeared to be doing nothing. She sat uncharacteristically slumped at her desk, by turns glowering and grimacing. What in the world was the matter, Paul-Henri thought, peeking at her from time to time. He predicted a blow-up, directed at him, as she made an attempt to offload her frustration or anger; it was time to make himself scarce.

"I'm going to rue Tabac once more," he said, jumping up and

reaching for his coat. "I know I've already canvassed twice, but there are a few houses I haven't been able to contact. Including Archie Pippin."

"That lowlife," growled Charlot. She sat up straight and put her palms on her desk. "This case has all the markings of Fletcher Barstow," she said. "That necklace would be catnip to him. And a murder on top of it? His favorite dish." She frowned. "It's a terrible shame that our best suspect is in prison."

"Fletcher does love a jewel."

Charlot nodded. "And obviously—would kill an old lady without giving it a thought. Archie Pippin, though? I think he would have managed to get the necklace off Lagasse and disappear into the night without her even knowing about it. Strangulation? Not his style at all."

"All right, sure," said Paul-Henri, with a note of petulance. "Won't hurt to talk to him, though."

"Of course not. Maybe check the papers, make sure there hasn't been a prison break."

Paul-Henri looked confused.

"That's a joke, Paul-Henri," Charlot said wearily. "Look, as soon as we get forensics back, we'll be able to do more. We can ask for prints and DNA of anyone who might have gone into the Lagasse house—delivery people, cleaners, friends, family—"

"Lagasse did her own cleaning. The family lives in Bordeaux and I haven't gotten the impression they came to Castillac often. And why would they need this necklace, anyway? They have their own jewels and plenty of money."

"You have confirmed this, not just drawn assumptions based on how they looked at the funeral?"

"Of course." Paul-Henri rarely expressed annoyance to his boss, or to anyone, at least directly, but he felt something loosening in himself and couldn't hold it back. "Do you think I have tossed all police procedure aside?"

"All right, delivery people and friends, then!" barked Charlot.

"So: Malcolm Barstow and Madame Tessier? That's your list of suspects?" His tone was sarcastic. Undeniably insubordinate.

Charlot's eyes got wide. "What's got into you?"

Paul-Henri didn't answer. He felt a sudden rage bubbling up that he had no idea how to handle, with only the vaguest notion that it wasn't really about Charlot at all.

"Go back to the neighbors. If someone saw something, we have to know about it," said Charlot, with gritted teeth. If there had been a vase sitting on her desk, she would've thrown it at Paul-Henri's head.

❦ 34 ❦

Snow flurries. Archie Pippin watched the Bresson house from a distance as he strolled down rue Camus, leaving a trail of footprints. He was a talented watcher, able to keep a close eye on something without being obvious about it. It would have helped to have a dog to busy himself with, and in fact he had often considered getting a dog for this reason. But he traveled too frequently. Castillac wasn't big enough to accommodate a man of his talents, and so he performed most of his burglaries farther from home. He couldn't be dragging a dog along all over the place.

The front door of the Bresson house opened and Jules stepped out, alone.

Exactly what Archie was waiting for. He obviously had no way of knowing when or how Jules would try to move that necklace, and so Jules's movements had to be monitored as best as Archie could manage. Surely Jules wasn't dumb enough to try to sell it locally, where it would almost certainly be recognized and also not get what it was worth.

The Bressons had no car; Archie expected that eventually, Jules would take a train in search of a better market. Archie—

quelle coincidence!—would take that same train. And pickpocket the necklace during the voyage.

He had prodigious pickpocketing skills, though he was a bit rusty because Castillac didn't have much of anyone worth pickpocketing. He wasn't going to steal just for the sport of it, it had to be something worth stealing, was how Archie thought of it. Thieves have morals too. Sometimes.

Jules was a fast walker and it was nearly impossible for Archie to give the impression that he was not following him—he had to hurry to keep the gap from widening. Jules had long legs and he did not. They went straight to the center of town, past the Cafe de la Place, down a street to pâtisserie Bujold. Jules did not slow down. Archie stayed a block behind, getting more and more curious about where he was going.

The snow came down a little faster. Some children ran past Archie, scraping a bit of snow off a car and throwing a little snowball at him, shrieking as they ran off.

Archie brushed snow off his arms and head. Jules went around a corner and Archie hurried to close the distance. What if Jules had the necklace in his pocket, right now? He might have decided it was safer to keep it on him rather than hide it in his house, especially with a kid around. Archie broke into a trot. If the right moment presented itself, he could run into Jules, pretend to slip in the snow, and check his pockets.

This might turn out to be a very lucrative snowfall, Archie thought with a smile, his eyes on Jules as he ran to catch up.

PAUL-HENRI DID GO to rue Tabac, he did knock on a few doors, but his heart wasn't in it. Archie Pippin wasn't answering, and he stood on the front step feeling angry at the man, whom everybody knew was a thief or worse, for not having the decency to answer his door.

Paul-Henri was aware this was a ridiculous reaction, but he

could not quell the feelings of annoyance. The business of the possible transfer continually hung over his head. He knew he was not behaving in a disciplined manner consistent with the ideals of the gendarmerie, but lately, his feelings about the gendarmerie were mixed.

Not just mixed—angry. An officer with his record! Whisked off to parts unknown, with no say in the matter? It was unconscionable.

He wandered down rue Tabac in the snow, losing focus on why he was there. He thought about Ninette, and how she had an attractive glow about her lately. He wanted to ask her out on a date but did not want to be rejected. Perhaps he would go and buy some more chocolate bars, and see what the temperature in the épicerie was that day. Maybe she would be warm and welcoming, and he could take his chance.

Using some willpower, he thought about the Lagasse case on his way to the épicerie, the snow covering his shoulders and cap. Did he think the forensics report was going to be helpful? He did not. He thought the killer had likely worn gloves, so that the marks on the victim's neck would yield no prints. Much more likely, all the DNA samples will belong to Lagasse and her friends and that was it, and they'd be right at square one. For a moment, he imagined telling this forcefully to Charlot, implying that she was being lazy to expect positive results when such results were highly unlikely.

Charlot, in his daydream, told him that of course he was right, what had she been thinking? And instead of being transferred, they switched places and he was the Chief.

Around the corner just ahead, a huge dog appeared, skidding in the snow, and Paul-Henri recognized it as Yves, the *bleu de gascogne* belonging to Madame Bonnay. She got frantic when her dog escaped, which it did routinely. Paul-Henri lunged this way and that, grabbing for its collar and slipping in the snow, finally— triumphantly—getting the dog under his control.

He had collected Yves so many times that he kept a leash attached to his belt, and quickly snapped it on the dog's collar, and with a deep Gallic sigh, turned away from the épicerie to take him home.

JULES WAS ONLY A QUARTER-BLOCK AHEAD—a quick sprint and Archie would catch up to him. He was mindful of the slipperiness of the snow, an advantage for the pretense of falling into Jules, but he had to be careful not to slip unintentionally before he even caught up to him.

The first few strides, Archie took it easy, then he gained speed. Jules was still walking fast and Archie understood, believing that if you had a valuable necklace in your pocket, you wouldn't want to saunter down the street at your leisure.

Closer, and closer. Jules did not hear him or at least show any sign of hearing him.

Then, just seconds away from skidding into Jules and nimbly emptying his pockets, Archie realized the most obvious truth: that whoever was in possession of that necklace was automatically a murder suspect. Simple as that. How he had managed not to grasp this sooner, he could not say. The lapse felt shameful and he wondered for a moment if he was losing his grip.

He stopped running and watched Jules turn a corner and disappear.

It would have been so easy to steal that necklace without killing anybody, he thought. Jules is an amateur, a murderous amateur.

Why didn't I think of it, with the old lady living right across the street all this time? Am I getting soft?

Archie was confident he could move the necklace in a very short period of time. But if it was ever traced back to him, he wouldn't be able to shake off suspicion—he hadn't completely lost his mind, he understood quite well that if it was a matter of his word against Jules's—that is, a known burglar against a family man with no record—Archie would lose without question.

Lose all the way to prison, which he had a particular aversion to, more so than your average criminal. He would need to think this through some more. Was there any way to have Jules arrested for the old lady's murder but keep the necklace for himself?

There had to be a solution. He was going to pour himself a glass of beer and think the situation through, instead of going off half-cocked. His first idea had been the best—to steal the necklace while the family was at the fête. That way, no one would know it was Archie Pippin who had it.

❧ 35 ❧

"Come on now," shouted Lapin, "shake a leg!"

He was standing in the middle of Lili Lagasse's living room, overseeing the transfer of her furniture to his shop. It was not going well.

Rodney and Shane were quick to say they could do anything, where money was concerned. And so, rashly, Lapin had hired them after running into them at the épicerie and lamenting that his usual moving guys were unavailable. They looked beefy enough, and were considerably younger than Lapin himself. But so far, the pair had taken more breaks than moved furniture. The van was not even half full and Lapin's stomach was telling him it was lunchtime.

"Go on, then, we can handle it from here," said Rodney. "It ain't like loading a van is rocket science. Go have your lunch. By the time you're done, the van'll be all packed up, done and dusted."

Lapin knew better than to leave the likes of Rodney Smith and Shane Fowler alone in someone's house. But his stomach let out another mighty roar, and he wondered, well, really, what harm could they do? The furniture wasn't worth much of anything, they'd have no reason to steal it. Why not let them take their time while he ate a lamb chop?

The door had barely closed behind him when Rodney and Shane went running upstairs, the same thing on their minds: if Lili Lagasse had this famous necklace? What else did she have?

The bureau had been emptied and the contents packed or disposed of. The armoire—empty.

"Give me a hand," said Shane, grunting as he lifted the side of the mattress. "I'll lift 'er up, you peek under and see what she was hiding under there."

Rodney saw nothing. They looked around some more, but didn't see any good hiding places. Rodney even checked the toilet tank but it contained nothing but water.

They trotted back downstairs, dispirited.

"Maybe we could have a snack at least," said Shane, wandering into the kitchen and opening the refrigerator. "Crikey, did the woman live on air?" The refrigerator was clean as a whistle and nearly empty except for a small container of yogurt with prunes, which Shane opened and dug into.

Rodney, meanwhile, had spotted a bottle of Bordeaux in a cupboard. "Thirsty?" he asked Shane.

And that was the end of the furniture-moving for that day. After they polished off the Bordeaux, they found their way into the cellar where more wine was stored, all thoughts of finding treasure gone from their drunken minds.

"You're very sweet to visit and keep me up to date," said Molly, as she walked back and forth with a squalling Olivier. She wished her friend had not come, that was the ugly truth of it. The baby's crying had her on edge. And this business of keeping secrets—it did not suit Molly at all. It was easier to live with when she was alone and not more or less lying to anyone's face.

Madame Tessier put her hands over her ears and then took them away. She tried to summon a tolerant smile. "I know you, my dear Molly. And I'm quite sure that a commonplace event such as having a baby isn't going to make you lose your taste for murder investigations."

"I always come out sounding like some sort of slavering corpse-monster," muttered Molly. "Really, murder is not something I have a taste for."

"Oh, you know what I mean. Is he quite all right?" Madame Tessier asked, as Olivier let out a piercing shriek.

"Just gas," said Molly.

"Well, you do seem more or less calm in the face of that... noise."

Molly smiled at her boy. "There's this feeling...let's see...ah... with a baby? There is no controlling the situation. His needs are greater than my will or my desires or...than anything really. So I might as well relax and go with the flow." She said these words but there was nothing relaxed about how she felt.

Not with Lili Lagasse's necklace hidden in the armoire in the annex.

Not with knowing perfectly well who killed Madame Tessier's best friend, and not telling a soul.

Not telling was intolerable. So was telling. How could she be responsible for sending her pregnant friend's husband to prison?

Olivier made a high-pitched sound that made both Molly and Madame Tessier wince. Molly skipped across the living room, bouncing him while holding his head steady, and in a moment or two, the cries finally died down.

"Well now, that's better," said Madame Tessier. "Come sit, and let's go over what we have."

Molly dropped into a chair, gently. "Do you have anything? I'm sure you've tried the neighbors?"

How much closure—if such a thing existed—was she denying her friend by not immediately going to Charlot with the necklace?

"Oh yes, I tried them. I got nowhere. I thought possibly Annette would know something, at the very least—you know her, works at the *mairie*? Lives right next door to Lili. She's a nosy sort, always peering out of her window from behind a curtain, you know the type."

Molly laughed. "Well, we're nosy too."

"Just be out in the open about it, is all I'm saying. Anyway, maybe you'll get something out of her. I had some expectations of myself, if I'm honest, but it turns out I have no talent in the interrogation department. Or wheedling, or whatever skill it is when you get people to talk who don't want to. For whatever reason."

"I heard from Paul-Henri that Charlot expects the forensics report soon," Molly said.

"Am I supposed to cheer about that? Some lousy fingerprints, a stray hair or something? Who are they going to match them to, is what I'd like to know! It's not as though the entire village's prints are on file. Our gendarmes sit on their hands while waiting for the lab report, staying inside where it's warm instead of out combing the village, doing their jobs. As though DNA will do all their work for them! The pair of them are lazy and bumbling, and I think I never noticed before—never took in the full picture of their ineptitude—because, selfishly, it wasn't my best friend's murderer they were failing to catch."

"I'm sure they haven't just been sitting around. And neither have you. So nothing at all from any of the neighbors?" Had anyone seen Jules out on the street on the night of January 18? And if so, why hadn't they come forward? Even if they hadn't seen him go in Lagasse's house, it would be suspicious. Especially if no one else had been seen. Especially if it were the middle of the night.

"Like I said, nothing, zero," said Madame Tessier crossly. "Honestly, I don't know how you stand it, Molly—not knowing if people are lying, holding back on you, or telling the truth.

Because I will tell you, I suspected each of those, sometimes all three at once. How on earth do you sort it out?"

Molly tucked a conked-out Olivier into his bassinet. His red hair spiked straight up, giving him a sort of punk rock look. She stretched and went into the kitchen to get something for them to drink and eat. "Well, it's hard to answer that. And for sure, sometimes I get it wrong. Listening is a high art—most people have no understanding of this, though I know you certainly do." She pulled out some *comté* and a bottle of lemonade and seltzer. "Sometimes we just don't have enough information ourselves to be able to judge. Sometimes we *do* know something, or part of something, and then what someone says contradicts that and we have to figure out who's right and whether the other people were lying or just mistaken. And sometimes...the best thing...is when you just get a feeling. Like—you can't prove it, not yet, but you have this sense, this uncanny perception, that someone is lying."

"And where does that feeling come from?"

"I have no idea," Molly said. "I've learned to trust it implicitly. But obviously it's nothing you can conjure. It happens or it doesn't."

Molly thought about the time she had spent with Jules and Ben out by the shed. No alarms had gone off, nothing had hinted to her that Jules might be lying, might be pretending to be someone he wasn't. She had found him closed off, hard to reach in some way...but Laurent was the same way, and the little boy certainly hadn't stolen the necklace or murdered anybody.

She wished Madame Tessier would go home and let her think it all through, carefully, step by step. Would Lapin be able to identify the necklace as belonging to Lagasse? Maybe...but he would never be able to keep it to himself. The whole village would know in five minutes if she showed it to him.

And why did she keep bothering about identifying the necklace when she knew perfectly well what the necklace was and to whom it had belonged?

Molly kept bothering because she was looking, desperately, for a loophole. For some other truth to be revealed, because the truth right in front of her was not a truth she wanted.

Molly brought over the lemonade spritzes and the plate of cheese and set them on the coffee table.

"Would you...have anything stronger?" Madame Tessier asked, nonchalant.

Molly paused. She knew that the French had much looser rules about when and where to drink alcohol than Americans, but it was ten-thirty in the morning and she gave Madame Tessier a questioning look.

"I find it helps," said Madame Tessier, her chin lifted.

Molly fetched a bottle of tequila and set it next to the spritzes. She ate a piece of cheese. In that moment, she wanted to catch Lili Lagasse's killer with every fiber of her being. She wanted him not only brought to justice but for him to suffer because of what he had done to Madame Tessier. And she wanted him to be someone other than Jules Bresson.

The women ate and drank without talking. Molly kept glancing over at Olivier because letting her eyes rest on him felt good and relaxing to her frazzled nerves.

Madame Tessier polished off her lemonade and tequila, then reached into her large handbag and drew out a package of butterscotch candies and offered them to Molly, who took one. "Perhaps it was simply my presence that made the neighbors uncomfortable. They all knew Lili and I were great friends—they'd seen me countless times on rue Tabac, on my way to and from her house. So...I sort of understand that finding me on their doorstep, wanting something, all full of emotion even if I'm not expressing it—the sense I got was that everyone—really, every single person I spoke to—wanted me out of their house as quickly as possible."

"I'd have expected better manners than that, given the circumstances. With all of them knowing her, and who she was to you."

"Eh, no one was rude, exactly, I'm more describing how I thought they felt rather than how they were acting. It's possible I was just letting my own emotion distort how things actually were."

"Some people get brusque when they can't help."

"Mm."

The women sucked on their butterscotches and thought some more.

"Pretty sure Ninette is pregnant," said Madame Tessier.

Molly was bug-eyed. "What?"

"Edmond."

"No! What in the world? *Edmond?!* I mean...hurray? I—how do you know this? Did Ninette tell you?"

"She did not. To be perfectly transparent, it's a guess."

"Oh."

"Don't give me that deflated 'oh.'" Madame Tessier laughed. "I would bet anything you like that I'm correct."

"Then how..."

Madame Tessier smiled wide. "Detective work," she said. "I pay attention. And at my age, I have years and years of experience. I know the signs when people get together, even when they think they're being so clever at hiding it. A flash in the eye, a kind of private smile that is actually plain to anyone paying attention at all. A blush—but the signs don't even have to be as obvious as that."

"Your skills are amazing."

Madame Tessier inclined her head. "Thank you. I may not know how to get anyone to tell me what they saw on January 18, but I do know how to read body language."

"And the pregnancy? How do you divine that, are you rummaging through her trash and finding pregnancy tests?"

"I'm not going to dignify that with a response," said Madame Tessier, but she was pleased—even smug—and not annoyed. "Just you wait. I'll hazard a further guess, though of course this is entirely made up—I think they'll be married once she tells Edmond. And probably be very happy together."

"Edmond and Ninette. It boggles the mind."

"You will lose your *devoté*."

Molly snorted.

They sat looking at the flames in the woodstove. Molly leaned over to check on Olivier and saw his little eyelids twitching as he dreamed. For a long moment, she forgot all about Jules and Lili and the necklace.

"Do *you* think the forensics is going to be helpful?" asked Tessier finally.

"Might be," said Molly. "Depends on whose DNA it turns out to be. If it's just yours..."

"By this point, don't criminals know not to put their mitts all over everything when they're committing a crime? It's not as though fingerprints are a recent discovery, for heaven's sake."

"Eh, a lot of criminals are stupid. Or—maybe stupidity isn't the main thing—it's recklessness. He knows he shouldn't touch anything with his bare hands, but he's so dazzled by how rich he thinks the necklace will make him, that he doesn't take precautions. He knows better but can't help himself. And these days, it's not only fingerprints he needs to be worried about. Like you said, a stray hair, a bit of dead skin—things that aren't controllable, unless you're going to break in wearing a HAZMAT suit."

"Might attract some attention."

"Mm."

Molly thought for a moment about the chunk of pottery she took to Charlot, wondering if it was sent to the lab or sitting in a drawer somewhere. Had Jules thrown that object and broken it? Why would he, if he had the necklace and got away?

Madame Tessier, only a little tipsy, said her goodbyes and took off on her bicycle. With a gust of sadness, Molly watched her go.

Was there a way for Madame Tessier to get the justice she

wanted and deserved, and for Amelie to have her husband and the father of her children at her side where he belonged? *How?*

But the painful truth was: Jules didn't belong at Amelie's side. Murder is murder.

AFTER MADAME TESSIER HAD GONE, Molly did a number of things new mothers do: she checked on Olivier multiple times. She made a cup of tea but did not drink it. She did a load of laundry. She looked out of the window and considered how her life was unrecognizable.

While she did these things, she was thinking over what Madame Tessier had said.

How no one on rue Tabac saw anything the night of January 18. Jules had managed to slip into Lagasse's house as easily as a ghost, unseen and unheard.

Well, wait, thought Molly. That's not necessarily true. More exactly: the residents of rue Tabac claimed they saw nothing on the night of January 18.

Seeing and claiming: two very different things.

Though of course, making that point got Molly no closer to anything useful. The necklace, tucked away in the armoire in the annex, was like a constant pressure, a sort of itch in her brain, that even when she was not directly thinking about it, caused irritation and anxiety. She could forget about it in her conscious mind—but her subconscious, and her body, never forgot for even a second.

She was deep in thoughts of rue Tabac when Ben returned from his run.

"I know it was the middle of the night," she said, as though she and Ben were in the middle of a conversation. "But it does seem sort of lucky that a person could break into a house and murder someone and get away without anyone hearing or seeing anything. The houses on rue Tabac are close together, this wasn't out in the countryside, after all. And from what I've heard lately, half the village is afflicted with insomnia, up half the night worrying about tourism and global financial collapse. Yet on that one night, that one particular, specific night—everyone is tucked in and sleeping like babies?"

"I don't—"

"And where on earth did the phrase 'sleeping like a baby' come from, anyway? Did someone with an actual baby think that up? I don't think so. I think it's all a grand scheme to mislead women about what having a baby is actually like."

"How many times was it last night?"

"Six. And I can't believe you slept through it all. Especially the last two when I was grumbling pretty loud."

Ben made a sympathetic face and put an arm around her.

"Anyway, he's out now, fast asleep with a full belly. Would you —I'd like to take an hour and go...."

Ben waited.

"Uh...I...I want to..."

"Want to what?"

"Well, I'm not entirely sure. Maybe all I want to do is ride the scooter for a minute and feel like myself again." She paused. "And maybe talk to one or two people."

Ben cocked an eyebrow. "What sort of people?"

"Just...people."

"Molly."

"What? Do you have something else to do? Can you watch Olivier while I'm gone?"

"He's barely a week old. And you got no sleep."

"I know that."

They stared at each other.

"I don't understand why you're resisting catching up on your rest and being with your newborn."

"It's just—" Molly looked at the floor. She was not a fan of this tone Ben was taking, but also, she felt guilty about wanting to go out, no matter how important the reason.

"I know you. Obviously you're not just wanting to go out for a breath of fresh air. You've got some thread of something you want to investigate, don't you? You want to leave the house and Olivier because of the Lagasse murder, is that right?"

Molly narrowed her eyes at Ben. Sometimes when he was right, she had an urge to do something ugly.

"Is that so wrong," she said finally.

Ben relaxed a little when she admitted it. "I guess not. I just... I worry about this transition a little, I'll admit. I mean the transition from obsessive investigator—and I mean that as a compliment—to this new job as mother, which takes up so much time and energy. All of it, really. How do you think you can do both? Isn't it—right now, anyway, with him so young—impossible?"

Molly took a deep breath. She nearly told him about the necklace—she opened her mouth to say the words but then closed it again. "I don't know," she said finally. "It's not...I'm not taking on the investigation in any comprehensive way, not like I would if there was no Olivier. Please, don't worry about that. It's only...it's only just a few people I'd like to talk to, really just one...I'll be back very soon."

Ben nodded. He spoke softly. "I wonder...does some part of you regret it? Having a child? I know getting used to it—after all the freedom you had—it must be—"

And then Molly was in tears yet again, her shoulders shaking. Which woke Olivier up and he started bawling too.

Ben blinked, amazed at what he had set off.

"It's not that at all!" Molly said through her sobs. "I love Olivier more than anything! Not an instant of regret and I'm honestly shocked you could think that!" She picked Olivier up and the two of them cried together.

Ben wanted to turn and run right back outside, but he did not.

"It's only that I want to do *all* the things," said Molly. "I want to be a good mother, I want to spend time with Olivier, and I want to solve the murder of Lili Lagasse. Is that too much to ask?"

"I don't know," said Ben, putting his arms around the two of them and kissing their heads. "I hope not."

❧ 36 ❧

Chief Charlot, right smack in the middle of working hours, left the gendarmerie and the massively annoying Paul-Henri and went to get a haircut.

This was not normal behavior for a woman who had always put work first.

"Just cut it off, all the way off," she instructed Marcel, one of the two hairdressers in Castillac.

"If you say so. But you have lovely hair, if I may be so bold. Might you regret it later?"

"That is not your business and I am not a person who regrets decisions," she said. Then she swallowed hard because too much saliva was pooling in her mouth. She swallowed again, nearly choking, and then managed to get control of herself. "Apologies, Marcel. I'm under a lot of pressure as I'm sure you understand. I had the idea that I could better focus on the work at hand if I didn't have to take the time to fuss with my hair."

"Murder does loom larger than hair, no doubt, even I would agree with that. But surely a little self-care does not go amiss?"

"Do we have a problem? Do you argue with all your customers this way?"

Marcel cocked his head. "Sometimes. Depends. It has been my experience, Madame—or I should call you Chief?—that very often a woman comes into my salon with an idea in her head that is...let's call it...unfortunate. Not really the right thing. You could describe these ideas as an attempt to solve a problem, but it's not the best way, or even a halfway decent way. The hair and the problem are most likely unrelated, and one cannot force solutions in that way. You see what I mean? And you know, it's entirely understandable, I don't point this out to criticize. The pressures on women these days! I have it very easy in the hair department, I am quite aware...and quite grateful." He smoothed a hand over his bald head and smiled at her. "It can be a relief not to have any say in the matter."

Charlot sat in the chair, glowering at Marcel's reflection in the mirror.

"All right then," he said. "So....you're looking for something... no-nonsense? Is that the vibe?"

"Yes. Exactly."

Marcel billowed the apron out like a matador with a cape, and fixed it around Charlot's neck. "You're a bit young for no-nonsense," he said, not cowed. "I'm just saying."

Charlot sighed. She had long ago, as a teenager, made peace with the reality that she was going to have a career and not a husband, not a family. At the time, it had felt more like fate than a decision. And her rise at the gendarmerie had been impressive and steady, so that she never regretted going down the career fork in the road, never looked back thinking she shouldn't have devoted herself so single-mindedly to work, or shouldn't have given up on finding a man who accepted her and understood her priorities.

But it was easy enough not to dwell in regret when she was successful. When she was getting commendations, moving up the ranks, becoming Chief at the youngest age anyone had ever been Chief, at least in Castillac. But now? Now it was a different story.

Whether she actually was or not, Charlot believed she was the laughingstock of the village. She imagined people were talking about her behind her back, saying what a failure she was, how inept. How the village of Castillac was continually beset with violence, with murder, with all manner of abhorrent crimes...and did Chief Charlot put a stop to it?

No. She did not. And she had no argument against that because she hadn't stopped it, pure and simple.

The crime kept coming, and in the eyes of the village, ridiculous as it seemed: a redhead from America was the best they had for defense.

Chief Chantal Charlot—*she's a joke.*

She put her head in her hands.

"I can't do a thing with you like that," said Marcel lightly. He fluffed her hair and looked at her in the mirror, head cocked. "So what do you think? A bob? They're back in. Well, they were never out," he said with a laugh. "Or are you thinking even more radical —a shag, or a pixie? How do you feel about bangs?"

Chantal had no idea. She had never paid much attention to fashion; she wore uniforms most of the time. She had only the barest familiarity with her own reflection. She stared at herself in the mirror as though finally trying to get to know herself.

Marcel shifted his weight to his other hip and waited.

"Just...short. Whatever you think best," she added, more meekly than was usual for her.

Marcel led her to the sink and sat her down, and began to wash her hair. It felt luxurious to Chantal to be taken care of that way, and she began to relax. Marcel used his skilled fingers to massage the tension out of her scalp, and of course plied her with lovely smelling unguents while he was at it.

Her body sank into the padded chair. The neck support added to her sense of relaxation, and she started to feel as though her body was floating.

"I can't find the necklace," she said, without meaning to.

"Hm," said Marcel. "If I had it? I'd be in Marseille. Or possibly out of the country entirely."

"All our inquiries have come up empty. It's like trying to find a needle in a haystack. So easy to smuggle, a little thing like that."

"Yes, for sure. That's why I say I'd have left France. It's not as though—well, I have no idea, I've got no experience with smuggling, you tell me—what's the best country in which to get rid of stolen goods? That's where I'd go. And hopefully that country wouldn't be too bad as a vacation spot, because after I sold it, I'd have the money for a luxury hotel room."

Chantal actually chuckled. "You think like a criminal, Marcel."

"Off the top of my head—and I swear I have no idea what I'm talking about—I'd say: Thailand, China, and Russia? Forget Russia, it's too cold and I don't want to pay black market prices for decent food. I'd say Thailand is the best option, what do you say? Always wanted to go to Bangkok. And those beaches..."

He kept massaging her scalp. The aroma of the oils was making Chantal feel drunk, in a good way.

"If he's in any of those places, I've lost."

Marcel shrugged. "Win some, you lose some. I guess your job's easier when someone steals a car. An itty-bitty necklace though? Nobody could expect you to get that back. At least not without some ridiculous luck."

Ridiculous luck, thought Chantal. Where do I get myself some of that?

MOLLY AND OLIVIER were dozing in front of the woodstove. Ben had agreed to watch Olivier later, after some hours working with Jules on the shed, and she tried to organize her thoughts about who to see, who to talk to, but kept falling asleep. Annette was worth a try. And who lived on the other side of Lagasse?

Her phone buzzed. She opened one eye and closed it again. Olivier was out cold.

I was up six times during the night, she thought, I *need* this nap.

But her curiosity, as it almost always did, won out. Molly struggled up on one elbow and reached for her phone.

JULES WANTS to show me a ruin, out route de P. Be back in time to make you lunch. Xx

MOLLY STARED AT THE TEXT. What ruin?

And in the next moment, moving more quickly than any recently post-partum mother in human history, Molly leapt up, put coats and hats on herself and the baby, found some shoes and a pair of tiny baby mittens, got Olivier in the car seat for the first time, and took off in search of Ben and Jules.

Ben should not be alone with that man, not in some secluded spot. Somehow the work on the shed had seemed all right, with her close by, but that too seemed like a bad mistake now that she saw it clearly. What insane denial had she been in for the last few days, to allow this to happen? To allow Ben to make decisions without all the facts?

Olivier reacted to his first car ride with wonder. He looked around in awe and did not utter a peep.

"You're an excellent wingman," Molly said to him, reaching back to pat his head. Then she floored the car and squealed out of the driveway.

"Okay that was a little much," she said. "Don't worry, Olivier, I'm calm, I'm collected, I'm going to drive like a church lady."

She had no specific address, so she was going to have to drive along the route de Périgueux and hope she saw Ben's car from the road. She racked her brain trying to remember if she'd seen a ruin out that way—rural France was littered with them, especially if you included outbuildings. She guessed that Jules wanted to show it to Ben because it had some relevance to rebuilding the shed. They must have ridden bikes so Molly kept a lookout for those.

But—did Jules have some other motive as well? Was this little jaunt just an excuse to get him out somewhere alone, where no one could hear his screams?

"Come on now," she said out loud. "No need to go full horror movie. I'm sure it's fine. Jules only killed Madame Lagasse because it was the only way to steal the necklace and not go to prison. He's got no beef with Ben. No reason to want to hurt him."

Molly did believe this. But still, the thought of having put Ben in danger, even if that chance was slim, was too much to bear. How could she have allowed Ben to be alone with a man she knew was a murderer?

Was motherhood literally making her lose her mind?

❧ 37 ❧

Madame Tessier got home from Molly's safely. She hung up her coat, turned up the heat, and made herself a drink.

The next few hours she spent in her armchair, remembering Lili, reliving some times of high hilarity they had spent together, and others of sorrow, and everything in between. The feelings of anger were, blessedly, at last receding...but not so much the feelings of grief. Missing Lili—it felt sort of like a burning wound in Madame Tessier's chest, as though she had been stabbed with a hot poker right in the heart.

A few more whiskeys. More memories. She laughed out loud a few times, cried yet more tears.

The phone rang and Madame Tessier at first thought she would ignore it, but the ringing persisted and she finally picked up.

"Âllo?"

"Madame Tessier, this is Marie LeBlanc, how are you today?"

"Never mind about that." Drunk, that's how I am, she thought with a snort. "What can I do for you?"

"Ah, it's more what I can do for you, in a way. I'm the notaire taking care of Lili Lagasse's will. You are mentioned. There is a

213

bequeathment, and I'm calling to let you know that I will do everything I can to make sure you receive it."

Madame Tessier was dumbfounded. Was bequeathment a real word? Hearing the word "will" and "Lili Lagasse" in the same sentence actually surprised her; even though she had been spending the afternoon grieving her friend, she thought: wait, Lili was dead? Her mind still refused to accept it completely.

Then her eyes welled up again, realizing that Lili had thought of her when she was still alive, and had made this gift to her, whatever it was.

It was all Madame Tessier could do to stop herself from breaking down in sobs.

"Would you prefer that I tell you over the phone, or would you like to come to my office?" asked Marie. "I will say, upfront, that I do not have the item to give you, at the moment."

And with that, Madame Tessier knew exactly what her friend had left her. She began to laugh, and the laughter was not drunken laughter but a pure laughter of love for her friend and an appreciation of a magnificent irony.

"It's the necklace, isn't it?" said Madame Tessier, once her merriment had died down.

"Indeed it is," said Marie. "She had mentioned it to you?"

"The bequeathment? No. She had not."

"Very often, people make bequeathments but do not inform the recipients. I suppose they like the idea of a surprise."

"Oh, it's a surprise all right."

"Of course I will be in touch if the necklace is recovered, and I certainly hope it will be, Madame."

Madame Tessier rolled her eyes and politely got off the phone, keeping her thoughts and opinions about the gendarmerie's chances of recovering that necklace to herself.

She poured another drink and settled back in the armchair. The room was swelteringly hot but she liked it that way. "To you, dearest friend!" she cried, lifting her glass in a toast. "Lili, you have outdone yourself this time! To give that necklace to the one person who was never interested in it—it's quite a stroke." She topped up her glass. "I thought—well, not that I gave it much thought, I should say I merely assumed—that you would leave the necklace to your nephew. Family things stay in the family, that's the usual thing, right? So I am gratified, more than I can say, that you considered me family. We really were. Let me toast you again." She held her glass up and clinked it with the imaginary glass that Lili's ghost held out.

"Am I rich now? That's something to think about," she said to Lili. "I wonder why you never sold the damn thing. Though I suppose I shouldn't be cursing it now that it belongs to me. Not that I expect to lay eyes on it ever again." She sat back and closed her eyes. "I hope your nephew doesn't feel ill-used. I know he did come for visits from time to time, and that should count for something. Though I hope the visits were not simply banking favor with his eye on the necklace. I suppose there's no way to know, is there?" She heaved a sigh. "Why is love like this? Why does loving someone eventually mean pain, one way or another? Well, I guess *you* aren't feeling any pain, not anymore." Madame Tessier squeezed her eyes shut, not wanting to think about the pain and the fear Lili must have suffered on the night of her murder. Hopefully the murderer hadn't been inept and it was over quickly.

"Tell me, Lili—why did you love that ugly thing so much? What did it mean to you? Was it really something your mother left you? Because you couldn't stand your mother, you told me so a thousand times."

She sipped her drink. Kept her eyes on the ceiling, in the corner of the room, as though she could see Lili hovering there.

"I suppose...this situation is inevitable. Unanswered questions, where the only person capable of answering is dead and buried. Even with your closest friends, or maybe because they're your closest friends—you never finish the conversation." She looked up at the ceiling again. "Your mother hurt you so. And that is the one thing mothers are charged with not doing. Maybe I didn't ask you enough about it, maybe I should have opened that conversation more times. There is always more to say, more to ask about. And now I will never know. Well, I can say this much: if that necklace is ever found—not that I'm holding my breath—I promise to wear it faithfully, just as you did. In your memory."

The hot room and the whiskey took effect, and Madame Tessier sank into sleep. When she woke an hour later, she remembered her promise to her friend and immediately took it back. "I know what I said. And I hope you don't think this is disrespectful. But if by some miracle the necklace is found, and it turns out to be worth a fortune, or even a fraction of a fortune, I'll be marching straight to that huckster Lapin and taking whatever I can get for it. Because Lili—that necklace is cursed. I think I always felt it, and that's why I never admired it like you wanted me to. I'm not saying I could see into the future...but it gave me a bad feeling always. And I wasn't wrong. Whoever it touches is going to suffer, one way or another, I'm convinced of it.

"So five minutes after it gets put in my hands, I'm off to see Lapin. I'll be walking on the beach in Nice before you can say boo, with a sea-view room at Le Negresco."

And then Madame Tessier laughed and laughed, with tears streaming down her face.

❧ 38 ❧

Molly had managed to spot Ben and Jules from the road, and shouted that there was an emergency at home, hurry—

"Okay, so what was that all about?" said Ben, once they were home.

They'd given Jules a ride and he had gone back to work on the shed. Molly was pacing, with Olivier in the carrier.

"So?" he said. "What's going on? Are you all right? Not about Olivier?"

"Olivier is fine. But no, I am not all right. Which—you'll understand, once I...." She paced some more, slapping her head with her fingers as though to rearrange her thoughts, to edit them somehow so that the facts were different facts, so that everything she knew was blessedly wrong.

Ben had never seen his wife so anxious.

Olivier grumbled and Molly began the intricate process of getting his little arms and legs out of the carrier so he could have a nap in the bassinet.

Then she faced Ben. She tried to speak. She tried but couldn't find the words, or found them but couldn't make herself say them

—and finally, at a loss, she gave up and went to the annex and fetched the necklace.

Without a word, she held it out to Ben.

He blinked. Then a double-take. "Is that—"

"As far as I can tell, yes."

"I thought—I thought something was bothering you. It was this?"

Molly nodded.

"Where did you get it? Are you sure it's Lagasse's?"

Molly took a long, slow breath in and closed her eyes. She was so embarrassed at having kept this from Ben for all those many days, and it was uncomfortable to go through the long-put off conversation. "Well, I haven't shown it to anyone, so I can't say it's been verified as hers. The only person I figured would be able to identify it for sure is Madame Tessier, and I didn't want to...but the description matches. It's unique, wouldn't you say? Not a popular design a lot of women are wearing. Not something you see every day."

Ben watched Molly, noticing how stressed she was. He waited for the rest of the story.

Molly paced some more. "I should have told you right off. I know that, and I apologize. I deeply apologize. I hope you'll understand—"

Ben was a patient man, but even he had limits. "What are you saying, Molly? *Where did you get it?*"

"The Bresson's," she said, so quietly Ben thought he must have misheard.

"The who?"

"I was at Jules and Amelie's the other day. Right before Olivier was born. I had...I felt a sort of...I was missing my mother," she said quietly. "And so I walked over, just for some company, you know? Some female...I don't know, I can't really explain. Something drew me there, I went. Amelie invited me in, she was very welcoming as usual. The house was cozy, I was glad to be there.

And then...Amelie and Laurent went in the kitchen to make tea. It wasn't like I took the opportunity to rummage through their things! All that happened was: I picked up this toy train and the necklace was inside and it fell out."

They stood still, Molly remembering the moment and wishing she could rewind time and have a piece of candy spill out of that boxcar instead of Lili Lagasse's necklace. And Ben trying to understand all of what Molly just told him, and what it meant.

"You know what I'm going to say," said Ben finally. His voice had no trace of criticism. He did not chastise. He did not lecture. Molly loved him in that moment more than she ever had.

"I should have gone straight to Charlot with it. After telling you. I *know*. But Ben..."

"Jules."

"Yes. Exactly. *Jules*. I mean—is there some other explanation I haven't been able to see? How else could the necklace have gotten into their house, if Jules didn't steal it?"

Ben was staring into Molly's eyes, his mind racing, trying to come up with any other possibility.

But he couldn't.

Molly realized that part of the reason she had waited to tell him was that she had a hope—a puny, meager hope—that Ben would be able to explain the situation in a way that shifted blame to...to someone else. Someone they wouldn't mind putting behind bars. It was magical thinking, she realized now. There was no possible way to explain away the horrible fact that Jules had stolen that horrible necklace.

And murdered Lili Lagasse.

As Ben said, as they talked it over for the next couple of hours —if it were only the theft? Perhaps they could wait, not report him immediately, figure out a way to keep him out of trouble. A theft, even of something as valuable as the necklace—they might have been able to work with that. Maybe.

But murder?

Murder was not, obviously, something you could explain away, sidestep, make excuses for. Even when the consequences for his family were impossibly painful.

"Well, then we're agreed?" Ben said at last, when they were worn out from coming at the problem from every angle they could possibly think of.

"Yes," said Molly. "We'll take forty-eight hours to work the case, and then we go to Charlot, no matter what."

Ben shook Molly's hand to seal the promise, then folded her into his arms and hugged her tight.

"You have such a big heart," he said. "And who knows, if anyone could pull a rabbit out of a hat, it's you."

She hugged him back. Molly was grateful for the compliment, and extremely grateful that he had not been angry at her for leaving him out of the loop and potentially hurting their reputation by keeping back evidence from the gendarmerie.

But she still felt sick over the prospect of what was going to happen to Amelie. They had given themselves forty-eight hours, but she had no ideas for how to spend those hours to find some alternative explanation for how that necklace got in that boxcar in that house.

Molly had no confidence about finding any rabbits anywhere.

THE NEXT MORNING, apprehensive but determined, Molly and Ben drank their coffee standing in the kitchen. They had agreed that Ben was unlikely to be in danger from Jules, so the work on the shed would proceed—Ben, of course, on his guard, not saying anything to alarm Jules, but carefully listening and observing. Ben would be looking at the other man in a new light, and it was possible something might surface that he hadn't noticed before—some slight admission, some flash of the other man's character, some something...

"I guess Olivier is okay with having a working mom," Molly

said, looking at the baby with love as he slept in the baby carrier, head against her chest.

"For a few days anyway. How many times did you get up last night?"

"Three." Molly yawned. "I'm fine. Adrenaline is magic."

"Mm. Well, with some luck...okay, a *lot* of luck...we'll get to the bottom of this mess and you'll be home later for a good lunch and a nap."

"I...I don't feel very hopeful. Even if Amelie offers an alibi for Jules, how can we trust it?"

"You trust her, don't you?"

"Absolutely. But...would she lie to protect him? Maybe. Would you lie to protect me?"

"Maybe."

"This is what I'm saying. Trust is...not a black and white thing. It's complicated."

"Law enforcement doesn't tend to think of it that way."

Molly nodded. "I understand. But I mean, we're all liars sometimes, right? If a person never, ever lies, I think people would think he's a weirdo, to be honest. Or worse. And I'm not even counting the answers to 'do I look fat in these pants?' kind of lie. Sometimes...sometimes a lie might be the most loving thing you could do for someone. Even if it's a whopper."

Ben looked at Molly and nodded slowly. "Complicated indeed." He kissed Olivier on the top of his head and poured one more cup of coffee.

"Also—back to the nuts and bolts—what alibi can Amelie give that would be convincing, thinking about it logistically?" said Molly. "Can she say 'the night of the Lagasse murder we were up all night and he never left the house'? Because if she slept even one wink, there goes any possibility of an alibi. I think if they had been up all night, we'd have heard about it before now. That's not...it's not usual behavior. You'd moan about being exhausted, if nothing else."

"Look, chérie, all we can do is ask questions and see where they lead. You're right about everything you just said. But we may not know everything, we may not be able to grasp—yet—what the best questions are to ask."

"Okay. Thanks. Tally-ho," said Molly, still pessimistic.

Molly had already texted Amelie and asked to meet in the park. She felt sweaty just thinking about seeing her friend, not sure she would be able to be with her and not ask all the questions.

For instance: did Amelie know about the necklace being in her house?

Molly believed that was impossible. Unless she had misjudged Amelie entirely—there was no possible way that she knew.

Was it Molly's job to tell her? What would be the fallout from telling her—would it put Amelie in danger?

Should she be helping Amelie and Laurent get away from Jules to some hidden place of safety? Should she urge them to move into the pigeonnier, just for now—or was that too obvious and not safe enough? Would Jules really do anything to harm them? Maybe she was completely jumping to the wrong conclusion, and murdering one person didn't have to mean he would murder anyone else.

What was Jules Bresson capable of?

Ben dropped Molly and Olivier at the park, and Molly settled herself on the park bench to wait. The baby was still sound asleep, even snoring lightly, which even in this fraught circumstance gave Molly a feeling of love and protectiveness. That protectiveness extended to Amelie and Laurent, even though the friendship was new, even with all the unanswered questions.

Molly took a breath to calm herself and tried to think like an investigator instead of a new mother. Jules had been nothing but even-tempered, every time she had seen him. Never any hint of violence, of mental disturbance, of having the capacity to kill a villager for money. Sure, he was a little distant. Hard to feel connected to. Not great with eye contact. But that was true for a lot of people who weren't murderers. Jules was polite and he was a hard worker. Did those qualities mean...well, what did they mean? Doubtless there were polite, hard-working murderers—these were hardly disqualifying traits. She understood that her entire line of thinking was basic and not fine-tuned enough. But she couldn't stop looking for loopholes, for some way to make it impossible that the husband of a woman she felt so much affection for was an actual killer.

It was overcast and much warmer; Molly reached under Olivier to unzip her coat and wriggle out of the sleeves, just as she saw Amelie round the corner, holding Laurent's hand. They crossed the plain little park—just a dirt basketball court, the hoop without a net, and a few benches around the perimeter. To Molly, the park was beloved because everything in Castillac was beloved. A big manicured garden would be all very well, but this was familiar and it was home, even if a bit ratty. She had a quick daydream of Olivier playing hoops there with his friends in fifteen years...

"Bonjour, Molly!" said Amelie with a wide smile.

They kissed cheeks and Molly greeted Laurent, who did not meet her eyes but mumbled something in return.

"I don't think I've ever once sat down in this park," said Amelie, as though she were embarking on a grand adventure. "Now tell me," she said. "What's on your mind? You sounded troubled in your text."

"How could you tell? I just asked to meet in the park."

Amelie laughed. Molly thought: is this the last time I will ever hear her laugh like that, carefree and untroubled?

"How did I know? Molly, your feelings are plain for anyone to see. It's part of your charm."

Molly was a little taken aback.

"This is a good thing!" said Amelie. "People know where they stand. I like this about you."

NELL GODDIN

Then, out of nowhere, Molly was blinking back tears. What is this new thing where I'm breaking down crying every five minutes, she said to herself, biting her lip and closing her eyes tight.

She was about to ruin this little family. And every cell of her body did not want to.

"Amelie," she began. "I'm wondering...how is your sleep these days? I know in the later part of my pregnancy, I was up during the night all the time with backaches or worries or whatever."

"My sleep? Oh, it's not too bad. Of course, like everyone, I've been worried about finances. So that keeps me up sometimes. This too shall pass, I try to tell myself."

Shall it? thought Molly.

"What about Jules? Is he a good sleeper?"

Amelie looked puzzled. "Um, well...actually...lately he's been having some trouble. He's under a lot of pressure, as you know, with the new baby and all..."

Molly watched Amelie carefully. Did she know anything?

"Why do you ask? Are *you* having trouble sleeping?"

Oh, if only she knew...

Laurent was picking up small stones and throwing them at the basketball backboard. Plink-plink-plink.

"How is Jules doing?" Molly asked.

Amelie did not answer at first. She kept her eyes on Laurent. She smoothed her dress over her bump and shifted her position on the bench.

"Not well," she said at last.

The two women looked into each other's eyes.

"I know we're not paying him much for the shed."

"You know how grateful I am—we are. It's..."

Molly heard something in that last word. A hesitancy, an admission...

"What is it?" Molly said, so gently.

"He's...he's troubled. I don't know why. I've asked and he

224

brushes me off. And he would be so upset if he knew I had breathed a word to anyone. I don't know what to tell you, Molly. I don't know if you've ever gone through this, where someone you love won't share and is apparently in their own private hell and they won't tell you what's going on so there's nothing you can do but watch them live in misery and hope they eventually pull out of it."

Molly took her friend's hand and squeezed it, and then threw one arm around her and gave her an awkward hug with Olivier pressed between them.

"Why do you ask?" said Amelie, and in her voice Molly heard dread.

There was no other word for it.

❦ 39 ❦

C hief Charlot was at first relieved and then not so much, as the results of the forensics tests—the fingerprints at least —were back from the Bergerac lab, first thing Friday morning. Faster than expected, and she told herself to be grateful for that. Police work was almost always painstaking; following procedure meant taking one step and then another step, based on evidence, not making wild leaps all over the place. As she had been trained, Charlot believed that what would catch the murderer of Lili Lagasse was data, such as just received from Bergerac, paired with diligent legwork.

Data, legwork, and a healthy dose of luck, Charlot thought.

According to the data collection by the techs on January 21: apart from Lili Lagasse, four other people had been in her house and left prints. The visits could be assumed to be fairly recent, since the victim kept an orderly house and any prints would be wiped clean during her regular housework.

Of course, the prints taken from Lagasse's neck had obvious prominence. The lab had succeeded, so all that remained was finding a match, and there was the murderer on a silver platter. To be thorough, Charlot wanted the identities of all four sets of prints matched to their owners.

Paul-Henri—who despite his insufficiencies, was not terrible at legwork—had determined that Lagasse had no housekeeper, and as far as he could find out, there had been no visits from a plumber, electrician, or any other household-maintenance worker in recent weeks or months. Nor any visit from a doctor. No deliveries of anything that would require a delivery person to enter the house.

In short, according to the thorough work of her junior officer, the only people who had come inside 49 rue Tabac recently were Lili Lagasse, Lapin, her friends, and her murderer. Whether the murderer was also a friend—that remained to be determined.

First order of business: take prints from Madame Tessier and anyone else who might have visited Lagasse at home. Madame Tessier herself would be the best source for who should be added to that list.

Which was all fine and well, standard police procedure. Charlot swallowed hard and nervously tapped her fingernails on her desk and then raked them through her new bob. The problem in front of her, which had been looming, but now she could no longer avoid facing: what was she going to match those prints against? One set was likely to belong to Tessier, and one to Lapin. And the other two? If the murderer was a first-timer, a man who had never broken the law or never been caught breaking the law —never done anything to get his prints into the system—what good was having those prints going to do? Even the ones from the victim's neck?

It wasn't as though she could set up a stand outside Chez Papa and take prints of everyone who walked by. She couldn't even force a suspect to give prints, not without cause.

Not that she had a suspect.

She stood up and walked around the gendarmerie. Sunlight came in strong through the window, but the room was not warm. She had personally followed up with tracing the necklace, calling all the places Paul-Henri had called, checking to see if any of them had seen it or heard of any efforts to fence it. She'd asked about any sightings of a large ruby as well, thinking that a clever thief might take the necklace apart to make it less traceable.

Nothing. Not so much as a hint of an inference of a rumor.

She and Paul-Henri had talked to everyone on rue Tabac multiple times, and no one had admitted to having seen or heard anything on the night of January 18. It was as though the murderer had worn an invisibility cloak and crept through the village unseen and unheard on his diabolical mission. And then hidden the necklace away, very effectively thwarting any effort to find him out.

Of course Charlot was not giving up. *At least Molly Sutton is home nursing that baby,* she thought with some satisfaction. *At least the gendarmerie doesn't have to compete with her to solve the case. It's simply a matter of taking the next step, and then the next one, just as it's always been.*

She sat back down and got out a pad to make some notes. It was quiet in the room, quiet enough that she finally wondered: where was Paul-Henri?

"I WAS GOING TO WAIT—"

"—at our age, we shouldn't wait for anything, ever," said Edmond, giving Ninette what he imagined was an amorous and inviting glance.

"We're not exactly old. And listen," she added, nervously, "there's something I need to—"

In two steps he bounded around the end of the counter and took Ninette in his arms.

"Edmond!" she said, looking over his shoulder at the door. She much preferred seeing him at night, when they could have privacy.

Not that she didn't love it when he left the pâtisserie behind and came up the street to visit her.

"I don't care if someone comes! I'm tired of keeping us a secret. I want to—to—sing from the rooftops, chérie!" He kissed her.

Now, Edmond was a man who took his life seriously; he was a straight-up perfectionist. He wanted, in everything he did, to be highly skilled, better than anyone. He had won prestigious awards for his pastry-making because of the effort he poured into it. Kissing was no different. He kissed Ninette to within an inch of her life, leaving her gasping for breath, her expression impossibly bright, her heart tearing along as though she had just run a race.

They both looked quickly at the door. The street was empty as far as they could see.

"I've got something to talk to you about," she said, trying to calm herself down. Without meaning to, she put her palm on her belly. "But I'm worried...about how you'll react."

Edmond smiled. "You're sweet. But whatever it is—*I'm* not worried. We will be all right, dearest Ninette. If there's any sort of problem? Let me help you with it." He leaned back against the counter and took her hand. "Tell me, what's the matter?"

Ninette didn't know how to start. She opened her mouth but no words came. She squeezed Edmond's hand. Then put his hand against her stomach and looked at him, half apologetic and half hopeful.

"I had no idea it was possible, Edmond, I promise you. I just said we're not old—and we aren't—at least—not old-old anyway. I absolutely thought it was too late for—" She pushed his hand into her belly and looked into his eyes to see if he understood.

Edmond was mystified. "For what?"

"I might be pregnant."

"You said what now?"

"I might be pregnant!"

Just then, Madame Renaud came in with a whoosh of cold air.

Edmond did not leap away from behind the counter—he wasn't kidding when he said he had tired of the secret and wanted everyone to know—

—Wait a second—

"—*did you just say*—"

Ninette nodded, smiling shyly.

Madame Renaud looked from one to the other and back again. "Bonjour Ninette, I was wondering if you had got in the mustard I've been waiting for? Or are you too busy monkeying around like a schoolgirl? And Edmond, if I may say—you belong at pâtisserie Bujold and seeing you here at the épicerie at this time of day makes my world turn upside down. Do you want to lose all your business to Fillon?"

At this, Edmond gritted his teeth and scowled. His face was flushed because of what he understood Ninette to have just told him. He turned his attention back to her.

"A baby?" he squeaked out, putting his other hand on Ninette's belly, his eyes wide.

She nodded.

"Oh sweet Mary mother of God!" he shouted. He threw his arms around Ninette, kissed her (expertly) on the mouth, and then came around from behind the counter and kissed Madame Renaud on the mouth too (just a dry peck).

"Did you hear that, Madame Renaud? Ninette is going to make me the happiest man in all of France!"

Ninette giggled. "I had no idea you even wanted—"

"Sometimes a person gives up hope because a thing seems impossible," he said. He wiped tears from his eyes, shaking his head, trying to believe it was really true.

"A baby?" said Madame Renaud. "You?"

"Me," said Ninette, not taking offense at the other woman's tone.

"Her," said Edmond, wrapping his arms around Ninette. He squeezed her tight and then dropped to one knee. "Will you marry me?" he said, holding both of her hands. "Please, do me the greatest honor of my life."

Ninette did not hesitate. "I will," she whispered, hardly believing what was happening.

Madame Renaud could hardly believe it either. As she rode her bicycle back to the farm, without the mustard she came for, she was laughing the whole way home and thinking about whom to call first with this most delicious bit of gossip.

❧ IV ❧

❦ 40 ❦

Charlot called Paul-Henri's home number: no answer. She called his cell: no answer.

This was highly unusual. She considered her junior officer a dolt, but he was her dolt, and she thought him reliable for certain things—answering his phone, taking on extra work without complaint, following orders, and showing up when and where he was supposed to show up.

Paul-Henri Monsour was not a man who colored outside the lines.

So where in the world was he?

Irritably, Charlot put away the forensics report and left the gendarmerie. Paul-Henri spent hours each day walking the streets and obviously she was going to have to follow suit in order to find him. It must be that his phone had died and he hadn't realized it.

She was annoyed, and she was anxious. Her feelings of failure had not changed even a little from changing her hairstyle—as Marcel had gently tried to warn her, and which had obviously been an idiotic attempt in any case. Now she worried that the bob made her look like she was trying to be fashionable, which she considered detrimental to being taken seriously.

Getting forensics back early had made everything worse, not better.

The truth was: she needed Paul-Henri to insult and harass, to make herself feel better. Sitting alone in the gendarmerie made her own shortcomings glaringly obvious. There was nowhere to hide, no one else to blame.

Where could he be? Was it possible there was a break in the case, and he was following some lead he had not been able to communicate to her?

Had that idiot somehow managed to find the necklace after all?

"IT's *YOUR* STORE, Ninette! You're the owner! You can close anytime you like. So please, my darling—let's not waste a minute! The mairie will close for lunch if we don't get moving. And I—I don't want to wait all the way until the afternoon to make you my wife."

"You are the silliest man," Ninette said, grinning, her face flushed. About closing the shop, she hesitated, picking up the sign but still hesitating, not hanging it on the door. Edmond was right, she did own the épicerie and answered to nobody; she could slap that sign on the door if she wanted to. Just as Edmond had been doing with pâtisserie Bujold for the last six weeks, she thought, with a flush of pleasure.

"Let's do it," she said, feeling a little like a middle-schooler cutting her first class.

"I love you," blurted out Edmond, and they laughed and then kissed. Later, Ninette told her friends how funny it was that he had asked her to marry him before he had even once told her that he loved her.

After the "closed" sign was in place, and door locked, the couple walked hand in hand to the mairie. The streets were empty as they had been so much of the time lately; it was cold and the skies gray, but Ninette and Edmond did not notice.

Ninette stopped suddenly. "Wait, hold on. I don't—listen, there's something you need to understand. At my age—well, at any age really, but *especially* at my age—things...things can go wrong. Women lose babies, Edmond. They have miscarriages, you know? Of course it's horrible, but it's common. And I don't...I don't want you to feel like you have to do this. To feel pressured to marry me. Because of that. I mean, I appreciate your honorable impulse, I really do. But if something *did* go wrong, which is entirely possible, and there's no baby...I wouldn't want..."

Edmond only smiled and shook his head. "Now that you've said yes, there is nothing that will stop me from marrying you. Come on, chérie, run!"

Ninette could hardly believe her ears. She wondered if she were having the most realistic yet impossible dream ever. But she nodded at Edmond and they ran down the street still holding hands. They made it to the mairie with only a moment to spare before the noon closing.

"Bonjour Edmond, Ninette," said Annette from behind the counter. She noticed they were holding hands and looked from their hands to their faces and back again, dumbfounded.

"We want to get married," said Edmond. "Can you believe it? She's going to make me the happiest man on God's green earth."

Annette was stunned. Edmond and Ninette? How had she not known of this? Was the mairie completely out of the Castillac gossip loop?

"Hello, Annette?" said Edmond. "What's required? It's a simple matter, yes? A form to fill out, that's about it? What is the fee? Where do we sign?"

Annette lurched into action, getting the forms and finding them a pen, and in a matter of minutes, Edmond and Ninette Nugent were pronounced husband and wife in the eyes of the French government.

After receiving congratulations from everyone at the mairie, the couple left, still holding hands, laughing and smiling so hard it looked as though their faces might crack.

Annette watched the big door close after them. Despite all the happy emotion she had just witnessed, she felt frozen inside.

It had been many days since the murder of her neighbor Lili Lagasse. Lili had lived right next door and she had been a real friend over the years. Only the day before she died, she and Annette had chatted on their front steps about how cold it was and how desperately they wished for spring to arrive.

It was nothing more than a conversation about the weather. Nothing personal, nothing deep. But nevertheless, it meant something to Annette. The subtraction of Lili from her life—by violence—was going to take a very long time to get over.

She stood still, her eyes remaining fixed on the door. The business of the mairie was wrapping up for the lunch break and she heard her co-workers getting ready to go out.

But Annette was rooted to the spot, once again reliving the night of January 18, when she had been up in the middle of the night, feeling anxious about her sister's little girl who had whooping cough, and also about whether maybe that tender place in her lower belly meant she had some kind of terrible cancer... She had been worrying about these things, unable to sleep, standing at the window facing the street, when she saw the man approach Lili's door.

She had seen him. And as much as she wished to, she could not unsee him.

She hadn't known it in that moment. Only the next day did the full truth come out: he was *a murderer*.

Standing not ten feet away. Annette did not know for sure whether he had seen her in the window, or caught the movement out of the corner of his eye as she jumped away out of sight. And maybe, she wondered, maybe she *had* known he was a murderer at the time, or at least sensed he was a very bad, dangerous person.

It was the middle of the night, obviously not the time for a friendly visit. The fear she felt, the instant she saw him—Annette could not put that aside, could not forget how the feeling had run through her body, how it felt as though her muscles and bones had turned to jelly, so that she was completely vulnerable, unable to defend herself or to run if he had decided to come into her house next.

Like a living nightmare, that's what it was. She wanted to forget the sight of him, as though if his image were not in her memory she would be protected from him—but she knew that was ridiculous. If he saw her, he saw her. It would take almost no effort for him to find out who lived next door to Lili. He obviously killed with ease. Maybe he even took pleasure in it—

—and ever since that night, Annette felt as though her insides were frozen solid. She knew she should go straight to Charlot and report what she had witnessed. She should, but she did not. Almost as though he had cast a spell of immobility on her; she was like a prey animal who believes the predator is about to pounce even when she no longer sees him, and her only hope is to remain perfectly still.

Because, logically, what would stop him from coming to her door next? She understood a little bit about how investigations worked. The Chief wouldn't arrest him right away, they would need time to gather evidence, they would need to interview him, to ask for his alibi, so on and so on....

And while those wheels of justice turned ever so slowly, he would understand that someone had ratted on him. Someone had been a witness. He would remember that flash out of the corner of his eye as she moved away from the window. And then it would be her turn. What would he have to lose? What was another body to him?

She *should* tell Charlot. She did not doubt this.

But she was a coward.

There's nothing wrong with having an instinct for self-preservation, she argued to herself. My telling Charlot won't bring Lili back. And plus, the man had been bundled against the cold, she couldn't even identify who he was, so what good would her coming forward really do?

"You coming? We're splurging and going out for lunch," said one of her co-workers.

Annette tried to answer but there was a big dry lump in her throat and she could only shake her head. Ah, if only it had turned out I had cancer, instead of being in this dreadful situation, she thought, watching her co-worker leave, laughing about something.

MUCH HUBBUB in the Libourne train station but of a harmless kind: mothers dragging small children along to get to the platform on time; teenagers smoking and leaning up against a wall as though they didn't have the strength to stand upright on their own; businessmen with briefcases and decent suits, reading the newspaper. The smell of coffee and cigarettes.

Paul-Henri waited patiently, standing off to the side where he could see most of the room, out of habit and police training wanting as many people in his view as possible. He was dressed in civilian clothes: a pair of dark brown slacks, a white button-down shirt, a sweater his mother had given him for Christmas, a coat, and a wool hat. He looked more like an accountant than a gendarme.

He hoped he would not be easy to recognize, at least to any residents of Castillac who might be in that station. Mostly, with mixed feelings, he understood that there would be no one out looking for him. But Paul-Henri had always been one to dip in and out of fantasy during the course of the day, and this day was no different. He imagined Chief Charlot sounding an alarm, and the citizens of Castillac volunteering to form a search party, fanning out through the village, making calls, posting sentries at the train station, calling Libourne and the airport in Bordeaux.

It was a satisfying image, but even so, he did not go on to imagine the next sequence, which would have been a home-coming to cheering villagers.

He carried a small suitcase and had his passport in an interior pocket of his coat.

Paul-Henri Monsour, junior officer of the Castillac gendarmerie, had left the village. And he did not plan on coming back.

❧ 41 ❧

"What has happened to this village, that's what I'd like to know," a disgruntled woman gave the door to the épicerie another shake, but the lock held firm. "I need some peppercorns to make the steak *au poivre* for lunch, so now what am I going to do?"

"And if you want a bit of bread to go with that, or God forbid a pastry? You'd best head to Fillon because pâtisserie Bujold is also shuttered tight."

"I just cannot."

"I know. It's an upside-down world lately."

Molly Sutton, baby in carrier, caught this last remark and nodded. She too had been to pâtisserie Bujold and found it closed. On market day, of all days!

The women praised Olivier, which like any new mother, Molly never got tired of. Then she headed over to Manette, hoping to hear a bit of gossip and maybe buy some good-looking leeks to go with it.

"I've been wanting to see you," Molly said, grateful that market attendance was sparse and she could have Manette all to herself.

NELL GODDIN

"Look at you!" Manette cooed, letting Olivier grab her finger. "Such a strong little man!" She leaned over and sniffed his head. "What is it about the smell of babies' heads?" she said, inhaling.

Molly beamed.

"So, you are happy, Molly? You always said you wanted a baby more than anything, and you got your wish! Is it all you hoped?"

"Words can't express," said Molly, beaming even harder—and then, because apparently the waterworks were ever-ready to turn on at the slightest provocation, tears rolled out of her eyes and she wiped them away with her coat sleeve.

"I know, my friend," said Manette gently. "The emotions, the hormones, the lack of sleep—it's a lot. All of that will settle down before long though, I promise."

Molly smiled through her tears. Then she caught a glimpse of Laurent and craned her neck to see which parent was with him.

It was Jules.

Molly felt—it was hard to describe to herself—something like an electrical jolt go through her body. The tears dried up instantly. She put her arms protectively around Olivier in his carrier. She waited until Laurent and Jules were far out of earshot, then said, "What do you think of the Bressons, just between you and me?"

Manette grinned. "Amelie—that woman is salt of the earth. Warm, smart, generous. I'm trying to think when they moved here...I liked her instantly."

"They're not from Castillac?"

"Oh no. I'd say they got here right around when you did."

"Hm."

Manette gave Molly a sideways glance.

"One last question," said Molly. She noticed, of course, that Manette had said nothing about Jules. "And then I want to talk about leeks. There's barely anyone here at the market. Maybe last week was the same, it's been so cold! So maybe you haven't heard any talk at all. But I wonder—have you heard anything about the

244

night of Lili Lagasse's murder—has anyone been whispering about seeing anyone out that night, in the vicinity of rue Tabac?"

Manette shrugged. "Not that I've heard. Though I can't say I've been paying much attention. My youngest has had a stomach bug and—oh it's fine, she's fine, it's only that my attention has been on my kids and not the murder. Are you making any headway with it? Do you even have the time and energy, what with your munchkin being so little?" She grabbed Olivier's little foot and gave it a little shake.

Molly felt some irritation at Manette's echoing Ben, but she brushed it away. "I'm not really investigating," she said.

They talked of leeks and when they would come into season, and about some recipes Molly had never made, a bit about stomach bugs, and diaper rash, and finally Molly wandered away to meet Ben for a ride home.

The clock was tick-tick-ticking toward the deadline she and Ben had agreed on, when she would have to take the necklace to Charlot and report where she had found it. Molly, uncharacteristically, was starting to feel as though this case—for so many reasons —was beyond her grasp, that there was no possibility of finding anything that would exonerate Jules.

And really? The whole time, since the moment of seeing the necklace fall out of that boxcar, she had known it would take some kind of miracle to save him. Molly knew an impossible scenario when she saw one. Amelie *was* salt of the earth; she was dependable and trustworthy. And Laurent was just a child, younger than his years at that. And it was tragic that their fate depended on a man who did not deserve their trust.

As was her way, Molly did her best to shake off the feeling of a dead end. While waiting on the corner for Ben, she made an effort to think as clearly as possible, making no assumptions. Was it possible that she and Manette were wrong about Amelie? Molly had been drawn to her so powerfully, but was that impulse clouding her vision? Could Amelie be in cahoots with Jules after all, could they be a sort of French Bonnie and Clyde?

Ben's dented Renault came into view, and like everything else that day, the sight of it and of her husband behind the wheel, made tears spring to her eyes.

Oh for heaven's sake, she muttered, wiping them away and reaching for the door, giving Olivier's head a sniff as she slid awkwardly into the car.

THE WHOLE FAMILY TOOK A NAP, and the afternoon passed, unusually, without much talking or crying. Thus fortified, Ben, Molly, and the littlest Dufort were all yawning but ready to socialize as they headed out to the fête that evening.

"All set?" said Ben, kissing Molly on the cheek and then Olivier on the top of his head, sound asleep in Molly's arms.

"Yes, I've been looking forward to it," said Molly, putting on something of a brave face. The village fête was a welcome occasion, no matter the season—but this time, the ticking clock of the deadline was so loud in Molly's ear, she could hardly hear herself think.

Olivier did not even wake as he was buckled into his car seat. Molly climbed in and Ben slowly backed up and headed down rue de Chêne. Molly stared ahead, thinking.

Ben knew exactly what she was thinking about, and stayed silent so as not to distract her.

After parking the car outside the community center, he turned to her. "Do we need to make a plan?"

"Hm. I wish something concrete would come to mind. How about we try to sit with the Bressons? That's all I got."

"All right."

"You've spent time with Jules, I wonder if he will show a different side, here with his family?"

"If they come. They may not."

"Everybody comes to the fête."

Ben shrugged. "If I had murdered a villager, I would not be coming to the fête. But I know what you're going to say: I didn't murder anyone, and so I can't draw any conclusions about the state of mind of someone who did."

"So you're just reading my mind now?" Molly laughed.

"You've taught me a few things I didn't get at the academy."

"I think that's a lie, but it's a very sweet lie and I thank you for it." She took his hand. "Pay some attention to Amelie as well. I know I've been her biggest fan—and Lord knows I hope I've been right about her—but I think we shouldn't give her an automatic pass. Well—no one should get an automatic pass, right? That's the most basic rule of all."

"Especially because we happen to like them."

"Right."

They sat in the car, thinking. Olivier was quiet, apart from some contented gurgling—so far he had proved himself to be a fan of car rides. Molly and Ben watched people streaming inside, hurrying to get out of the cold.

They exchanged glances, and without a word, entered the fray. Molly tended to Olivier while Ben watched the crowd. He waved, he kissed cheeks, he acted like it was any other fête night—but Molly knew better. She could see how sharply he was observing everyone, how he gave the bisous and sounded like his usual wry and thoughtful self, but underneath, she could hear him working. Could see him watching.

Molly scanned the room once they were inside. Kids raced around underfoot, a woman in a wheelchair careened by, a small group was on stage playing music. The comforting smell of grilled duck and potatoes. A few couples were dancing and some children ran around them, playing a version of tag.

In short, the usual fête-night bedlam.

And then, almost like a ghost, Amelie appeared at Molly's

side. Her smile wide and warm as usual. Holding Laurent by the hand.

"I'm so happy to see you," said Molly, feeling a pang of guilt. "Sit with us?"

"Of course," said Amelie. She looked over at Jules and Ben, who were already engrossed in a discussion about roofing tile. "I'm so glad they're getting to be friends," she said. "It means a lot. I really appreciate what you've done for us," she added quietly.

Another stab of guilt for Molly but she smiled through it. "It's always amazing to me, how babies don't freak out with all this noise. I used to marvel at people bringing their little ones to Chez Papa, and they'd just sleep soundly through the whole thing."

"They feel safe in all this company," said Amelie, and Molly cocked her head and considered this. Jules was standing only a few feet away and his presence made Molly feel...well, she wasn't sure how she felt. Nervous, certainly. Was there fear mixed in? Possibly?

The truth was—when Molly dug all the way down, past the usual sort of thoughts that can crowd into our minds to keep the real truth from us—she didn't even blame Jules for taking the necklace, not really. Like all of life—it was not black and white. Sure, thievery was wrong on its face, and of course she believed that. But the Bressons were struggling financially, and Jules's primary intention, his motive, was to provide for his family. As it well should have been. It was not that Molly believed stealing was a reasonable response to that pressure, only that she could understand how that pressure—with so much love mixed into it, and sense of responsibility, and people you loved counting on you—might make you bend some of your rules.

Might make you do something that was wrong, but for the right reasons.

She could imagine Jules thinking: what did an old lady need with a valuable necklace anyway? She had a house, she had an income, she was safe. His family was not safe. His family needed help.

Molly looked over at Jules who had his arm protectively around Amelie; he was staring into the crowd, eyes seemingly unfocused.

Of course stealing was still wrong, even if she understood the motive behind it. But murder...there were no excuses to be made for that, not unless it was in response to a direct attack and you feared for your life. An old lady asleep in her bed? No. Absolutely not. No justification, period, end of story.

That Amelie and Laurent and the unborn baby would have to pay for his terrible deed...a wave of nausea swept over Molly as she watched Jules and Ben talking.

Tick-tick-tick towards the deadline. She got a quick flash of Charlot entering the Bresson house and leading Jules away in handcuffs, with Amelie and Laurent in shock, devastated.

"You are way out in the cabbages!" Molly heard Amelie say, and her body jerked back to the present moment.

"Sorry," said Molly. "The lack of sleep...I'm a little out of it."

Amelie reached for her hand and held it under the table, which moved Molly so much. She squeezed Amelie's hand and took a deep breath.

Ben put a plate of duck and potatoes in front of her. "I'll bring you salad when you're ready," he said, disappearing again into the crowd. The music went faster and Molly saw a blur of children go tearing by, one wearing a paper crown and another a mask in the shape of a frog.

"Well, salut, beautiful mother," said Lawrence, sliding into the chair next to Molly. "I wondered if you'd be coming out. What does Oliver think of the proceedings so far?"

"He's been asleep the whole time."

"Yet he'll have you up in the middle of the night multiple times?"

Molly laughed. "It's how they work. They get hungry." She

bent and kissed Olivier for the hundredth time that day. He was deep asleep and his little body completely relaxed, which made Molly relax more than she would have without him.

Hubbub near the door. Some shrieking. Molly and Lawrence craned their necks and saw Ninette and Edmond come in, smiling broadly, holding hands, the very picture of wedded bliss.

"Hold on a minute," said Molly.

"You've lost your admirer," said Lawrence, amused at her surprise. "You haven't heard? They're married."

Molly's eyes got wide. "They *what?*" Did Madame Tessier really know everything about everything?

Lawrence jumped up. "I'm going to go congratulate them. Molly, you really have to get out more," he said and winked at her. Then he knelt down beside Molly. "Sorry, I meant to tell you before—I have a message from Matthias—"

"Where is Matthias, anyway? Doesn't he know that attendance at the fête is compulsory?"

"Fever and sniffles," said Lawrence. "Listen, he told me to tell you—" Lawrence lowered his voice and spoke into Molly's ear "—he heard from somebody, I guess Florian?—the forensics report has come in. Including fingerprints from Lagasse's neck. Which is terribly creepy and I wish those words didn't just come from my lips. But there you have it."

Molly shivered. She looked past Lawrence into the crowd, trying to find Jules.

"That's huge," she said quietly, and Lawrence nodded. "Thank Matthias for me."

Molly couldn't look in Amelie's direction. She swallowed hard, feeling the walls closing in around the Bressons, even while Amelie had no idea.

$$\text{❧} \quad 4 2 \quad \text{☙}$$

Archie Pippin had wasted no time—he was a pro, and he knew what needed to be done and in what order. He positioned himself on rue Camus so that when the Bressons left, he saw them go. It was cold, but after these weeks of frigid weather, he was used to it. He stood a few steps down an alley, where he could see the door to the Bresson's house but was not visible to most people on the street, dressed of course in dark, warm, unremarkable clothing, including a wool cap with a brim that hid his face.

When he heard someone coming, he bent to one knee and pretended to tie his bootlace. In his pocket, Pip had the tools of his trade; he expected no trouble whatsoever with the break-in portion of the evening, since in his experience, people with little money do not spend it on fancy locks and other security measures. In his inspections on earlier occasions, he had seen nothing but the cheapest lock and no other measures taken.

After a cold and tedious forty-five-minute wait, he had watched the Bresson family leave the house. They moved slowly down the street in the direction of the community center, the child in the middle holding a hand of each parent, the poor wife burdened by another pregnancy. Pip shook his head. Some people have all the luck, and some people don't: that was more or less his world view, though he gave himself credit for having the smarts to improve his natural position. It was luck, certainly, that led him to be looking out of the window the night of January 18 at just the right time, and for the clouds to let just enough moonlight through—at that exact right moment—so that he could see Jules Bresson break into Lili Lagasse's house. And it was smarts that had placed him on rue Camus the night of the fête, watching the terribly unlucky Jules Bresson leave his house for probably many hours, giving Pip all the time in the world to snatch that necklace for himself.

With a satisfied expression, Pip let himself into the house as easily as if he had been given a key. All that remained was to toss the place and find the necklace. The place consisted of so few rooms, he might, with any luck, be on his way to Marseille while the family was still eating their dessert at the community center.

SHE DIDN'T UNDERSTAND the reasons why, but Amelie understood about her son that he was easily overwhelmed by sound, by movement, by light—and so fête night, with music, dancing, and Castillac's version of a crowd, was not Laurent's idea of a good time. He *wanted* to attend. He wanted to be part of it, to run wild through the groups of adults and laugh and play, like his classmates. But once there—the lights, the noise, all the bodies—it was too much. About an hour in, long before dessert was served, he was sitting with his head bent, rocking, saying "put it back, put it back, put it back" and none of the strategies Amelie tried could ease his anxiety.

When Laurent started with these repetitions, Jules found it unbearable, so he was off somewhere else, leaving Amelie to try to soothe her son. Her techniques sometimes worked, but not that night. The sensory input was too intense, coming from too many directions at once. She realized it was time to go home, dessert or no dessert. She stood, asking Laurent to follow. She signaled to her husband, who was still talking to Ben about matters of construction and demolition, and the family went out into the night, where it was cold but quiet.

It was a silent walk home, except for Laurent saying under his breath, "put it back," timing the phrase with his steps. Amelie felt like screaming, but she had enough control over her emotions that she stayed quiet. Jules glowered and Amelie could feel the tension in her husband, could feel him winding tighter and tighter.

And then he lost it. "Shut *up!*" he shouted at Laurent. "It's the same thing, over and over, do you want everyone to lose their minds?"

Laurent froze. Amelie quickly put her arms around her son, and even though he was too old and too big to be carried, she gathered him into her arms and picked him up. Laurent's body was stiff; he did not relax into her, and she held him awkwardly as though holding a statue, taking short steps towards home.

Jules's face had a complicated expression: part chastened, part still enraged. His mouth was turned down cartoonishly and his fists were clenched, though he followed Amelie, and along with the rage there was also a sort of meekness in the mix.

Finally their house came into view. Amelie set Laurent down and they hurried to get inside where it was warm.

But the door was unlocked—not how they left it—and when they went inside, they gasped.

"Oh no," said Amelie, hand to her mouth.

"No," said Laurent. "No, no, no. I don't like this."

Jules said nothing. He began straightening up the little living room, picking up books and putting them on the small shelf, gathering up train tracks and putting them in the toy chest.

"My train," wailed Laurent.

"Who would do such a thing?" said Amelie. She went to the phone and picked it up.

"No!" said Jules.

Amelie shrank back. "What do you mean, no? We've been robbed! Paul-Henri—"

"I don't want him here!" He picked up some more train track and threw it in the chest. "They're incompetent and I don't want them in our business. What would anyone steal anyway? We don't even know if anything was taken."

Laurent sat down on the floor in a funny position he used, his knees bent under him as he perched atop his feet. He began to rock. He was muttering something else, something new, but too softly for his parents to hear what it was.

Amelie put her hand on her baby bump. The baby was moving less and less as labor got closer. Silently she said to it that everything was all right, they were safe, and the family would be going to sleep soon.

But of course, once in bed, none of them slept. Each Bresson worried about something different, and they were awake well into the night in their own private unhappy worlds.

MOLLY SAW THE BRESSONS LEAVE, and it worried her. She found Ben and whispered in his ear, and asked him if he thought they should be worried for Amelie. Again the unanswered question: what was Jules capable of?

Can any of us answer that question about the people we love? If they are under unendurable stress, especially of their own making?

It felt different, being at a fête with a baby. Molly was still getting congratulations, people peered at him and complimented his ginger hair, and blessedly, Olivier seemed to approve of the proceedings because he had been sound asleep the entire time.

He even managed being shifted in his carrier from Molly to Ben, waking up for a moment and then dropping back down.

Molly stretched and took a spin around the community center, chatting with people, trying to enjoy the night instead of feeling burdened by that necklace and the impending resolution of the murder case. She passed Annette, who was sitting with some friends eating duck and roasted potatoes. Molly stopped and squatted down beside her.

"Bonsoir, Annette," she said, and the women kissed cheeks. "I've been meaning to pay you a visit," she said, quietly enough that the others at the table wouldn't hear.

Annette looked pale. She shrugged her shoulders and looked away.

"Sorry for jumping right into it—I wanted to ask if you happened to see anything the night of January 18th, when your neighbor was killed."

Annette pulled her lips over her teeth and held them there. She looked up at the ceiling.

She did, Molly thought. But will she admit it?

"Anything at all?" said Molly.

Molly was hoping that Annette would say she had seen a teenager out later than he should have been, or a stray dog wandering down the street. Anything, anybody—but not Jules Bresson.

Annette shook her head and told Molly to go get a plate before they ran out, the duck was too delicious to miss.

With some effort, Molly stood back up. She thanked Annette, not believing her for a second, and kept moving through the crowd, a little dance in her step because the music had a good beat that could not be ignored.

Madame Tessier appeared, wearing a wool hat with a paper flower tucked into the brim.

They kissed cheeks and then Molly stood, suddenly stupefied, unable to come up with any conversation.

"Are you quite all right?"

"Sleep. Not enough."

"Oh, that," said Madame Tessier, waving it away. "Your baby is an infant, what did you expect?"

"That's a little harsh."

"I *am* rude," said Madame Tessier, laughing, and then throwing her head back and leaning into a bubbling kind of hilarity that made Molly laugh too, even though she was annoyed. "Gracious, now on top of being rude, I'm going to wake the baby. Listen—I came to find you because I've got news."

Well, no matter how much sleep she didn't have, any kind of news was always music to Molly's ears, and Madame Tessier's was usually the best. "What sort of news? Come, let's go out in the hallway where we can hear ourselves think. I hope this news is good," she said. "Or at least juicy."

"Oh, it is. For *me*," said Madame Tessier with a snort, following Molly out of the big room. "It's about Lili's will. What do you think she left me? I'll give you one guess."

"The necklace."

"You take all the fun out of everything."

Molly laughed. "So? Are you pleased?" Some children ran by holding lollipops.

"Of course I'm pleased. I found it hilarious. A joke from beyond the grave! Though of course I will never actually have it in my possession, which is a terrible shame."

Molly swallowed hard. At least that would be one good thing, she would be able to make sure Madame Tessier received what her friend had left her.

"I thought you hated that necklace."

"No, my dear, not quite. What I hated was what it represented."

"Which was?"

Madame Tessier sighed. The music got louder and she tapped her foot to the beat. Molly waited. Her eyelids got heavy and despite the music she nearly fell asleep while Madame Tessier collected her thoughts.

"You see, Lili had a complicated childhood."

"Didn't we all," murmured Molly.

"Listen, this isn't really—you're obviously on your last legs and there's too much going on—we'll continue this conversation later. Someplace quieter. After you've slept."

"Now you've got my curiosity piqued."

"Good," said Madame Tessier, and she stood up and then melted into the crowd.

✼ 43 ✼

Somehow he'd managed to fall asleep, but towards two a.m., Jules woke with a start, his body clammy with sweat. Quietly he slid out of bed and went to the small bureau, knelt down, and eased the bottom drawer out as quietly as he could. The wood squeaked a little—he should have soaped it earlier—but Amelie did not stir.

Jules had not dared to check for the necklace before bed, partly because he was afraid of how he might react if the thief had found it—which of course he almost certainly had. Amelie would have known something terrible had happened. He was not ready to tell her about it.

About any of it.

Hopelessly, Jules reached to the back of the drawer, feeling for the necklace; he knew it would not be there. The clothing that had been in the drawers had been on the bedroom floor when they got back. The thief had been thorough: the Bressons did not have much, and every last bit of their belongings had been strewn about.

Now, too late, he saw that in their small house there existed no safe hiding place. He had shoved it in the back of that drawer because it held summer clothing, and he figured Amelie wouldn't be rummaging in it anytime soon. He had meant it as temporary, a place Laurent wouldn't get into because clothing didn't interest him.

Jules let out a long, despairing sigh. He should have realized that if someone knew he had the necklace, it would be easy pickings to break in and take it. He should have hidden it somewhere in the village, in a drainpipe, behind a loose stone, or even better —in the forest, under a rock or up in a tree.

But who knew? Who had been watching? Who had seen him?

Jules sat back on his heels, his shoulders slumped. He felt as though barely any air was getting into his lungs. His whole life, as he saw it in that moment, encompassed in an instant, was a colossal failure.

Stealing the necklace, committing the murder—even if he hadn't meant to—and then losing the necklace...these were only the most recent events...magnificent mistakes, all of it.

Unlike Archie Pippin, Jules did not much believe in luck. He thought people succeeded or not according to their wits and hard work. And so his self-judgment was harsh. He stayed sitting on his heels in the dark room for a long time, listening to the sound of his wife breathing as she slept, and asking himself if there was any way out of the terrible situation he was now in, thanks to his pathetic ineptitude. Should he simply kill himself and relieve his family from being dragged down with him?

Was there any way at all to salvage this mess?

THE NEXT MORNING when Amelie woke up, Jules was gone. He had left a note saying he was headed over to La Baraque to work. There was no other comment, no signature, just one sentence saying where he was going. Amelie stood with the note in her hand, staring at it as though staring might make some other words appear, words that would express some feeling Jules had—love for her, and for his son. Some stray bit of affection.

Anything at all.

Jules—as Amelie understood correctly—was not thinking about her or Laurent at all. He was thinking, exclusively, about the necklace, desperate to find out who had taken it and how he could get it back. He would have to steal from the thief who had stolen from the robber, that was all there was to it.

He was glad that part of the shed wall needed to be taken down, because the more physically demanding the job was, the better his various anxieties were managed. He was starting to feel some relief as the pile of stones got bigger, and he worked up a sweat even in the cold.

But then he saw Ben on his way through the meadow, and his spirits sank. Jules much preferred to work alone. He did not want another person around, watching him or getting in the way, and expecting to carry on conversation.

"Did you enjoy last night?" asked Ben, looking at Jules's progress and smiling. "I think I did the macarena one time too many. My back is so stiff I could hardly get out of bed."

Jules shrugged. "I'm not much for dancing."

"Neither am I, when left to my own devices. Well, looks like you've been at it a while."

Jules nodded and swung the pickaxe, sending out a spray of chunks of rock and mortar.

"At least I heard some good news," said Ben, maintaining his casual tone but watching Jules carefully. "Apparently the forensics report is back already. It usually takes forever, you know? But I got word that Charlot has it in her possession. And that it is extensive."

Jules suddenly understood the old saw about one's blood running cold. He stopped swinging the pickaxe. "What's that mean, extensive?"

"Just that they got good prints from a variety of locations.

Including...the victim's neck." Ben had shifted his weight to the balls of his feet, ready for anything.

Jules did not look at Ben but went back to the pickaxe and landed a mighty blow. A spray of debris. Ben took a step back, then another.

"Great news," Jules said, and swung the pickaxe again, even harder.

Ben backed up some more. He watched the other man, could feel his anger, and even more, his fear. Ben could almost smell the shift in Jules's scent to something like prey, about to flee, or fight.

❧ 44 ❧

Charlot made her way to the Barstows yet again, thinking again how sorry she was that Fletcher Barstow was in prison (all jokes aside, she had checked: no prison breaks) and she would not have the opportunity to build a case against him, Castillac's most prolific thief. But Charlot had another idea, involving Fletcher's son, and she thought it had some promise.

If her junior officer was AWOL, she would simply have to do all the work herself. Maybe it was better that way.

Malcolm answered the door, lucky for her, and said that Mrs. Barstow had taken the girls to Bergerac to a place that served fish and chips. The house was quiet.

A lecture sprang to mind and Charlot nearly opened her mouth and delivered it, asking the boy why he stayed in that house, why he didn't take off to a big city and make something of himself, show his family that walking the straight path worked better than the criminal one. But as she and Malcolm went into the living room, she saw him lean down and pick up a doll from the floor and put it on a table, and the situation suddenly made sense: he stayed to look after his little sisters.

"So Malcolm," she began. "I could use your help." She felt him

NELL GODDIN

withdraw. She put some effort into arranging her face in a friendly expression. She smiled.

He shrugged and waited to hear what she had to say.

"It's the Lagasse murder. Of course you know about the stolen necklace. And it doesn't take any special training to see that if we can find the necklace, we can find the murderer." She sat down on a worn sofa and put her palms on her thighs. Her hair kept swinging into her face and bothering her.

Malcolm waited.

"So what I'm proposing, Malcolm, since you seem to know everyone everywhere, and you're friendly with all kinds, I was thinking..."

Malcolm knew what she wanted, but he was going to wait until she said the words out loud.

Charlot drew in a long breath. Why was this so hard? Why wasn't Paul-Henri here taking care of this?

"I wonder if you, with your particular skills and knowledge, would be able to find that necklace, or at least hear rumors of who has it. You know everyone, like I said. You put your ear to the ground—I bet you'll find out. Maybe the necklace is still here, in the village. Or maybe it's been moved to another city, another country. Go undercover. Find out."

"You have a lot of confidence in me," he said with a smile, leaning back into the sofa cushions, hands behind his head.

"I do."

"You make it sound like I'm hanging with thieves all the time. That's not my life. And I'm not a snitch."

"I'm not saying you are. We're talking about a person's life here. I don't think you like murder, Malcolm."

He looked down at the floor and shrugged. She was right about that.

"What I *am* saying," she continued, "is that you have entrée to a particular world, in what could be a very useful—and lucrative—way."

"What's lucrative?"

"I'd pay you, of course."

"How much? Do I get the money only when I produce the necklace? Or how does that work?"

Charlot smiled at him. "You're no dummy, Malcolm Barstow."

She laid out the details of her proposition, and Malcolm, who was indeed no dummy and knew potential with little downside when he saw it, readily agreed. Though he pretended, just for form's sake, to be on the fence for a little while just to make Charlot sweat.

❧ 45 ❧

Ninette had enjoyed the fête more than any fête in her life. She had felt like a queen as she received congratulations on her marriage from the entire village—and the more surprised they seemed about the wedding, the more gratified she felt. And they hadn't even told anyone yet about the baby on the way. She anticipated even more joy to come, not a feeling she had ever had before; she was so used to getting up seven days a week, having her coffee and croissant, and running the épicerie. A decent life, but not an especially joyful one.

There was so much good news, so much happiness, and all so suddenly—Ninette thought she might burst.

People go through life thinking the future is so predictable, she thought, that they know more or less what's coming. But it isn't so. Who would have imagined that she would find love at her age, with someone she'd known her whole life?

The next morning, Ninette kissed the sleeping Edmond with passion, and he woke with a deep gratitude and wonder he had never felt before; the morning quickly turned into a morning of love even though they had stayed up late and enjoyed a night of love only a few hours earlier.

After an hour, Ninette sighed happily and said, "Now then, cheri, I know it's early but I've got to go home—well, my little place isn't 'home' anymore, is it?" Ninette laughed. "I've got to go pick up a few things. And put the 'closed' sign on the door," she said, grinning. "Indefinitely! People can get their chocolate bars somewhere else for a little while."

She slipped out of bed, showered, and was gone. Edmond sighed a contented sigh, smiling to himself, still in shock at his great good fortune. Love and a baby, at his age! It was a miracle, there was no other way to see it. He closed his eyes and fell back asleep, into a dream of sailing on the sea with Ninette by his side, dolphins jumping alongside the boat.

Ninette made her way down the street, pulling her coat tight against the relentless cold. The winter sun was just coming up. She was thinking about that morning, and about the night before...she was so deep into savoring those memories that she was not aware of her surroundings. She walked without seeing what was in front of her, without hearing anything but her thoughts.

Jules stepped out of an alley just after she passed by.

He took her by the arm. He was not rough but his grip was firm.

"Bonjour, Ninette."

"Well salut, Jules," she said, wonderingly.

"You're going to come with me," he said. "Please don't shout, I will not hurt you."

"What are you talking about?" She laughed, though it was clear Jules was not fooling around. Her mind was tearing along, zigging and zagging, trying to understand what was happening— but no explanations came to her.

Walking quickly, he steered her the few blocks to the church in the center of the village. It was not a remarkable church—not architecturally significant, not considered beautiful by anyone, even the priest—but the bells that rang on the hour were the village's clock, and that sound served as the backbone of the day, something all the villagers relied on for a predictable reassurance that time was passing as it should.

The front doors were unlocked, as the priest wanted anyone to be able to enter if they felt moved to, and Jules and Ninette slipped inside. It was Sunday morning, but so early the priest was still in bed asleep.

"What is going on?" said Ninette. Her mouth was suddenly and drastically dry. "What—are you having some sort of problem, Jules? Is Amelie all right?" She tried to pull away but he held on tight. She wrenched her arm, harder, but he did not let go.

"Don't do that," he said in Ninette's ear, and his tone scared her. He held on to both her arms and half-dragged her down the aisle and then to the side, to the small door and the stairs to the belfry.

"Jules," said Ninette, trying to keep her voice steady. "Jules, I never did anything to you. You—you can't, not now, when my life is suddenly so good! Not now!"

Jules did not answer. He didn't take in what she was saying, he was so tangled up in his thoughts.

He pushed her through the small door. "Start climbing," he said. "I said I'm not going to hurt you. I'm...look, just keep going up. I'm sorry. But you have no choice about this."

She did not move and he shoved his elbow into her back and she hopped up a few steps.

"I told you—I'm not going to hurt you. Don't make this harder than it has to be."

"I'm afraid of heights."

"Then close your eyes."

"Jules, please. Talk to me. I know we don't know each other well, but whatever it is, I can help."

No answer from Jules.

Ninette saw no alternative so she started up the stairs. The only light was sunlight filtering down from the very top; it was hard to see and she stumbled.

Jules said nothing. He pulled her to her feet and they kept going, slow step after step, and it felt to Ninette as though she were walking straight to her death. Jules had gone off the deep end, that was clear. Her mind filled with scenarios of how things might be about to play out. Everything she imagined was dark and terrifying. The steps seemed to go on forever. Ninette was breathing hard.

"Let me rest a second." She gasped and leaned against the wall.

The space they were in, the stairwell, was narrow, with wooden walls; the top was the equivalent of three stories high. There was only room to go up or down in single file. Ninette put a hand on her stomach and clamped her teeth together. This crazy man was not going to ruin her life. Not now.

She would get out of this somehow.

MOLLY, Ben, and Olivier were driving into the village. They met no one on the road. Strictly speaking, the forty-eight hours had run out the day before, but that was the beauty of a self-imposed deadline: it could be extended. They had decided to see if the fête brought anything new to light, any possible way that Jules could be exonerated or at least a case made for leniency—not that either Ben or Molly could imagine what that could look like. And if they found nothing, straight to the gendarmerie on Sunday morning, no more extensions.

It was Sunday morning. So now the time had come.

In the car, no one spoke.

Molly was wrestling with a hollow bad feeling because a murder had happened in her beloved village and she had been unable to solve it—well, she did solve it, but the solving was no good either, and she was about to cause her friend a great deal of pain. She felt she had failed to bring justice in the usual way, where villagers felt relief, a sense of things returning to how they should be. And Molly knew how much she had disappointed Madame Tessier. As for Amelie... how she was going to take the news that Molly had found the necklace in her house? Not told her? And of course, Jules's arrest, which would happen within the hour.

She couldn't help wishing she had never found the stupid thing, or even that she had shoved it back in the boxcar and pretended she hadn't seen it.

Meanwhile, Ben dreaded having to face Charlot with evidence that should have been brought to her many days earlier. There would be questions about that, at some point, and he had no good answers.

Olivier was gurgling and cooing; as far as he was concerned, the more time in the car, the better.

At the edge of the village, Ben slowed down; a man was running straight down the middle of the street. He waved and then veered down a side street. They saw two women standing on a corner, talking with their hands, obviously worked up about something. A woman walked very quickly, holding the hand of a young girl.

"Things seem a little jumpy," said Molly. "You'd think someone planted a bomb or something."

"Sometimes, Molly, your imagination—"

"Sorry, I'm just trying to work out why people seem...you can feel the energy, Ben, right?...they're upset."

Ben decided to park closer to the center of the village instead of going down the side street to the gendarmerie. Once out of the car, they could see and hear a crowd, in the Place. On a Sunday morning, right after a fête? Odd. People usually slept in. Hardly anything was open, and the church hadn't seen a crowd this size in years.

Quickly Molly slipped Olivier into his carrier and the family hurried to join the group in front of the church.

"Molly! About time!"

"Huh?"

"It's nearly nine!"

"What?"

"The bells!" The woman pointed to the belfry.

Molly could see two people standing under the bell. There was a sort of guardrail, about waist high, wooden, possibly flimsy.

"Is that Jules?" Ben asked the woman.

"Yes, and he's got Ninette! He says he's not letting her go until he talks to Charlot. I think it's a love triangle, personally. Poor Amelie! I always thought there was something off about him, ask anybody, I've always said so."

Ben looked at Molly. She shook her head, meaning, *I have no idea what we do now.*

He raised his voice. "Has anyone called Charlot?"

"Our useless Chief?" someone called out.

"Why bother?" shouted someone else.

"Half a minute and the bells—"

But that person's watch was not quite accurate, a little slow. The big church bell rang, with a pause in between gongs as always, nine times, the sound such a part of the fabric of village life that even in this strange, unsettled moment, they felt a kind of safety from hearing it.

Jules and Ninette had dropped down out of sight at the first gong. It would be unbearably loud up close.

"Ben," said Molly. "Can you make any sense of this? What is he doing?"

He shook his head.

"Hey Jules!" someone shouted. "She just married someone else, you're out of luck!"

A few in the crowd laughed, but it was forced, the laugh of

people hoping to feel that the situation was humorous when they knew that it was not.

Everyone stared at the railing to see if Jules and Ninette would reappear.

They waited. The crowd started to murmur.

Ben asked if Jules had said anything, had he made any demands? Were they sure Ninette was up there against her will?

Nobody seemed to know anything.

Then Jules stood, alone. "I want to speak to the Chief!"

Louder murmuring, with people guessing his reasons or making smart remarks, some quiet, some starting to understand the situation for what it was.

Ben jumped up on a bench and told the crowd to stay calm. Then he shouted, "Jules! It's Ben. We'll find Chief Charlot for you. Don't worry!"

Then, to the crowd, he said in a quieter voice, "Don't taunt him. This is not a joke."

Some nervous laughter. Though people were having different reactions and obviously different thoughts, something about the crowd felt as though the mass of people had its own energy, its own role to play in what was unfolding, almost as though the crowd—not the individuals in it—wanted drama, was waiting for something terrible to happen, and even wishing for it.

Molly squinted at the belfry, trying to catch a glimpse of Ninette. Then she bent and kissed the top of her son's head. She had no reason to think Jules had a gun or that Olivier was in any danger, but she worried anyway, a new kind of worry that she recognized as part of what it means to be a mother.

The necklace was in her pocket. When Charlot arrived, as surely she would, any minute, Molly could give it to her, tell her it had been found in Jules's living room, and the arrest would be made.

Case closed, at last.

Molly did not relax at the thought; there was too much that

had to happen between now and then. As long as Ninette came out of the belfry safely, that seemed to Molly, at this point, like a good enough resolution. It would cost Amelie, there was no avoiding that. The situation—that was, Jules—had now spiraled so far out of control, it was beyond Molly's help.

BEN HAD CALLED and texted Charlot: no answer.

"I'm sure she's on the way!" he yelled up to Jules. "Is there something I can do? Do you need help? Can I bring you anything?"

The crowd was quiet for once, listening for Jules's answer. Still no sign of Ninette.

"Charlot, I have to talk to Charlot," Jules shouted.

Olivier woke up and began to cry.

Molly said to Ben, "I have to feed him. And the sound of a crying baby won't help the situation, I'll be back as soon as I can —" Molly comforted Olivier as she walked quickly back to the car, where at least they would be out of earshot of the belfry. Enough minutes had passed that she was less in shock, and she considered what Jules's demands might be. Something for his family, she thought. Some promise, from some authority, that they would—what?

He had to know he was going to prison.

With a sudden stab in her chest, she feared Jules would jump. And for some crazy, misguided reason, force Ninette to jump with him.

But was Jules that deranged? Molly didn't think so. She had never thought so and her mind hadn't changed. It made more sense that Jules had taken Ninette hostage because he wanted to extract something, something it was in Charlot's power to give... as his last, desperate act before his arrest.

But what promise could Charlot make? Since Jules had stolen the necklace and committed a murder in the course of that theft, there would be nothing for him. He had exactly zero leverage, even including the hostage, since Molly did not believe he would really hurt Ninette.

But then—would she not give the hostage any consideration at all, if she were in charge? How could you gamble with someone's life?

She could find no way to take a softer perspective or find leniency for Jules. No way he could be able to stay with his family and take care of them the way he said he wanted to. Molly shook her head at the hopelessness of his situation.

Jules Bresson was caught, and he was going to leave that belfry in handcuffs.

End of story.

What remained—what had to be their focus now—was getting the newlywed Ninette safely on the ground.

❦ 46 ❦

Amelie Bresson stood in the bathroom splashing cold water on her face. Laurent was in the next room, lining up pirates and dinosaurs.

She knew Jules wasn't having an affair. He wasn't moonlighting in some factory somewhere, or working a night shift as a watchman. She could go on and on, listing all the things he wasn't doing...but what *was* he doing? Where did he go at night? And this morning, for the first time, he was gone when she and Laurent got up.

Amelie was tired. The birth of her second child was coming very soon, if all went well, and what she wanted to do was rest as much as she could while she still could, and enjoy these final days before the newborn claimed most of her attention and energy.

She brushed her hair, which thanks to pregnancy was thick and glossy. She got dressed and saw that Laurent had dressed himself. "How about a treat?" she said, with false gaiety. "Let's have breakfast at Café de la Place!"

"Where is Papa?"

"Out...working."

Laurent did not believe her. He had a finely tuned ear for

when a person was not being forthright. He said nothing but set a pirate holding a sword next to a stegosaurus.

"I'm not hungry," he said.

"Well, let's go for a walk, then. Come on now, this is not a negotiation. Here's your hat."

Amelie bent, awkwardly, to tie the laces on her boots, then slipped on her coat. The air outside felt like a slap in the face, but Amelie welcomed it. The cold helped her think more clearly.

Laurent was glum as they trudged towards the center of the village. Neither of them saw Pip, who had stepped out of an alley and followed, staying a half-block behind them.

If the necklace wasn't in the house, Pip had reasoned, then one of them must be carrying it on their person. And the best choice for that, he guessed, was Amelie. He thought Jules a coward, first of all, and second? Who would assault a pregnant woman? Who would even guess that a pregnant woman would be carrying something so valuable?

I would, Pip thought, smiling to himself, and keeping a professionally correct distance between himself and his prey, as he waited for his chance.

OLIVIER CONKED RIGHT BACK out after being fed, and Molly quickly made herself presentable and hurried back toward the Place. And whom should she meet coming the other way but Malcolm Barstow.

"Malcolm!"

"Salut, Molly." They kissed cheeks quickly. Malcolm smiled at Olivier and then the friends looked at each other.

"This looks bad, huh?" said Molly.

Malcolm shrugged but his expression was dour.

"Charlot get there yet?"

"I didn't see her." He had been on his way to Archie Pippin's, thinking that if anyone knew where the necklace was, it would be

Pip. He thought about telling Molly what Charlot had hired him to do, but his natural sense of secrecy won out.

"You know Jules at all?" Molly asked.

Again, Malcolm shrugged. "Nah. Not really. You know he's got Ninette up there?"

Molly nodded. "And Ninette is pregnant."

Malcolm's eyes got wide. "Huh? But she's old!"

"Not old enough, apparently." Molly remembered that the pregnancy had only been a guess of Madame Tessier's, but she didn't correct herself. She was thinking so hard about what was happening, trying to see paths forward, that she nearly drooled on Olivier's head.

"Listen," she said, with some urgency. "I trust you, Malcolm."

Malcolm nodded.

Molly looked around to make sure no one else was around. Then she reached into her pocket and took out the necklace. "Here," she said. "Yes, it's what you think it is. Keep it hidden. Get it to Charlot as soon as possible. Go to her house if you have to. No, I don't know where she lives, I'm sure you can find out. And tell her—tell her it came from me, and that I found it at the Bresson's. That's right, at Jules's house. And obviously—tell her Jules is in the church, and he's got Ninette and won't let her go."

Malcolm stuffed the necklace into his pants pocket without looking at it. He paused for an instant to take in everything Molly had said. And then he gave her a wink and disappeared down a side street.

She appreciated that he hadn't asked any questions. Malcolm's wide understanding—his ability to take in confusing, new circumstances and then act—was going to make that kid a real success someday, Molly thought. With a deep, fortifying breath, she strode toward the Place. It was time to have a chat with Jules.

🎍 47 🎋

The Place was filling with more and more villagers—there had to be close to two hundred people there now, milling about, pointing up at the belfry, talking and talking. Jules had said nothing more and at the moment was hidden from sight. So was Ninette.

Molly slid in next to Ben. "What did I miss?"

Ben shrugged. "I've tried to engage him but he hasn't responded. All he says is that he wants Charlot."

"Where is she, anyway? And Paul-Henri? It's weird."

Ben could only shrug. The noise of the crowd was a low murmur interspersed with silence. Everyone waited, eyes fixed on the belfry.

"Shall I give it a go?" Molly asked Ben.

"Absolutely," he said. "Want me to take Olivier?"

Molly considered. "Not yet."

She walked to a spot where she had a little space around her, staring at the ground for a moment as she collected her thoughts. She put her hands on Olivier's legs and held them. Did Jules trust her? She wasn't sure. The only thing she did know about him, or

281

at least believe, was that he cared about his family. Molly didn't think Amelie was wrong about that.

Just as she was about to shout up to the belfry, Edmond appeared beside her.

"I got here as quick as I could," he said. His hair was sticking up and he looked as though he had just rolled out of bed. Which he had.

Molly just grasped his hands and squeezed them. "I'm going to try to talk to Jules. Just—just stay calm. Hard as that is."

She couldn't waste any more time. "Jules!" she shouted, trying to make her voice have some softness, some warmth, even though she was shouting. "It's Molly!"

Everyone's faces were tilted up, watching.

She prayed that her French was flawless, for once.

"Hey Jules, I've got a question for you!" She waited a short moment. "Will you come down so we can talk?"

A pause. Then "No!"

A murmur of disapproval from the crowd.

Molly turned to Ben. "Can you move through the crowd and tell people to keep quiet? I don't want Jules reacting to their oohs and ahhs."

"On it," said Ben.

Molly waited some moments for the message to make its way through several hundred people, all with their eyes on the belfry or craning to see how Edmond was reacting. Molly peeked at Edmond as well. His eyes were on the belfry, his expression inscrutable.

"Jules!" she called out, again trying for a particular tone in her voice. It was a difficult note to hit, sounding almost relaxed, not intense, to try to communicate that same relaxation to Jules. She knew the only way out was for him to calm down so he could think about the situation rationally.

Maybe that was a hopeless goal, but it was all she could come up with.

Ben put his hand on her shoulder and she felt his support, his belief in her.

"Jules!" she called out again, a little louder. "What do you want? I can make sure Charlot knows."

Jules's head popped up above the railing. "Get her!" he called back.

At least he's answering me, Molly thought.

Edmond stood very still beside her, his eyes never moving.

"Is Ninette okay?" Molly called.

They could see Jules turn and look down at Ninette though they could not see her. He said something to her but they could not make it out.

Jules turned back to face the crowd but he said nothing.

Molly's mind was racing. How to reach him? She had no power to offer him anything, not the way Charlot might—though how did hostage negotiations normally work? Was it all right for her to lie, to promise him whatever he asked as long as Ninette was released?

Was it moral to lie to a murderer?

"Molly," Edmond said. "I want to go up there."

Molly startled. "That's a terrible idea."

"I have to."

"Listen to me. What you want or don't want isn't the point right now. I understand your anxiety. Seriously, I do. But—"

"Charlot!" yelled Jules.

But there was no Charlot. A murmur from the crowd as people wondered where she was. Paul-Henri was usually everywhere in the village, and what had happened to him?

Edmond seemed to understand. Molly noticed that an oven with the temperature slightly off made him lose his mind, but in this real crisis, he was calm. Edmond's face went impassive again and he went back to fixing his gaze on the belfry.

Molly took hold of Olivier's feet and squeezed them. She had believed that an idea would come to her, some flash of knowing the right thing to say—but the flash had not come.

SOME IN THE crowd began making bets on outcomes. The positive ones did not have good odds.

A cry from up above.

"Ninette!" Edmond shouted, waving both arms.

Neither Jules nor Ninette were visible.

"Any ideas?" Molly murmured to Ben.

He shook his head. "Not really. Just get him talking. Stall for time."

"The longer this goes on, the worse the ending will be," someone said, and that sentiment was passed around the crowd with the growing sense that it was truth. People managed their fear by expecting the worst.

"This would go better without the audience," Molly told Ben.

"I can't see how we're going to clear the Place. I don't have the authority."

"Where in the world is Charlot?"

Ben just shook his head.

"Should you go up there?" Molly asked. She didn't want him to, didn't think it was safe. But he did have training, after all.

"I'm considering it," he said. "I don't want to spook him."

They gave each other a long look, and so much was contained in it—fear, determination, love—

"Hey Jules!" Molly called, as softly as she could and still be heard.

She thought she saw the top of his head at the railing.

"How about you tell me what you need, and I can text that to Charlot?"

"Why doesn't she come?" he called back, popping his head above the railing.

"I don't know!"

A long pause.

"Is Ninette okay?" Molly called.

"She needs medical care," yelled Jules. "I need Charlot."

"Can you—can you be a little more flexible, Jules? I know you don't want to hurt anyone."

No response.

"I know what you care most about is your family."

No response.

"Can Amelie come up? Would you let her help Ninette?"

No response.

Molly was starting to sweat. It was harder than she anticipated, trying to talk someone down, literally down the winding belfry stairs. She could not find a way to lure him into hitting the conversational ball back over the net.

"I'll go find Amelie. Should have done that before now," said Ben, giving Molly's shoulder a squeeze before taking off.

Well, it was time to show a few cards, Molly thought. Nothing else has worked, so what do I have to lose?

"Listen, Jules," she called. Her voice starting to show the strain of shouting. "I know you've been feeling up against a wall. Debt is a terrible load to carry, I completely get it. I've been there!"

She paused. She could still see the top of his head.

"And I can see how that load might...might make me consider doing some things that I wouldn't have, otherwise."

The crowd was quiet, the village hanging on her words. It was exhausting, shouting these long sentences.

"And maybe you think Charlot can at least make things all right for your family, if you just face the music. Taking care of your family—that was always the point."

She heard a small "yes" from the belfry.

Jules put his face in his hands. What had he thought taking Ninette was going to accomplish? It was utterly pointless. He felt the hope of the idea draining out of him; it made him nauseated.

He felt doomed, as though the mistakes just kept coming and coming and he could not find a way to stop them.

Then a commotion broke out. Amelie had come into the Place, and the crowd was shouting at her and pointing at the church and Molly couldn't hear whether Jules said anything more.

Edmond did not move but kept his eyes on the belfry.

Ben led Amelie to Molly. Laurent looked like he'd seen a ghost.

The crowd was loud with people arguing over what should be done; Charlot and Paul-Henri were still nowhere to be seen; Archie Pippin, realizing the moment was lost, slipped down a side street out of sight.

❧ 48 ❧

And then, at last, more yelling from the other end of the Place: Charlot had appeared, and some clapping broke out along with some less polite greetings.

"Oh, thank heavens," said Molly when she heard. She squeezed Amelie's hand, hardly able to meet her eyes.

"I'm confused. What is going on?" Amelie said. "Jules is up there?"

Charlot did not approach the church but made her way through the crowd, asking for Ben Dufort.

"Will you come with me?" she asked, once she found him.

Ben nodded, and the two of them, current and former chiefs, set off for the church.

"Molly—?" said Amelie.

Laurent stared at the ground, his face pale. He did not murmur any of his usual phrases and stood very still.

Molly was worried for Ben, for Ninette, for Amelie, for Laurent—she was holding so much anxiety for so many people at once. She began to cry, to her great dismay and annoyance.

And then—it was an odd thing, remarked on for years after—people felt a sudden shift in the weather. The cold front that they had been suffering for so many weeks simply dissipated, all at once. The sun came out and it actually felt warm. The air, while not balmy, had a softness to it, a taste of spring. The mood turned along with the temperature, and the crowd—and Molly—felt a blossoming hope that things were going to turn out better than they had imagined a minute ago.

The crowd unzipped coats and took off hats, lifting their faces to the sun. They waited, and listened. Those closest to the church could hear the steady progress of Charlot and Ben going up the stairs, heard Charlot call out to Jules that she was on the way, that she was bringing help for Ninette, and that he was not to worry, everything was going to be all right.

Molly and Edmond put their arms around each other.

"How's Olivier," he said quietly.

"It's his first hostage negotiation. Can't say it went all that well. But maybe now..."

"Everyone is going to be fine," said Edmond. It was a wish as much as a prediction, they both knew that, but Molly nodded anyway, with a tight smile.

The other thing remarked upon later was how well-behaved the crowd was. Once Ben and Charlot entered the church, there was no clapping, no jeering, no noise. A strange sort of patience ensued. Hardly any fidgeting. Hundreds of eyes pinned to the belfry, everyone praying that this time, Charlot did her job well.

AFTER WHAT SEEMED AN ETERNITY, someone yelled, "They're coming out!" and just after that, the church door opened and Ben, Charlot, Ninette, and Jules walked out into the bright sunshine. Jules was in handcuffs. Ninette seemed to be all right; at least, she was walking without any trouble and did not appear to be in distress.

Jules was not resisting: looking down, shoulders slumped, the fight gone out of him.

Edmond raced through the crowd and took Ninette in his arms.

Amelie stood next to Molly, as frozen in place as her son. Molly slipped an arm around her.

"What—" Amelie managed to say.

"It's a long story," said Molly. "Obviously, this is very tough. Maybe you would come over, you and Laurent, and stay with Ben and me for a little while?"

Amelie shook her head. Of course she had known that something was wrong, had known it for weeks. But hearing that Jules had taken a hostage, and then seeing him led away in handcuffs—these were never any of the options that had occurred to her as possible, and her mind was struggling mightily not even to understand, but to accept that what she had just seen was actually real.

❦ 49 ❦

"If it's okay with you, I'd like to go for a run," Ben said, keeping his voice low in case their guests—Amelie and Laurent—were still sleeping.

"Of course." Molly knew running was the main way Ben handled stress. And yesterday they'd all had a whopping, heaping helping of it.

Molly's main way was cogitating, researching, eavesdropping—anything that brought her closer to understanding a situation, criminal or otherwise. As she made breakfast, she went over the events of the day before, her heart breaking for Amelie. Seeing your husband led away in handcuffs had to be right up there as one of the worst moments of one's life.

Though of course, things could be worse: strangled in your own bed came to mind.

"I thought I would make a real American breakfast!" said Molly, and cringed at the over-jolly tone of her voice. Amelie had walked slowly into the living room without speaking. She appeared to still be in shock, and Molly noted this and tried to think of what would help.

NELL GODDIN

"Here's some coffee. How about some bacon and eggs? Is Laurent still asleep?"

"No. He has the covers pulled over his head, muttering to himself. Yesterday..."

"I know. Awful for him to see that."

"He doesn't understand. And I can't help him with that, because neither do I." Amelie had been avoiding eye contact but then turned and looked at Molly, slowly shaking her head.

Molly took a deep breath. The night before, it had taken some convincing for Amelie and Laurent to come to La Baraque. And once there, nobody had been in any shape for hard conversations. They had all repaired to their bedrooms and shut the door.

But now it was time. Way, way past time.

"Do you want to eat and then talk, or talk and then eat?" asked Molly gently.

"Talk now."

Another deep breath.

"Okay. First let me say: you mean a lot to me, Amelie. And it's been a terrible struggle trying to figure out the right thing to do. Not to make it about me and my feelings."

Amelie showed no reaction.

"All right, so... of course you know that Lili Lagasse was murdered, back on January 18. People in the village knew that she owned a valuable necklace—she talked about it all the time, so this was no secret."

Still no reaction from Amelie. Molly chewed her lip for a moment before continuing.

"The whole world is under financial pressure, as I don't need to tell you. So that necklace...anyway, the fact that Lagasse was murdered is not in dispute—she was found strangled. And the necklace, which she always wore, was missing when her body was discovered."

Amelie sank into a chair and looked down at her bump. She

292

was due next week. She shook her head again, unable to take in what Molly was saying.

"The thing is," Molly said quietly, "when I showed up at your house that day, just before Olivier was born? Lili Lagasse's necklace fell out of a boxcar. Out of one of Laurent's trains."

A long, heavy silence fell across the room.

Laurent was still in bed, Ben was somewhere out on the road. Neither Molly nor Amelie could find any words. They both wished they could somehow go back and change history—but what would they change? The two of them had done nothing to get to this horrible point. They were not the people who had set any part of this story into motion.

Finally, Molly said, "I'm so sorry. I wish I hadn't found it. I wish I had told you the minute I did find it."

Amelie did not look up. She was so still that Molly had a flash of her sitting to have her portrait painted, a ridiculous notion given all that was going on.

The orange cat suddenly appeared—Molly hadn't seen it in weeks. She glared at it as it headed for Amelie's ankles. But the cat simply wound herself through Amelie's legs and purred.

"Jules did not murder that woman," Amelie said, lifting her head. One hand stroked the orange cat.

Molly hid her shock by moving back to the stove and turning the bacon. She understood a little, maybe—that Amelie was protecting herself from the truth. But what to do next? Molly decided arguing the point would be a mistake, at least for the moment.

It was a common enough human impulse, she thought, to dislike a certain set of facts, and want new ones. Everybody's done it, she told herself. Me included. Amelie just needs a little more time to get used to reality.

She broke some eggs into a bowl and scrambled them ferociously, listening out for Olivier who was due to wake up hungry at any moment.

. . .

BEN CAME BACK and went out again. The weather had in fact turned, and so Molly, Olivier, Amelie, and Laurent took a walk through the meadow, but despite the sunshine, all of them were glum except for Bobo. Molly was waiting for Amelie to say she wanted to visit Jules in jail, but so far, Amelie had not mentioned it. They were headed back to the house when Molly got a text from Matthias.

JUST HEARD—JULES fingerprints a match

SHE HESITATED and then showed her phone to Amelie, who read the text and then squeezed her eyes shut as though to erase what she had just seen.

"Okay, talk to me, Amelie. Any idea why Jules would have been in her house?" Molly asked. She was wondering about the location of those particular prints—were they on the broken piece of pottery? The front door handle? The location mattered. Obviously if they were taken from Lagasse's neck, it was all over.

Well, it had been all over for weeks, that was the truth of it. Molly criticized herself harshly for dragging it out. It had been pointless and sentimental and she should have known better. Should have gone straight to Charlot with the necklace and gotten this entire dreadful business over with.

Olivier started to fuss. Molly didn't want to feed him right then, she wanted to stay with Amelie...but she was getting used to the fact that what the baby needed, and when, trumped everything else. She made her apologies and went inside to feed her son.

Sitting in the rocker in the bedroom, Molly did her best to sweep any thoughts of Jules and Amelie and murder and necklaces out of her thoughts. She sang "Swing Low, Sweet Chariot," not exactly on key, but with vigor. She stroked Olivier's back, closed her eyes, wished for better things to come to everyone she knew, and eventually Olivier was full and sleepy.

"He's out cold, let me put him in the bassinet and then we can talk," Molly said to Amelie. After settling the baby, Molly sat by the stove—the weather had warmed up, but they still wanted a fire, maybe not so much for warmth as for comfort.

"So," she began. It was time for tough love. Wasn't it? "I—"

"Wait," said Amelie. "You don't understand, and I need to explain. I haven't said anything yet because finding the words...it's going to sound..." She shook her head and blinked hard.

Laurent was on the floor between them, tracing his finger on the rug pattern.

"Jules did not kill that woman," Amelie said. Her tone was even, she was not strident—she sounded as matter-of-fact, as confident, as a person possibly could.

Molly looked at her friend with sorrow. She shrugged and held out her palms as if to say, if I could change how things are, I would.

"I know it looks bad," continued Amelie. "He looks guilty. I understand that. I do hear what you've told me, I understand that the evidence is piled up against him. But I am telling you—with every fiber of my being—I am sure that Jules did not kill anyone. Because that is not the kind of man he is."

Molly looked carefully at Amelie. Who was she to argue what kind of man Jules was? Molly didn't know, she had barely spent any time around him. All she knew was that a woman was dead, Jules had her necklace, and now his prints were inside her house.

"Okay. So how do you explain..."

Amelie shook her head slowly. "I can't. Like I said, I see how it looks." Then she looked at Molly and made a small, hesitant smile that nearly broke Molly's heart. "You're the ace detective," she said. "You figure it out."

She hesitated to leave them alone, but Molly gathered up Olivier and told Amelie she would be back in time for lunch. She texted Ben to let him know where she was going, strapped Olivier into the car seat, and drove to see Madame Tessier.

Molly had debated which person to see first, Tessier or Annette. She felt unenthusiastic about both prospects, if she was honest with herself—but Amelie was so certain, and Molly had so much respect for her, that she had to turn over these last two unturned stones and see if anything that would help Jules was under them.

"I knew you'd show up today," said Madame Tessier after the requisite bonjours and cheek kisses. "How is Olivier faring, with you tearing around the village same as always?"

"It is not the same at all, believe me. But he only woke me twice last night so I feel fairly human today. I won't keep you long. I wanted—"

"Well, hold on just a minute, Molly. You have some explaining to do. What is this I hear about you having the necklace in your possession, and for quite some time, and not a word to me about it?"

Molly looked down at the floor. "Yes. I'm sorry. You'll understand why I couldn't...I'm glad at least that you'll get it, and it hasn't been lost—"

"—lost is not really the term. I think you mean stolen—"

"Can I sit down? And how about a cup of coffee?"

"Are you supposed to—"

"—don't you worry about that. It helps me think. And right now, I *need* to think. Listen, Hélène—can I call you Hélène?"

Madame Tessier looked surprised but pleased. She nodded.

"First, if you would finish what you started to tell me at the fête. About Lili's childhood?"

"Why does it matter now?"

"I don't know. I don't even have a theory. But I need to get all the facts I can lay my hands on, and see...just, please, tell me what you know about this complicated childhood of Lili's. So I can get the fullest picture I can of who she was and what formed her."

Madame Tessier looked up at the ceiling and collected her thoughts. "'Complicated'—perhaps I chose the wrong word. The situation was rather simple, actually. Stark, and cruel. I hesitate to...you see, the family was...oh, I apologize, it's taking me a minute to organize my thoughts. It's—what she endured—it's upsetting to think about."

"Take your time." Molly was getting that little tingle, a feeling of electricity going up her spine, that in the past had meant something important was about to happen.

"You see, Lili was the middle child. Her older sister was the apple of her father's eye, and the younger brother belonged to the mother. I say 'belonged'—I mean, emotionally belonged. It was a family divided into two teams: the father and the sister, and the mother and the brother. Lili wasn't on either one."

"An outcast."

"Yes. It was...it was quite difficult for her. It was not simply that she got less attention. She was an object of scorn, a sort of scapegoat I guess you would say. She eventually found happiness once she left home, moved here to Castillac and made her own friends, her own life."

"Not a rare scenario, I guess." Molly considered. "Sometimes I think a lot of us feel we were born into the wrong families. Never quite fit in."

Madame Tessier nodded. "Lili told me this only one time, and then never wanted to have the subject brought up again." She took a deep breath. "Her family would go for outings, sometimes overnight, or over a weekend. And leave Lili behind, to fend for herself. They would lock her inside the house so she couldn't get out."

Molly swallowed, then shook her head.

"There was food, the house was warm enough—it wasn't that Lili's immediate survival was threatened. But. Just imagine how it felt to a girl, a young girl, to be left behind in that way. Ignored, really. And trapped inside like a prisoner."

Molly felt a little sick to her stomach. "I am so sorry she had to endure that."

Madame Tessier nodded. "She didn't tell me about it for many years, but one night, after a bit too much grappa, which we got in Italy on a wonderful trip, she finally told me the whole story. And then you see, the necklace made more sense. Or it made different kinds of sense..."

Molly cocked her head. "Different kinds?"

"Well, one way to look at it is that inheriting that necklace from her mother gave her a feeling of belonging, at last. Made her feel deserving of a gift—it gave her the idea that she was valuable too. But perhaps that was not really it, maybe that's too pat. Maybe what that necklace did was serve as a reminder of her family's cruelty, and how she wanted to live a different kind of life."

Molly nodded. The two women looked at the fire and thought about Lili.

"I'll tell you, at Lili's funeral? I wanted to say something to her brother and sister, standing there so smug in their fancy clothes. But right then...what in the world could I have said that would matter? So I said nothing. That's going to be one of those decisions I second-guess for the rest of my life."

Molly nodded.

"I have so many more questions, so much I still want to talk to her about," said Madame Tessier softly.

"I can't understand how you have a child, and then act that way. So much of poor parenting I do understand: the frustration of feeling out of control, of limited resources, even old grudges and hurts causing a parent to lash out at a child or even neglect them, in the moment," said Molly. "I'm not defending those things—but I can see how they happen. But what you're describing...it's so cold. Not the action of someone who lost control, who is overwhelmed. Leaving a child behind overnight—" Molly's throat closed and she shook her head, unable to finish.

Madame Tessier was nodding. "Maybe you noticed how Lili decorated her house with all those patterns of green leaves? She told me it was because when she was alone, she would close her eyes tight, even when she was already in the dark, and imagine she was in the forest, at dawn. And her imagination was so vivid, she said she could actually hear the leaves moving in the breeze. She told me she felt the color green had saved her sanity, which in my opinion is a remarkable thing to think."

"Is that why the brooch?"

"You noticed? Oh, of course, you notice everything. Yes, that was a present from Lili. I don't think she even realized...it was just that she was so attracted to the forest, to leaves, always. We took many walks together, on the trails around here."

Molly and Madame Tessier sat in quiet for some time, digesting all of this.

"And I'll tell you this," Madame Tessier said finally. "When Lili finally shared this with me, after we'd been close friends for many,

many years…if her parents had still been alive? I'd have gone to Bordeaux and knocked them both on the head. And happily gone to prison for it."

"I'd have cheered you on," said Molly, and she wasn't joking.

❧ 51 ❧

"It was the necklace you were talking about," said Amelie to Laurent. It was not a question because she knew the answer. For weeks he had been saying "put it back, put it back, put it back" and she had never imagined until now there had been sense at the heart of what seemed like nonsense.

I should have listened to my boy, she thought, rubbing her arms and looking out of the window. If I had found it first, and been able to talk to Jules...

Amelie knew there was no talking to Jules. There never was.

But that didn't make him a murderer.

She was sitting on the floor of the bedroom in the annex. Molly had done a good job of making it a welcoming, cozy space for guests; the rug was soft, the sheets crisp, the comforter warm. Laurent was still in bed, all the way under the covers, but she knew he was hiding, not sleeping.

"Molly says we can stay as long as we like. What do you think about that?" she asked him.

"Stay," said Laurent, from under the covers.

"Maybe we could go home and get some toys?"

"Do they have a TV?"

"I'm sure they do, somewhere." She smiled a weary smile. "But don't be thinking because of everything that you're going to spend every minute watching TV."

"Papa is in trouble."

Amelie looked up sharply. It was not like Laurent to speak so directly. "He is," she said. She said nothing more because she knew nothing more, and her son would not be interested in vague reassurances based on nothing.

Amelie looked out of the window again, at the stark branches and gray sky of winter. She wished for spring to hurry. And for Molly, somehow, to pull off the impossible.

MOLLY WAS TIRED. She was beyond tired, tired in a profound way she hadn't known was possible. It wasn't so much the interrupted sleep and the new demands of the little person she carried everywhere, though of course that wasn't nothing—it was the weight of everything, emotionally, that was wearing her down.

The financial situation in America had not improved, and so there were still no bookings for the gîtes at La Baraque, nor any inquiries. The tension was unabated among the villagers, who worried about tourism being dead and never recovering, whether they depended on tourism directly or not. Molly did not want a different job—running investigations and a gîte business suited her perfectly, especially with mother now added to the list of hats she wore—and she resisted giving any thought to what else she could do. Not yet, not until there was no other choice. But all of this pressure, even if she was consciously deciding not to focus on any of it—it was exhausting. And of course, on top of all that, the Lagasse case.

All she could do that day was plod onward, chasing a trail that was ninety-nine point nine percent hopeless. She only kept plodding because she wanted to be able to tell Amelie that she had tried, had looked under every rock, interviewed anyone and everyone...and because when it came to investigations, Molly wanted every loose thread accounted for, even including the ones that seemed like total dead ends.

After saying *à toute* to Madame Tessier, Molly sat in the car for a few minutes, turning over what the other woman had told her and bouncing the slightly fussy Olivier in her lap.

So Lili Lagasse had a rough childhood. Not that unusual. Okay, maybe rougher than most, unusual in degree. Still...what was to be made of that? It sounded as though she had moved to Castillac and left the rest of the family behind, made her own life. A good outcome, all things considered.

Molly did not dismiss or minimize the effect of what had been done to Lili. She understood that cruelty to a child is not simply shrugged off and forgotten. But what did any of this history have to do with her ending? Her family was rich, they would have no reason to come to Castillac and try to get the necklace that had been in Lili's possession for so many years. The brother and sister had inherited all the money—and if the necklace had a particular sentimental value, why wait so many years—decades—before trying to get it back? Molly was not even certain the necklace had come from Lili's mother; Molly understood that Lili had told Madame Tessier that it had, but she wondered if that had been a wish instead of the truth.

What if Lili had bought the necklace with her own money, as a symbol of what she could do on her own? As a way to show herself she didn't need her family's money, she could have nice things without any help from them? Though it was hard to see how she could have saved enough to buy something so valuable.

Molly lay Olivier on the passenger seat for a moment and rubbed her temples. He stopped fussing and looked at her. She looked back at him.

"Beautiful boy," she said, putting her hand on his soft cheek.

Olivier burped.

Molly laughed and picked him up again, giving his little body a squeeze before getting out of the car and buckling him into the car seat.

Next and final stop: Annette.

Molly couldn't guess what Annette might be holding back, but at the fête she was pretty sure she was holding back something, and before heading home to La Baraque and Amelie, Molly had to try one last time to find out what it was.

ANNETTE HAD SPENT the last few weeks, since her neighbor's murder, only leaving her house to go to work and come home. Straight to the mairie and back, using alleys and side streets, trying to stay out of sight as much as possible. It was as though she were the perpetrator, instead of...that man she had seen on the night of January 18. Now known to be Jules Bresson.

As Annette saw it, she was not out of the woods yet. Bresson was in the Castillac jail, which was obviously a tremendous improvement over being loose in the village. She could breathe a guarded sigh of relief, but she was not going to feel completely safe until he was in prison and far, far away from the village.

Because Annette knew that jails can be broken out of. Who knew what gang of criminals Bresson hung out with, who could probably get into a jail as easily as he'd gotten into poor Lili's house. The gendarmerie was practically no better than a couple of slapstick comedians, utterly useless at their jobs. So that Monday, the jailing of Bresson notwithstanding, Annette had followed the same protocol of sneaking through the back alleys to get to the mairie, and not going out to lunch once there.

Annette was alone behind the desk when Molly rang the buzzer, and she very nearly didn't let her in—everyone knew the mairie closed for lunch, what was Molly thinking, anyway? But the sight of her with that baby in the carrier melted Annette's heart just enough that she opened the door.

"Bonjour Annette! I know, it's lunchtime, thank you for your understanding, I only want a quick word with you—"

Annette wished she hadn't opened the door.

She made some cooing noises at the baby, trying to distract Molly.

"Are you on lunch break? Is there someplace we could sit down? He's little but I swear he's made out of bricks. Heavy bricks," said Molly with a laugh.

Annette led her to a small room and they sat on uncomfortable folding chairs and looked at each other.

"Well, I appreciate this," said Molly. "I won't beat around the bush. I got the idea the other night that maybe you might have seen something—someone, rather—on the night of Lili's murder. Now don't protest—I'm not judging you, Annette, for keeping quiet. Believe me, I understand there are plenty of reasons—"

"—do you, though? Understand? I live alone, Molly. All by myself. No one to protect me—"

Molly nodded. "Right. I completely understand that there might be moments when living alone is difficult—"

"Difficult? No. More like terrifying. And the night of January 18 was one of them."

I knew it, thought Molly. She *did* see something. She waited, letting Annette take her time.

Annette looked at her hands sitting in her lap. She didn't want to tell anyone anything. But something about Molly...the words started tumbling out without Annette actually intending to speak.

"I'm up in the middle of the night—oh, most nights. Terrible insomnia. Fall asleep like a baby and then it's two a.m. and I'm wide awake, can't fall back asleep no matter what I do."

Molly nodded sympathetically but did not interrupt.

"That night..."

A long pause. Molly used every bit of willpower not to say anything. She knew that urging people on usually made them clam up.

Annette sighed and looked out of the window. She scraped her bottom lip with her teeth.

"Who did you see?" Molly finally said, very gently.

Annette swallowed hard. "A man. I was standing at my living room window, you know? Just looking outside for some reason, I don't know why. I didn't want to turn on any lights and wake myself up even more, so I was standing there in the darkness. I had come downstairs thinking about having something to eat but changed my mind."

She took in a long breath and blew it out.

Molly clamped her teeth together to stop herself from yelling at the other woman to just get on with it.

"And so I was standing at the window, and I saw the man coming down the street and then up to Lili's door."

"Did you recognize him? Was it Jules Bresson?"

"It was cold, he was pretty bundled up. I don't know. A man." She shrugged and then wrapped her arms around herself. "I think he saw me. I jumped back, then closed the curtains—it was just an impulse—to stay hidden, you know? But he saw it. He knew that the person in this house had seen him."

Molly nodded sympathetically.

"Or anyway—I think he did. That's why I haven't said anything. I don't want him coming to my house next."

Molly nodded again. She tried to think of any identifying characteristics of Jules.

Then Annette said, "So he got a key from under the flower-pot, and in he went."

Molly nodded once again, thinking. Jules wasn't that tall, sort of average height. No beard. Nothing, when dressed in winter clothes, to distinguish—wait a second—

"Key? He got a *key?*"

"Under the flowerpot on the front step. Most of us on rue Tabac don't lock our doors, not unless we're going away for a real journey. But Lili always did lock up, even just for a trip to the épicerie—"

Annette kept talking but Molly did not hear her.

A key.

She could think of no possible way that Jules would know about that key. He didn't know Lili Lagasse at all, if Amelie was telling the truth. Had never met her. There was no way for him to know about the existence of a key under the flowerpot.

The much, much more likely scenario was that Jules was not the only man to enter Lili Lagasse's house on January 18.

52

One more stop before home.

Molly texted Ben that she was almost on her way, there was a possible break in the case. After parking outside the gendarmerie, she clambered out of the car, unbuckled Olivier, laboriously got him into his carrier, and knocked on the door before pushing her way inside. Or, she tried to get in, but the door was locked.

It was the middle of the afternoon, and nobody was at the gendarmerie?

"Okay, here we go again," she said to Olivier, laboriously taking him back out of the carrier and buckled him into the car seat. She tried calling Charlot—no answer.

Since when did the gendarmerie not answer?

She decided to go home and talk to Ben in person.

In under fifteen minutes, she was standing with her back to the woodstove, talking with her hands, as Ben looked at her, eyes wide.

"It's not really cold out," she babbled. "But I'm so in the habit of standing here to stay warm that I just walked straight to the stove. And it's not even lit. Because it's not that cold."

"Uh, okay? Are you all right?"

"No! Yes! I'm about to drop dead, actually. Thank God Olivier is the best deputy in the world. We need to get him a little gold star."

Ben was holding him and he looked down and kissed Olivier on the nose. "He does seem to be crying a lot less lately. It's you who's going off the deep end."

Molly just smiled. "He was good as gold today. And I was all over the place. Okay, you ready? I apologize, I'm feeling extremely scatter-brained, sort of like the world is tilting."

"Are you—should I call a doctor?"

"No, no, there's nothing wrong with me. It's everything else," she added with a laugh. "Where are Charlot and Paul-Henri? Because there's been...a bit of a crack in the case. And they need to take it from here."

"What do you mean, a crack?"

"Is Amelie—?"

"You want her to join us?"

"I do." Molly sank down on the sofa, all of a sudden feeling as though her bones were made of jelly. She wanted a nap more than anything she had ever wanted in her life.

Ben brought Amelie into the living room with Laurent. To Molly they looked like sad refugees, people who had no home and no easy prospect of getting one, their former life in smoking ruins. But she had news, and maybe-just-maybe, that news would change everything.

"I'll get straight to it," said Molly. "I talked to Annette, Lili's neighbor."

Amelie and Laurent both sat on the floor; Amelie with her eyes on Molly, and Laurent tracing the pattern on the rug as he liked to do.

"She saw a man go into Lili's house the night of the murder. I can't swear to it—not yet—but I don't believe the man she saw was Jules."

"Didn't Charlot already speak to Annette?"

"No doubt she did. Annette has been terrified that the man would come after her next—she believed he saw her looking at him from the next-door window, and knew there was a witness… anyway, she didn't breathe a word to anyone out of fear. But now that Jules is in jail…"

"But Molly," Ben said. "Jules's fingerprints were in that house. Even if there was another man, how does he explain that?"

In her fatigue, Molly felt a flash of irritation. "I'm not claiming to have every last bit figured out. But don't you see? If Jules wasn't the only man who went into that house in the middle of the night, then we don't know what went down. Maybe you could go to the jail and talk to him, hear his side of it."

Amelie looked at Laurent before speaking. "As I told you, I can't believe he would…I don't believe he hurt anyone. Who is this other person?"

Molly could do nothing but shrug. "We don't know. Yet."

"But how do you know that the man Annette saw was not Jules?" asked Ben.

"Not because of how he looked. He was dressed for the cold weather, which makes everyone look sort of the same. But there's something else. The man Annette saw took a key from under a flowerpot on the front step to let himself in. Which means that man is likely someone Lili knew, someone she trusted, someone whom she had told about the location of the spare key."

"Only three of the four sets of prints have been matched," said Ben. "So what you're saying fits with the evidence so far."

"Lapin, Madame Tessier, Jules…all matched to prints inside Lili's house," said Molly. "With one remaining set unaccounted for. And thanks to Madame Tessier, I have at least a general idea of who that set might belong to."

Ben, Molly, and Amelie were lost in thought, playing out scenes of the night of January 18, trying to understand how the events unfolded and what parts people had played. Laurent kept on with his tracing, over and over. He was talking to himself, moving his lips without making any sound.

❧ 53 ❧

I t was an almost unbelievable story. Or—it was not at all, once you knew the underpinnings, the history, the various forces that had led to the final breath of Lili Lagasse. Thanks to Madame Tessier, Molly had that information. She understood the structure of the Lagasse family and how it had operated. It was true that Lili's brother and sister had no interest in the necklace; they had plenty of money, just as multiple people had observed. Once Lili left Bordeaux, they had more or less forgotten about her.

But their children—Lili's nieces and nephews—they were another matter altogether.

So often, perhaps even most of the time, destructive patterns in families repeat over the generations. It was no different for the Lagasses. The older sister had three children, now grown. During their childhood, one of those children had been favored above the others. The youngest, Philippe, was the outcast. As far as Charlot was able to determine, Philippe had not been abused in such a dramatic way as his aunt had been, but as he described it, he had been sneered at, left out, mocked—and when the other children were given very generous gifts of money over the years, he was given nothing.

At age twenty-six, Philippe was broke, and he was desperate. And so he concocted a plan that seemed simple and impossible to mess up: he would pay his Aunt Lili a late-night visit and take that necklace away from her. A pity he would need to get rid of her to prevent her from ratting him out, but eh, she was old, what did it really matter?

Phillipe had let himself in and strangled her without remorse. But as he was in the process of doing it, he heard someone downstairs. Quickly he had hidden himself behind a curtain. He waited. And when the house was quiet again—only a few minutes later—he stepped out to find the necklace gone. Gone! After all the trouble he had taken! The necklace had been right there, he had touched it with his fingers as he was squeezing the life out of her, why had he not snatched it before hiding behind the curtain?

How had he managed to flub the easiest theft in the entire world?

At the end of what had been a very long day, Charlot sat at her desk in the gendarmerie trying to dodge what felt like an emotional tornado headed her way. In one sense, she was able to witness the tornado moving towards her, sucking up everything in its destructive path. She closed her eyes, hoping that would make it go away.

It did not go away. Swirling through her mind were the details of case after case, where she had been slow on the uptake or missed a crucial detail.

She opened the top drawer of her desk and her eyes settled on the piece of pottery Molly Sutton had brought in many days ago. The glaze was a lovely green and there was a faint smudge on it.

Charlot had taken the pottery from Sutton and shoved it in the desk and forgotten about it. She hadn't consciously decided not to send it to the lab. But obviously it had not been sent. It possibly had Philippe Arpin's prints on it—he had admitted to flying into a rage after finding the necklace was missing—in any case, the forgotten evidence was one more failure.

It wouldn't have made any difference, one way or another. Even if his prints were on the pottery, that wouldn't have proven anything. The point was not that, but this: Charlot had taken possible evidence and not treated it with respect. That chunk of pottery was an i that was not dotted, a t that was not crossed.

The tornado came closer. It spun and whirled and threatened Charlot's very sense of reality.

She should resign. She did not deserve the job of chief. Maybe she should follow Paul-Henri to wherever he had got to.

But at least Philippe Arpin was in jail, he had confessed to killing his aunt, and the case was satisfactorily closed, though without much help from herself. With some belated digging, she had found that Philippe had a history of antisocial behavior—harming animals and setting fires—a history that would have been an obvious signal to bring him in for questioning and determine his whereabouts on the night of January 18.

But she had not done that digging, not until Sutton had already solved the case.

Charlot sat up straight, tried to pull herself together. Maybe... what about that cold case, the missing girl, from before her time... Elizabeth Martin. Could she redeem herself by finding out what happened to her, even if was far too late to save her life? She could take the lead, show the village that she wouldn't rest until all the cases were closed, every villager accounted for and justice served...

Charlot put her head in her heads, regretting for the millionth time the fashionable bob as her hair fell into her eyes.

. . .

NELL GODDIN

As the twinkling lights in the scrawny tree outside Chez Papa came into view, Ben reached over and squeezed Molly's leg.

"You do realize the village is at the point of making you Queen. And I am behind that a thousand percent. I'm so proud of you, Molly."

Molly beamed. "I'm pretty proud of myself, if I'm honest," she said, laughing.

Inside, the mood was raucous. A cheer went up when Ben, Molly, and Olivier came through the door, leading Olivier to burst into tears.

Molly hesitated. Did she belong at home with her baby? Was this nothing more than an exercise in ego, coming out at night to receive congratulations and compliments?

She decided yes, it probably was, and so what? It was also a happy moment to spend with her friends, and happy moments had been scarce in Castillac lately—she had no intention of missing out on one.

Frances was grinning her head off at the end of the bar. Nico said, "Kir?" Molly shook her head. "Not yet, I'm afraid! But give me whatever she's having," she said, pointing at Frances.

Lapin walked up, his chest out, with a broad smile. "I'm not sure why they're all cheering for *you*," he said. "When clearly *I* am the man of the hour!"

"Finding the body does not trump finding the murderer," said a woman who overheard.

"I didn't just find the body!" said Lapin. "I knew about the key!"

"Well, why didn't you tell that to Charlot weeks ago?" the woman said.

Lapin opened his mouth and then closed it again.

"We got him in the end," said Molly. "And of course, your information speeded things along."

"I'm lost," said a small man at Molly's elbow. "I thought Jules Bresson—?"

"He was. But—"

"—Jules *did* break in, and he stole the famous necklace," interrupted Lapin. "But Lili was already dead! At the hands of her nephew, Philippe Arpin. I was able to finger him," he said, puffing his chest out, "because when he hired me to take care of Lili's estate, he told me where the key was. So Charlot had his fingerprints taken and that was it, the sniveling creep confessed before she even sent his prints to the lab for verification! And of course, they did match the...the..." Lapin thought of the finger-prints on Lili's neck and shuddered, unable to say anything more.

Molly watched the faces of the crowd listening to Lapin's story. Eyes were wide, heads were shaking. All over the room, people were talking over the details of the case.

Molly looked for Edmond and Ninette, but they were not there. Barely left the house anymore, someone said with a smirk. The épicerie and Pâtisserie Bujold both closed, and how long was this going to go on? Florian and Selma were not there either. She was due any minute, as Castillac's population explosion contin-ued, and the couple wanted to rest up for the big event.

Just as Molly was considering heading for bed, the door opened and Madame Tessier came in.

"The usual," she said to Nico, who reached for the Irish whiskey.

"I've got the best joke to tell you," she said to Molly, grinning. "While you were running around finding Lili's actual murderer—and I'll pile on all the thank-yous after I tell you this—I took the necklace to Bergerac, to a jeweler I know. Not to sell, but for an appraisal."

Madame Tessier paused, giving the moment all the drama she could muster.

"The necklace is a fake," she said, and tilted her head back and roared with laughter. "The jeweler didn't even have to put it under that magnifying glass. It's nothing but paste. Isn't that glorious?"

Molly started to protest. She wanted to say, but then Lili was killed for nothing!

"Oh, Molly—I don't think Lili would regret it for a second. She had that necklace made for herself and it gave her joy every single day."

Molly nodded. She sort of understood and just felt glad that Madame Tessier looked like herself again.

"There are worse things than death, Molly Sutton," said Madame Tessier, and the two friends lifted the glasses and clinked them to that rather unsettling idea.

GLOSSARY

Chapter 1
rue...............................street
pigeonnier...................pigeon house (this one turned into gîte)

Chapter 2
épicerie........................small grocery store
gendarmerie.................police station
n'est-ce pas...................right?
pâtisserie.....................pastry shop

Chapter 3
jambon........................ham

Chapter 4
le bébé........................baby
pichet.........................small pitcher
mon Dieu...................my God

Chapter 5

pâtissier......................pastry chef
petit cafe....................espresso
bien sûr.......................of course

Chapter 8
le maitre....................teacher (literally, master)

Chapter 13
à table.....................come to the table (dinner time!)

Chapter 16
bisou.........................kiss
Chapter 17
réligieuse.................cream puff shaped like a nun

Chapter 18
pineau.....................a liqueur

Chapter 21
cecio et pepe.............cheese and pepper

Chapter 22
mec..........................guy (slang)

Chapter 24
département............section of France
priez our vos morts.....pray for our dead

Chapter 28
ferme ta gueule...........shut your mouth! (rude)

Chapter 30
fête...........................feast

Chapter 35
    quelle....................what
    comté.....................a kind of cheese (so good!)

Chapter 37
    mairie...................town hall
    dévoté...................fan

Chapter 45
    cou-cou.................French way of saying yoo-hoo

Chapter 52
    à toute.................short for à toute à l'heure, see you later

ACKNOWLEDGMENTS

Thanks so much to Nancy Kelley, Lisa Carlisle, Nellie Baumer, and Julian Baumer. A pleasure to work with you all.

ABOUT THE AUTHOR

Nell Goddin has worked as a radio reporter, SAT tutor, short-order omelet chef, and baker. She tried waitressing but was fired twice.

Nell grew up in Richmond, Virginia and has lived in New England, New York City, and France. She has degrees from Dartmouth College and Columbia University.

www.goddinbooks.com
nell@goddinbooks.com

ALSO BY NELL GODDIN

You can get Nell's books at goddinbooks.com, at all major online retailers, or ask for them at your local bookstore.

Sign up for news and discounts at goddinbooks.com